The Seed Vault

H. B. Viegas

Forelight Fiction

First published in 2026 by Forelight Fiction

ISBN 978-1-9194073-1-9

Forelight Fiction, UK

For my son, the fearless runaway who always found his way back

THE SEED VAULT

PART ONE: OUTLIERS

Prologue – (Birgit) Seeds

Fyr, Svalbard archipelago, June 2131

I knew you'd leave from the moment I became your mother. You had no sense of danger, no natural survival instinct. I spent my days pulling you out from under chairs, carpets, cushions, terrified someone would sit without looking, and accidentally crush you. When you started toddling, I set up a chime on your bracelet and attuned my ear to any silence longer than usual, ready to grab you from outside, before hypothermia kicked in. I thought I had cracked it. I had to keep listening for the chime. If it slipped away, I dropped everything and came searching for you.

Was life that difficult? Our routine followed the best parenting manuals. Feeding, hygiene, playtime, affection. I never chose to be a mother. But once I became yours, I threw myself into the project and never looked back. I'm a food scientist. That, I chose. Science and enforced practice made me a mother, rather than instinct. I thought I was doing a decent job. Was I wrong? What else did you need? Home-cooked food, pristine socks, blind dedication? Could I have stopped you from leaving, without becoming someone else?

It's too late for regrets. These halting messages are my best attempt to deflect the pain, to explain, to apologise.

One day, I hope you'll understand. Another project needs my full attention. The most important project in my career. When I started working in food science, I was full of optimism. Today, I no longer think people want a solution. Hunger is collateral damage, but there are other priorities. There are *always* other priorities. Perhaps you'll forgive my single-mindedness when you're old enough. If you had the power to end world hunger, what would *you* do? How ironic that you ran away just as we reached a breakthrough.

The Finder is here.

I need to leave.

I may have failed at being a mother, but I dare not fail at the rest.

Newsbreak: Switch to New Food agreed by over 100 nations

The Third Bengaluru Convention has ratified drastic measures targeting the farming industry, one of the largest contributors to greenhouse gases. The shift to New Food is part of the wider set of new standards to limit global temperature rises to under 8°C (46°F) compared to pre-industrial levels. In previous years, similar measures included the ban on fossil fuel extraction and embargos on industry and commerce in non-essential sectors. More than 100 countries, representing most of the world's population, have now signed the switch to New Food. This initiative aims to convert agricultural land into dense woodland to absorb heat from the atmosphere, supporting major global investment in plant genetics and vertical labs producing New Food.

Chapter One

(Hildr) Void

Fyr, Svalbard archipelago, June 2149 (eighteen years later)

She sat quietly on the beach, watching the lava ridges stretching to the Arctic Ocean, the bright sky looming like a low ceiling. Her eyes teared up. Cloud shapes flickered on her pupils. Fyr. She was back on the island. She recognised the dense, black volcanic sand under her tense fists, the smell of lichen and moss, the gentle sound of waves washing up against the shore, the clean crisp air. Even the sky, she could sense the exact time of the year producing these pale blue hues. Early June, afternoon, Fyr's southern beach.

Further along the coastline, silhouettes gathered by the shore. They looked as if they were dancing. She could hear no music. Turning her head to the Beranger, she traced the mighty volcano with her eyes. The wind picked up, a whoosh spreading over the rugged coast, clumps of moss stirring with its whispers. She heard a thud.

She turned back to face the sea.

A man was sitting on the sand, across from her. Around her age, maybe younger. Barely an adult. Dark skin, deep-set eyes, patchy stubble.

"What's your name?" the man asked.

He was wearing a white T-shirt, loose khaki trousers, and a stiff hooded cape over his shoulders. No technology on his body. A void.

She steadied her thoughts.

"Hildr."

Maybe she shouldn't have revealed her real name?

It had come out like a reflex.

"I'm Bas," the void said. His long, messy hair was full of black muck, as if he had slept on the beach for weeks without even washing in sea water. "Did you just arrive, Hildr?"

She wondered if he had seen the van dropping her off at the beach. He had the daring, intense stare of someone with nothing to lose.

"I'm looking for ... someone." Hildr looked up, hoping to find the right answer hanging from a cloud. Her tabs were gone. Nowhere to search for help.

"Looking for whom?" Bas asked.

She couldn't trust a void, could she? Her gaze flicked back to the sea. A quiet scream stayed trapped inside her head.

Bas pointed at the group of people dancing by the water.

"One of them?" The dancers were performing a head-banging, arm-yanking loop, with little grace or coordination. "Just joking. No one's looking for that lot."

The group knelt on the ground, swaying, hands half-buried in the sand. Hildr squinted but couldn't catch sight of a full face.

"Who are they?"

"Voids," Bas said.

"What are they doing?"

"Dancing."

"You're a void too." She cursed herself. "I mean, no one on Fyr wears technology any more, so everyone is void."

"No, that's not technically correct," he said, emphasising the *tech* part of the word. "The guards still have citizen-chips. Me and the others, yeah ... we got rid of the sensors, trackers, virtual tabs popping up in front of our eyes, all that crap."

"Why?" She couldn't resist probing his twisted logic.

The question made Bas frown.

"Because technology cut us off from our real bodies, our real minds. What kind of question is that? I'm an outcast from the algorithm, like you."

Hildr absorbed the shock of the label.

"Me, an outcast?"

There was genuine doubt in her voice. She felt as if she were waking up after a long, drug-induced coma, asking a total stranger about the state of the world; looking into a mirror to remember who she was and not recognising her own reflection.

"You have no tech either," Bas said, stating the obvious. "Doesn't take much to guess you're not in the model."

She looked at her bare hands and wrists, touched the back of her neck, her uncovered ears. He was right. All her technology. Gone. She'd had to give it away. She was a free agent, untethered, outside the AI model's predictions.

Void.

"Did you say you were looking for someone?" Bas said. She regarded him in silence. "*Who* are you looking for? There aren't many people left on Fyr."

Small, thin, lithe.

Just a boy.

"Ula," Hildr said. "I'm looking for Ula Svenson."

Bas shrugged and glanced over his shoulder, at the towering mountains. "From the farmers? They live near the volcano's mouth. Not easy to find, mind you. That's the whole point of setting up a *farm* on the highest mountain on Fyr. They missed the memo about ditching crops, planting trees and eating New Food. I don't give a shit about politics, by the way."

Hildr's lips sketched a faint smile. This was probably a good thing. They would have disagreed on many levels.

"What *do* you give a shit about?" she asked.

The question lit a spark in his eyes. "Helping migrants. That's my job. I've helped more than fifty people out of the sea since I arrived on this beach. It's not an easy job, mind you. They stumble out of their submarines half-dead, after weeks of pedalling and panicking about underwater pressure, Arctic seaworms, ships and drones. Have you seen a sub in real life? The most amazing and scary piece of engineering *ever*. Honestly. I'm learning to pilot one, by the way. Call me 'Captain'. Just joking. Don't get into a submarine if you don't know what you're doing, okay? It's dangerous. You'll suffocate if you stay underwater for too long, and you'll suffer from decompression sickness if you come up too fast. Hopefully, not at the same time. Just joking. We need to keep our spirits up round here. When new migrants arrive, I say hello in the local Fyr dialect and hand out New Food cartons."

Naive. Good-hearted. Talks too much.

"Where do you get New Food from?" Hildr asked.

"The guards at the removal centre give us their spare cartons," Bas said. "The algorithm doesn't mind the voids.

It's the new migrants they target. They don't want more people risking the journey from the continent. Unless loads of USK citizens die, or Mondo chucks out New Food faster, no one can get a chip. They're not allowing anyone else into the model."

"And after helping migrants, what are you going to do?"

"Dance?" he grinned.

"You can't stay on this beach forever."

He tilted his head left and right. "Why not?"

She frowned. "It'll be too cold in the winter."

Bas crossed his arms. "I didn't ask your advice. I don't care about the cold. One problem at a time, okay? It's not even winter yet. Why would I care about the cold? Mind your own business." He paused, changing tack. "Or you can help me, how about that? More subs will arrive any time." He nodded towards the sea, an inscrutable shade of blue.

She had to get going.

"Do you know the best route to the Beranger?" she asked.

She hadn't been on Fyr for a long time.

A smattering of black sand fell on her lap. The dancers had moved closer, doing frog-jumps, waving and calling them to join the awkward choreography.

"Can you dance?" Bas said.

Hildr sprang up, patting black dust off her trousers. "I need to go."

Bas's eyes widened.

"Moose's crap, are you for real?"

Walking steadily, Hildr projected her torso forward, compensating for the sand pulling against her feet. She visualised the coordinates in her head, the map she'd studied for weeks.

Bas followed her along the beach.

"Who *are* you? I've never seen anyone as tall as you." He had a point. The top of his head barely reached her chest. Her shadow dwarfed his, despite the wide cape over his shoulders flapping against the wind. "I can keep secrets," Bas continued. "Have you removed your chip to join Ula and the farmers? People say they still have supporters on other islands. Is that true? Hey, can you please slow down?"

"Ula has something that belongs to me."

Hildr squinted at the path veering off the beach, estimating the distance. Was it the right path? So frustrating, not having a map. She didn't recognise the natural landmarks, the faded mountain routes, the island's novel secrets.

Bas touched her forearm.

"That's not the best way to the volcano, by the way."

He led her behind a dune. A dozen tents came into view. Loose garments flapped against the breeze, hanging from clotheslines, including several hooded capes like the one Bas was wearing. Discarded New Food cartons lay scattered on the sand. Strategically placed rocks prevented old paper books from spiralling with the wind. Bas crouched to get inside one of the tents and came out with a rucksack. Through the open flap, Hildr saw an assortment of energy bars, a water bottle, a tangle of rope, and a musical instrument.

"What's that?"

"A ukulele," he said. "I have nutrition and entertainment. Grab one of the capes. They double up as thermal duvets. We may need a tent too. The journey will take us about two days, depending on the weather."

Hildr pressed her brow.

Entertainment? He would delay her.

"You don't need to come with me to the Beranger," she said. "Just some pointers would be great."

He chuckled. "Turn right by the skull-shaped rock, that sort of thing? There's no skull-shaped rock on Fyr, I'm afraid. How about if I walk you to the cleft behind that dune? From there, you can follow a route up to the volcano's mouth, where Ula and her group set up their *farm*. I heard it's more like a boy scouts' camp, by the way."

He was hugging the rucksack between his arms, as if it were a close friend.

So thin. So fragile. So eager to help.

She would feel awful if something happened to Bas.

"Are you sure? What about the migrants, your altruistic job, the submarine piloting lessons?"

"Someone will cover for me," he said. "No one is irreplaceable."

"I thought you didn't like politics." Hildr was half-smiling.

Bas glared at her. "I said I didn't like the farmers' stupid theories. That's what I meant by politics."

"You said *no one is irreplaceable*."

The mantra from old tech companies. Artificial intelligence had replaced most jobs.

"So what?" He looked annoyed. "We've heard that line so many times, we don't think about what it means any more. It's just a convention, a habit, a rule of thumb. Most definitely *not* politics." He zipped up his rucksack. "There haven't been new subs arriving lately, anyway. Maybe the buoys are intercepting them again. No one expects the Devs to let more people in."

"That's your job, right?" she said.

Now he looked upset.

"I'm addressing a basic injustice. I didn't choose to be born in Uskania, and the migrants didn't choose to be born overseas. If there's nothing but luck separating us, why did I get a citizen-chip and not them?"

"If everyone could be a citizen, the chip would be worthless. There would be no essential nutrition, no minimum income, no free healthcare."

"I renounced those things when I became a void. When my time comes ..." Bas lifted his chin and made a swiping gesture with his hand. "I'll lie down and die, like every living creature on Earth." He looked at her with suspicion. "You know, defending the algorithm is kind of weird, for someone in your position."

"You prefer *dying* to accepting your good luck?"

A hooded cape hung on a rope. Hildr snatched the padded fabric, tucked it under her arm, and started hiking.

Bas wrapped his fingers around the straps of his rucksack, following her in small jumps. "What I prefer doesn't matter ... doesn't matter a jot." Each of her steps covered three of his. "We're a grain of sand on this beach, a mere accident from our shitting God."

Hildr shook her head, smiling.

"You've gone religious on me now. Did you just say *our shitting God*?"

Hilarious.

She shook her head again.

They were making progress. Early evening, Arctic summertime. Permanent daylight. The sun shone behind strewn clouds of regal pink and red. Ahead of them, black mountains slammed against the sky, a stark contrast of light and shadow. The Beranger was magnificent, beautiful, arresting. Soon, she would find Ula and recover what Birgit had given her eighteen years before. She wasn't sure if bringing Bas along was a good idea, but "our shitting God" might have a plan.

Uskanian archives: Extract from parliamentary session before the islands' unification referendum

STEWART (Conservative Party): Would my honourable friend explain how she intends to protect migrants displaced by climate change without neglecting our own citizens, thus causing further social unrest?

ROBINSON (Prime Minister): International co-operation has always been a necessity for small nations, and as such my intention is first and foremost to abide by the new UN statute.

CLARK (Scottish National Party): May I remind the honourable gentleman who posed the question that once migrants are embedded in our legal framework, they will become citizens. Hence the fallacy of pitting people against outsiders; the strategy has a circular nature, much like the chicken and egg conundrum?

Chapter Two

(Axel) The Finder

Iceland, June 2131 (eighteen years before)

Axel was sitting on his bed eating lunch when a new user tab popped into view. A woman with windswept brown hair and almond-shaped hazel eyes stared into the distance. *Carla*, her nametag flashed underneath. Too stunning to be real. The USK algorithm knew his tastes and used its knowledge to good effect.

"Good afternoon, Mr Jóhannsson," Carla-the-bot said, voice as smooth and seductive as her face. "According to our data, you were born on Fyr. Can I assume you're well acquainted with the island?"

The world was fucked up but he didn't make the rules. New Food, an energy-efficient home, a life without scavenging in the dirt, in exchange for his personal data. That was the deal. Every citizen-chip fed the AI model.

"It was an accident," Axel said, chewing on a rib. Barbecue sauce slid down his chin. "Viking by heart, born on Fyr by accident." The spicy, salty taste almost made up for the fake meat consistency.

Carla mimed a coy smile. Not bad for a machine.

"I'm sorry, were you making a joke? I'm getting better at humour every day, but some jokes still elude me."

She was spoiling his meal.

"Is this a national census?" he said.

"We don't need a census, Mr Jóhannsson. We have everyone's data. National duty would be a better description. We'd like you to investigate a new case on Fyr."

Maybe it was a glitch.

"You've got the wrong person. I'm a freelancer. I find voids on behalf of real people. Lovers and enemies, anyone with a score to settle. I don't work for the model."

USK paid peanuts. Fake peanuts. Not worth his time.

"We know everything about your assignments, Mr Jóhannsson. According to our data model, you're the best Finder for this job."

Interesting.

"Who do you want to find?"

"A little girl. Her name is Hildr Olsen. She's the adopted daughter of a corporate citizen living on Fyr."

"A kid going void?"

Kids loved technology.

"That's correct. She wore her citizen-chip on a bracelet, and yesterday she removed it by compromising the strap with a sharp, cutting object."

Axel smelled something fishy.

"Why do you want to find her?"

"We're not as interested in the girl," Carla said, "as we are in her mother, Dr Birgit Olsen. She's a Swedish scientist working for Mondo Foods, leading a new plant genetics project in the Svalbard seed vault."

A fake bone was attached to the side of his rib, surrounded by a strip of glistening white fat. Mondo Foods might be monopolist bastards, but they made clever stuff like this.

"Gotcha. You can't access personal data from corporate citizens, so you need a Finder to poke around with the excuse of looking for her daughter. I'm not interested, thanks."

He closed the tab.

Fyr, of all places. He had sworn never to set foot on the island again. It would take more than a lousy job offer to convince him.

A new tab popped up.

"That wasn't very polite, Mr Jóhannsson."

Axel sighed, wiping sauce off his mouth.

Holding the fake rib with one hand, he activated his bee camera, releasing it from inside his watch face. "Why don't you ask someone on Fyr?"

So many islands in the Svalbard archipelago. Why had the scientist picked the gutter?

"The algorithm wants *you*," Carla said.

The bee camera buzzed in front of his face.

"I can't travel right now."

"Why not? According to the data, you are in perfect health. You don't have any ongoing commitments in Iceland. No live jobs, no family. You meet two friends face-to-face once a month, and four acquaintances online occasionally. I can see you were recently in a brief romantic relationship, but last week she told you she wasn't interested in being intimate any more."

Axel slapped the bee camera against the mattress.

The bot was getting on his nerves.

"Hello? Mr Jóhannsson? I lost visuals." Carla's eyes scanned left and right, looking for a focal point in the darkness. "Would you like a further incentive to travel? If you accept this job, USK predicts higher advertising revenues for your video channel. Fyr has a special place in our collective imagination."

The bot's repertoire of facial expressions included a patronising smirk.

"It's a fucking rock in the middle of the Arctic. Seagull turds and scum."

The algorithm knew everything about him. That's why they had him covered in cameras, mics, and health nodes. They knew he hated Fyr.

"Don't think about the negatives," Carla said. "Think about the money."

"Pay me ten times your usual fee, and I'll think about it."

His physical health might be perfect, but his mind was still recovering.

"That is an unreasonable proposal, Mr Jóhannsson, and you know it. Why don't you ask Dr Olsen to bump up your fees?"

"Are you asking me to spy on behalf of the algorithm, and lie to my client?"

Corporate citizens usually paid well. The bot was right about that.

"Ethics have never been a problem before. What happened to your camera?"

Axel lifted his hand from the mattress.

"Why the Mondo scientist?"

The bee camera spiralled upwards, like a real bug.

"Mondo Foods are paying Uskania to use the seed vault in Svalbard. They signed a confidentiality agreement with the Trust managing the vault. We've asked for more information about their new research project, led by Dr Olsen.

They declined to provide it. Please note you mustn't share these details with anyone."

"I need to know what I'd be looking for," Axel said.

"You'd be looking for Hildr Olsen."

Not enough. "Why do you care about the research?"

"USK is negotiating a new contract with Mondo Foods," Carla said, "including a discount on New Food shipments to the islands."

The story started making more sense now. USK wanted information about the research to get leverage on food prices from Mondo. The world was running out of food. Best to grab a good deal from the source.

Still, none of his business.

"I don't know why the algorithm picked *me*. I don't care about New Food, corporate secrets, or international politics. I'm not one of the fuckwits on a crusade to save humankind from their own stupidity."

"You're a service provider, Mr Jóhannsson. You don't need to care." Carla focused her hazel eyes on him. "Would you like a further incentive?" Fake breathing rustled in his headphones. "I can get you meat. Real meat."

Sexy.

"Tell me more," he said.

"A weekly delivery to your flat in Reykjavik, for one month."

"Make it a year."

A meaty job deserved a meaty deal.

"Your counterproposal has been accepted. Leave without delay and wait for further instructions when you arrive in Fyr. You will be matched with Dr Olsen for the finding job. Film everything inside her lab. Get her to talk about her research. We will edit out sensitive information from your public stream.”

“Can you make it beef?”

“Sure thing. One last detail. Beware of Ula Svenson. The farmers have been causing trouble in the island, smuggling food and materials out of USK cargo.”

Ula wasn’t a farmer. Not many farms left, after the switch to New Food. The main question was different though.

“How come USK doesn’t stop them from stealing our food?”

“It’s all in the data,” Carla said. “The farmers are popular. Waves of new voids have been cropping up on the island, and regular pushbacks have radicalised citizens against data surveillance. If we do another sweep of illegals now, we’ll be increasing their ranks. Ula and her followers pose no immediate danger. They’re trying to set up a farm on the Beranger.”

A *farm*? No proper soil. No power supply. Where were they going to grow food – in the volcano’s mouth?

Axel got Carla to agree the beef cuts and bought his ticket to Fyr.

This was how the algorithm kept citizens under control. Studying their data, modelling options, targeting the ideal approach, manipulating. He knew returning to Fyr wasn’t a good idea, yet he had been swayed. How the hell had that happened? For the next few nights, he would be dreading old nightmares.

All flights to Fyr had been grounded so the journey now took two days in choppy seas. Axel boarded the catamaran and headed upstairs, towards the back, sitting at the end of a crowded row of seats. The ship was bobbing with the waves, and a strong bleach odour rose from the linoleum floor. Years before, Fyr had been a desolate volcanic rock northeast of the Svalbard archipelago. No one would have thought of setting foot there, let alone living on the island. Then temperatures in continental Europe spiked, the numbers living North swelled, and suddenly every inch of land mattered.

At least there was a reclinable seat and a paper bag.

He didn't miss being seasick.

An invitation to play Robot Apocalypse Chronicles arrived on a new tab. *Declined.* Multiplayer games were for people who enjoyed company.

He felt a tap on his shoulder. Someone sitting in the row behind him. Without turning, Axel slid his headphone backwards, exposing a bare ear.

"Are you a USK citizen?"

North American accent, with a hint of wealthy corporate citizen.

"Yeah."

He missed talking to tourists as much as seagulls shitting on his head.

"Awesome," the tourist said. "Is it a nice place to live?"

Axel looked back. Worse than he thought. The guy was smiling, as if they were best friends. Perfect white teeth and ginger hair. Axel leaned forward in his seat, avoiding the breath warming the back of his neck.

"No."

"Haha, thanks for the honesty. I'm heading to Fyr, where they piloted the beta version of the USK software."

That's how it had started. People from continental Europe had had to quarantine on Fyr. A few tents and little contraception. The excitement of kicking out politicians led to more people joining from Iceland, Scotland, Greenland, until Fyr grew into a collection of estranged people hoping to build a New World based on surveillance technology.

"It's a dump," Axel said.

"They were pioneers," the tourist said, as if his lousy travel guide made him an expert. "The first to get citizen-chips."

But Axel knew the rest of the story.

"Still a dump," Axel said.

They'd got fed up with being tracked. Citizens on the island wanted the lost paradise of simple living, claiming technology was a *bad* thing, while new migrants wanted nothing more than a citizen-chip pinned on to their skin – food, housing, a life without misery. The world was full of ironies, eh?

"I always wonder," the ginger tourist continued, "how you see the world in your little mind tabs. I find it fascinating, allowing a clever algorithm to decide everything for you. Such a neat solution, when democracy is falling apart in the rest of the world. Is there a way you can share your mind tab with me, show me what you see?"

He hated tourists.

"It's not a *mind tab*. My mind has no tabs. It's a user tab. We use moisture projectors or pair the chip with standard screens, like everyone else. Only USK citizens can access our tabs."

The tourist lowered his chin to the padded fabric of Axel's seat.

"But what does it feel like …? To have an AI model tracking your every movement, every turn, every decision, even your thoughts when you use voice-free speech?"

Here it was. Everything that was wrong with tourists. Feeling entitled to share their opinion of Uskania without having a fucking clue. The feeling of being constantly watched, probed, nudged, made him want to punch the walls sometimes. Axel was entitled to hate the algorithm only because he knew all the drawbacks and had made his decision. Closing the borders and keeping citizen numbers low meant they weren't sucking everything out of the planet as if there was no tomorrow.

"Everyone is being tracked," Axel said. "You're the slave, not me."

The tourist shrugged. "I'm corporate, dude. I earn my own money. Your freedom in exchange for pennies from the state? Not worth it, IMO."

Axel stared at his perfect manicure, the safari shorts, the spiky haircut. He could afford to travel all the way to Uskania, that much was clear. Idiots with the last corporate jobs thought they were *special*. They didn't realise how little it took to end up in the gutter. The smell of spoiled milk flooded his nostrils. A man in the front row was retching into his crumpled paper bag. Behind them, another passenger moaned. Immediately to his left, a woman started gagging and throwing up on the floor.

"Exactly how I feel about this conversation," Axel said. "Shut your trap, or I'll rub your face in her vomit."

For a moment, he thought the tourist was going to throw up too.

He didn't bother him again.

Day two. The paper bags ran out. Lines of runny puke swayed back and forth on the linoleum floor, drawing branches without leaves, pushed by the incessant rising and falling of the bow. The catamaran stopped seven times before Fyr. Scotland, Norway, slowly making its way up the Norwegian Sea and the Svalbard archipelago. Passengers hopping off looked like people given a reprieve at the gates of hell. Those carrying on to Fyr continued retching. The seats around him were free. Unpopularity was a blessing.

As the pneumatic hulls hit the pier of Fyr's old town, the remaining passengers lined up to watch the mooring, glad to leave the stench behind. Axel wondered what business they had in the island, what made anyone come to this place of their own free will. They were like sheep in a flock, heading up the steep ramp. Axel walked fast, hands in his pockets, as a cool, refreshing breeze washed over him. Ahead, the black slopes of the Beranger volcano, the sun barely rising in the sky after its long knock at the horizon. June was white night season. The sky wouldn't go dark.

Shadows surrounded him soon enough. Sniffing the port's litter. Loitering by the pier. Creeping out from under blankets. Left. Right. Behind. Shadows everywhere. Instead of the vast solitude of the Arctic Circle, people shuffled from under clothes, sleeping bags, rubbish bins, crawling out of every hole. Illegal migrants. If they lasted the long queue to get a USK citizen-chip, they'd be entitled to a living wage, housing, and New Food cartons. No wonder they kept arriving in their dinghies and subs, despite the risk of drowning or being caught and sent back to the mainland.

The port building was smaller and dirtier than he remembered. Boxed corridors of cement with faded blue tiles. They meant nothing. He felt nothing. Too many years had gone by since he'd hidden in Fyr's smeared public spaces, trauma pushed aside by numbed senses. Outside the building, a ragged man wrapped in a soiled blanket looked up from a heavy paper tome. The cover was ripped, but the book's title glared on Axel's tab. The Bible.

An urge grew in his stomach.

Fyr.

Axel ran back inside the port building, followed the signs to the bathroom, and stumbled into a toilet cubicle, retching.

The seasickness had finally caught up with him.

Robot Apocalypse Chronicles (RAC), chat feed

@Gamer_grapefuit: Did you know the new RAC level is based on Uskania? It's the country formed when Iceland, Scotland, Ireland, Norway, and Greenland decided to band together. The level starts with the last elected president getting a monumental kick in the ass after she's caught accepting a bribe.

@Ash2116: Yeah, who trusts politicians anyway.

@Gamer_grapefuit: So they scrapped the whole government and handed the islands over to an AI logistics software piloted in the commercial sector. Just because the robots don't look scary doesn't mean they won't kill all the humans.

@Ash2116: Muhahahaha.

Chapter Three

(Hildr) Cathedral

Hildr and Bas walked side by side on Fyr's black volcanic beach, two oddly contrasting figures, his lithe and delicate, hers tall and muscular, as if they had met to prove the power of difference. The dancers' camp was now a blurred spot in the distance. How many tents had there been? How many dancers? They had no tech to hold the facts together.

Veering off the beach, they reached a barren slope, the first of a set of three peaks. Silver-grey blades of rock and dark-brown blots of volcanic sand peppered a short climb. After the climb, a single-storey dwelling stood against the mountainside, square-shaped, concrete walls smeared with multi-layered stains of yellow and green, as if acid rain had poured over them for years. A crooked iron chimney topped the parched walls of the ruined building, and a round, rusty tin can stood in front of its entrance. Bas went around the crumbling structure. Hildr stayed at the front. The corrugated-iron roof leaned against what had probably been a window. Dark wooden slabs were piled on the sand next to the entrance, like dominos. Inside the building, exposed walls in dull colours, grey panels juxtaposed with black squares. No sign of human presence, no life, no odour.

The only sound came from Bas's footsteps at the back of the building.

Time dragged on.

"Let's go," Hildr said.

Bas returned to his place by her side. "An old weather station, abandoned," he said. "Someone used to live here, not long ago. There are still white bedsheets hanging from the ceiling."

"Were they using bedsheets as screens?"

He nodded, continuing the hike. "It's unbelievable what people do to get away from reality." His tone was gloomier than usual. "I once knew a man who lived between three hanging bedsheets, one in front of his face, one on his left and one on his right. He installed them near a bucket, a sink, and a food blender, each of which he used twice a day. He said the first cartons of New Food were tough to digest. Best to use powdered versions and blend them with water. When he wasn't drinking his New Food shakes or urinating in the bucket, he spent the rest of his day on betting games and shoot-em-ups, which he projected on the bedsheets. You could approach him from the back to refill the water in the blender, but he would not turn to face you. He was happy like that. Or so he claimed, when we spoke online. He didn't want people in his real life, interfering with his virtual persona."

Hildr observed his reactions through the corner of her eye.

"Sounds ... sad." He was probably quoting from an old children's book, one of those with misguided moral stories. "Are you suggesting the problem was the technology?"

Voids believed technology was to blame for all the sadness in the world. They wanted to return to a time when people had lived happily off-screen. A time that had never existed.

Bas looked at her, sighed and stared into the distance.

A minute passed.

"It was my father," Bas said. "The hanging bedsheets. The man with the blender. It was my father. He worked at the removal centre until my mother's death, then gave up on real life."

The revelation seemed significant.

"Is that why … you've removed your chip?" Hildr asked, hesitantly. "Was it a kind of revenge for your father's lack of … engagement?"

Now he couldn't reach him online either.

"No, not revenge. That's so lame. I don't care how he spends his time. He's happy in his own way. I removed the chip because it brought me no joy. I don't care about social games, winning credits, crap jobs. Those are distractions. I want to live a real life, speak to real people, make a real impact. Even if it means being cold in the winter."

Hildr looked beyond his words. He was speaking his mind. He genuinely believed in a "real life" outside USK, a life with purpose, perhaps a career, property, air travel. Bygone times. Telling her his father's story had made Bas's brown eyes a tiny bit brighter. Chestnut sharp. No need for sympathy, only acknowledgment. She bit her tongue. USK's entertainment apps had been proven to help citizens suffering with loneliness and bereavement. No real money was ever gambled, and the kick of adrenaline and dopamine proved beneficial to their recovery, although they had to be weaned off the games afterwards. How could she explain this to Bas?

"I'm not sure I follow you," she started, treading carefully. "We're the lucky ones. We live north. We extracted what we could from the fossil fuels boom. The old sovereign fund buys us New Food, despite people going hungry in other countries."

"You must be joking."

She glanced at his outraged face and reconsidered her tactics. To continue this conversation, she would have to reveal what she knew. Voids were hard-headed. Everyone knew that. She must stay quiet. Hildr kept walking, westbound, surveying the rugged rock surface, the fractures like scars gained over millennia, mulling over her thoughts.

Later that day, they reached a wall of grey with a patch of blood red in the middle, as if a giant had taken a knife and sliced the mountain down the middle to reveal its entrails. At lower latitudes, the sun had set. Here, the clouds emanated a steady brightness, the Arctic's white night slowly turning a dull orange.

"It's late," Bas said. "We need to rest before the climb."

"I'm not tired."

"That's impossible. We've walked for at least six hours. You need to learn to listen to your body."

"Fine."

He was obviously undernourished – walking too slowly and stopping too often. Despite this, his company soothed her and took her mind off the stress of the mission. Hildr spread out her padded cape on the ground, removed her trainers and sat, shivering, arms crossed in front of her chest. A chilly breeze lifted the loose grains of sand, carrying them in the air, spreading light-grey dust on her dark skin. Bas removed an energy bar from his backpack. Her mouth instantly salivated. She wasn't used to being hungry, but she had to be starving by the time she reached the farmers. She needed Ula to believe she had been kicked out and left without food in this Godforsaken land.

She couldn't stop staring at Bas's energy bar.

"Are you hungry?" he asked.

She shook her head.

He squeezed the exposed side of the bar and pulled both ends apart, breaking it in half.

Hildr gulped her portion in one go.

"Wow, that was fast." He munched on his half a while longer. "When was the last time you ate? Actually, I have a better question. When did you remove your citizen-chip? You haven't told me that either."

Stop the questions.

She picked at the traces of sand between her toes. "I don't know."

He narrowed his eyes. "You don't know?"

Hildr scratched her toes, the sole of her foot, the dry skin on her legs, feeling his eyes on her, demanding an answer. Under her trousers' hem, near her right ankle, thin white letters became visible on her skin. The sentence was written in baroque, hand-drawn serifed letters, along her lower tibia, bright and sharp.

Do the right thing, the letters wrote.

"I feel a bit dizzy," Hildr said.

"Don't worry," Bas said, unable to see the tattoo from where he sat. "Low-calorie lock will give you a permanent feeling of confusion, low energy, drowsiness, but you won't die. The removal centre leaves food out every week. The guards have known me since I was a kid."

"What kind of food?"

"Energy bars. New Food cartons. Even cooking ingredients sometimes. Rice, oats, beans."

The image aroused her.

"Can you cook?" She pulled the hem of her trousers down, covering the white tattoo.

"Of course. I love old food."

"What can you cook?"

"Porridge, rice, beans, you name it. I know we're only supposed to eat New Food, but the planet won't collapse with the amount of old food we eat on Fyr." He let out a dry chuckle. "I don't care anyway. I'm just trying to survive."

She lay down on her cape. "You're only making it hard for yourself."

A steely seriousness lit up Bas's face.

"What kind of comment is that? I've told you many things about me." His tone of voice changed, as if opening a new page. "Who are you? Why are you looking for Ula Svenson? Are you joining the farmers, or are you plotting against them?"

"What could I plot with empty hands?"

"I've met many who admire Ula. I recognise them by now. You're not one of them. In the jungle, there are no conspiracy theories. Lions kill because they're hungry or scared. You're more like a lion, aren't you? What are you scared of?"

A trace of a smile lingered on Hildr's mouth.

"What do you know about the jungle?"

"There are jungles in India, where my ancestors came from. Hey, you're changing the subject again. Do you believe in Ula's theories, that food corporations are hiding our old food in secret underground farms? Or are you an undercover agent for USK, trying to catch the farmers?"

She organised her story inside her head, studying the words, measuring what she could tell him.

"I don't believe anyone is hiding old food. But some people in the other islands believe there is something ... underneath Svalbard."

"Plants?"

"Not plants. Something else."

"What?" he asked.

She had trapped herself.

"Something," she repeated.

Bas frowned. "Fungi? Plankton?"

"Whatever it is, it's leaking into the Arctic Ocean, and feeding the worms." She was tying the loose ends of evidence in front of him, hoping he would build the bridge himself and jump over the chasm dividing them.

"Who thinks that? Who the hell are you?"

Would Bas believe her, if she told him what she knew? Did she *need* him to believe her? No. Only Ula and the farmers mattered. Only they could tell her where Birgit's messages were hidden.

Above the black cliffs of the Beranger volcano, the clouds were getting darker. Hildr took a deep breath.

"I really appreciate you sharing your food with me, Bas. But I ... I can't ... speak right now. You're right, I'm tired. I'm exhausted. Not only from the walk, but from ... this." She nodded at the nature around them, the stark orange sky, the stunning Arctic landscape in the twilight. "It takes a lot of energy to process the world without technology, to organise my thoughts without tabs. I will tell you everything tomorrow. I promise."

Bas lay down on the cape, next to her.

"I remember my first days without tech," he said. "Permanent dizziness, insecurity, a feeling of helplessness … it's tough. Dancing saves me every day." They lay down, side by side, staring at the sky, making out the stars in the white summer night. "You need to find your own way to cope." A subtle whoosh from the Arctic Ocean filled the gaps between their silence. "I'm tired too. We both need sleep." The questions had stopped. A nice surprise. She could rest. For now. "It's cold, and it's not even winter. We should have brought a tent." He turned the other way. "Goodnight, Hildr."

The wind whistled against the mountains.

The sea sang its lullaby.

Her confusion was real. She felt vulnerable, exposed, at the mercy of the elements. She had to find the farmers. Her story was so implausible, she had to keep it hidden. The girl who could end world hunger. Ula had to trust her; she had to believe Hildr was on the farmers' side. Repeat a lie often enough, and you end up believing it.

Bas's breathing became deeper. Hildr turned towards his back, shielding him from the northerly wind. She tried to guess the dreams inside his head.

A man surrounded by white sheets.

In the morning, she woke up to rhythmic, muffled sounds. Ripped strips of gauze floated in the light-blue sky. Bas was dancing by the waterline, slowly twisting his torso, pulling his hands up in the air, one by one, down and up again, in a circular motion, full of expression and pathos. He stepped on his tiptoes, bringing his knees up to his chest, then ran, arms open wide, quivering, a flamingo landing on the water.

Turning, Bas spotted her.

Watching.

He spun a full circle and pretended to fall.

The dancing had stopped.

"The jogger was here," he said.

He was on his knees, leaning over a lump of black sand. Hildr got up from the padded cape and walked over.

Bas traced a path in the air with his finger, along the seafront. "Do you see the footsteps?" She lengthened her tall neck, following the line drawn by his finger. "Fresh and well defined. From this morning. He was running along the shore and stopped briefly here to look at us, while we were sleeping. Sinister."

"Who's the jogger?" she asked.

Bas grimaced. "We reckon he lives somewhere along this beach, near the gorge. We see him every day, running in his tattered tracksuit. Long grey hair, long grey beard, arms folded. He usually runs away when we try speaking to him, never gets too close."

"He runs every day? Where does he get the energy from?"

"There are different theories. Some say he's a penniless hermit living on the mountain, scavenging abandoned subs for dead bodies to eat. Others say he's a rich, eccentric, corporate citizen who came to retire at the end of the world."

"Which way is the old town?"

When she closed her eyes, she still saw the steep narrow streets, the colourful houses with handwritten signs, the dusty road finishing on a black beach.

Bas was staring at her.

"Town? What town? There's the migrant removal centre and the residential block for guards and cleaning staff, nothing else." Hildr felt a fluttering in her stomach. Bas was still looking at her. "Now you really need to tell me your story," he said. "Fyr's old town was destroyed before I was born. Where have you been for the last eighteen years?"

Hildr kept a lid on her mental turmoil, rubbing her forehead, straightening her back.

"Sorry ... it's too early. My ... my head isn't working properly. I think I dreamed it. I know the town isn't there any more, of course. Let's carry on." She ran back to the capes, packed their things, handed him the rucksack and set off, rushing.

How come she hadn't remembered?

Why was the old town so vivid in her memory?

The lack of tech was messing with her brain.

The jogger's footsteps carried on, along the coast. After a curved beach section, they could finally see the tallest mountain on Fyr. The Beranger volcano. Not long to go now. She strolled ahead of Bas, avoiding him. The ground under their feet turned into a basin of cooled magma. Man-sized rocks grew into solid walls. The path was blocked except for a narrow passage ahead. Hildr plunged in sideways, twisting her hips, fighting the claustrophobia of being surrounded by rock. Light came through. She heard Bas behind her, entering the passage. Less of a struggle. He was so thin.

Close to the exit, she stopped and gasped.

In front of her, soared a cathedral of bleak natural beauty, a hall holding a vast expanse of dark water sheltered from the Arctic Ocean, vitreous green at the edges and ominous grey in the centre, mirroring the barbed outline of the mountain surrounding them.

"The Dead Whale's lagoon," Bas said, reaching her. "Isn't it incredible?"

The ground around the lagoon was covered in rocks filled with exploded bubbles, gas once trapped in magma that had burst into millions of tiny craters, turning the bedrock into a perfect lunar landscape. Clinking sounds replaced their previously muted steps on the sand, the tinkling of pebbles amplified by tall walls. Traversing the narrow rim around the lagoon, Hildr noticed a black shard shining brighter than the others, glassy surface reflecting the sky's hues among dull grey detritus. The shard was too large, too straight, too polished to have come out of a volcano. She got closer. Many similar effigies had been erected in other islands. This one was written in Fyr's dialect and translated into English:

We too shall flow into the water we've stolen from the glaciers.

Feeling a sense of bereavement, she walked around the dark lagoon slowly, without speaking. She lent Bas a hand, helping him to cross a long tongue of water. As she delivered him to the other side, she looked down. Soft ripples formed over a ghost buried underwater. White vertebrae stretched from the surface far into the depths.

"The whale," Bas said. "Amazing, isn't it? I always thought they looked like the bones of a dragon."

She was hypnotised.

"It's giving me goosebumps," she said.

"Flesh is much creepier than bones. I've found dead people inside submarines, purple and blotched like blobfish."

Hildr frowned, taken aback. "Why are you telling me this?"

He was trying to shock her.

"Are you scared of death?" he said. "We're made of flesh and bones, not artificial neural networks and alloys. When we die, we'll rot with the nature around us. No cremation or alkaline hydrolysis on Fyr, just natural composting. Small human bones dangling alongside the old whale."

Dryness scraped at the back of her throat. No technology meant no instant diagnosis, no medicines dropped by drone, no virtual doctors, no active prevention. Why would someone refuse science and technology and return to the dark ages? A plank had been laid down across the last sandbar in the Dead Whale's lagoon. Bas's turn to help her. Hildr took his hand, their joined arms reflected in the dark water below; the glacier's tomb, a streamer connecting past and present.

They stepped out of the cathedral together.

The Uskanian school for Devs, excerpt from award-winning documentary

The teachers pull open the blinds. Three emblematic scenes from the creation of Uskania are revealed on the large, stained-glass windows. The unification referendum, bringing the Nordic islands together as a single nation; the launch of the USK software, with its powerful AI engine; an incubator with nova babies opening in delicate, tulip-like petals.

Here, at this boarding school in Reykjavik, genetically engineered citizens (or "nova" people, as Uskanians call them) learn to perform the few jobs still needed by their advanced-tech society. They will become software developers, data scientists, drone and infrastructure supervisors, high-end tourism managers. In the Devs' wing, nova teenagers study fermion computing, machine learning, and traditional software development. These students will one day be responsible for maintaining the AI model at the heart of the USK software and ensuring that future generations have enough food. For outsiders, Uskania is a dystopia. For those attending this school, it's a fully realised utopia. It can be hard to tell the difference.

Chapter Four

(Axel) Shadows

Axel sat in the bathroom cubicle in Fyr's old port building, taste of sick still in his mouth, a sludge of New Food bars frothing in the toilet. What a waste of energy. He kept the cubicle door closed, hearing people coming in and out of the bathroom, footsteps, hand dryers, liquid gushing out, taps, body parts. He wasn't used to this any more. A misanthrope, alright. The label suited him. What was there to like about being surrounded by people? AKA the human plague. He sat quietly in the cubicle, just to be alone, migraine banging behind his eyes, Rodin's Thinker statue rising from the throne.

Why are you always so bitter and miserable, Axel? The past is the past. Look around you. A nice flat in a swanky part of Reykjavik. Chocolate cake slices stacked up on your bedside table. An almost proper job and thousands of people following your videos. A naked woman in your arms. You should be happy. Do you know what happiness is, Axel? Happiness is the ability to look around and be thankful for what you have. He wasn't going to put up with it any more, just to have sex. Fyr. After so many years.

This place messed with his head.

He pulled the cubicle door open, splashed water on his face, put his head under the tap, and shook it like a dog. Looking in the mirror, he saw the whites on black in his parting. Hard to hide. Comb left. Comb right. Older than his years. No escape from this place. Using his sharpest razor, Axel shaved off thin lines where his beard had grown back, a circle split into eight sections re-outlining his Helm of Awe. The Vegvísir tattoo on his arm was always crisp, a talisman guiding him through rough weather. Dark hair. Dark beard. Blue eyes. Brutal jawline. He was a Viking, straight from Norse mythology. Those were the only roots worth remembering.

Carla had asked him to wait. With a little help from the algorithm, he would be matched with Dr Birgit Olsen. From there, it would be up to him to find the kid and Mondo's secrets. The port was jam-packed. Rough sleepers everywhere, on top of chairs, under staircases, crouching in corners. He hadn't slept properly for two nights, but he couldn't rest yet. In the main waiting area, the screen which used to spit out arrival and departure times had turned into a news reel. Videos, memes, pseudo-private messages, each new comment pushing out the last one. As he walked past, a throng of voids gathered for a new video. The bright rectangle beamed a livestream of a white woman dressed in gardening overalls, moving her lips, sound off, subtitles under her chest. Ula Svenson. The leader of the farmers.

They had been raising their game. In April, a shipment of USK tech components had been intercepted by a rogue towboat, laden with explosives. The following month, one of USK's data centres in Greenland had blown up. Ula Svenson claimed both attacks. No one thought the farmers were nutjobs with a romantic view of cow dung any more. They were getting attention, railing against New Food and technology. A little guerrilla distraction. How exciting. No real farms involved, of course. The farmers swallowed New Food, like everyone else.

Axel tapped the buttons on the vending machine. Peanut butter, molasses, oats with berries. New Food energy bars. The flavours were familiar, the ingredients not so much. Everything grown in labs, instead of fields. He found a quiet spot at the back of the east wing, away from the screen, the farthest corner from the wide window overlooking the pier. Less than ten minutes later, a corporate ID number appeared on his tab, auto-completing with name and corporate sponsor.

Dr Birgit Olsen.

Mondo Foods International.

Here we go.

Within a click, Birgit was in front of him. Blonde, pale as a ghost, as if she'd hidden from the sun all her life.

"Do you have children?" she asked him, icy blue eyes staring into the distance.

"Sorry?" he said, startled. "No."

She was sitting on a sofa, in front of a wall covered in scribbles made with white ink. He tried to decipher the scribbles, but Birgit kept rocking back and forth, her bee camera struggling to follow, zooming in and out of focus. Plant drawings, long lines of letters and numbers.

"They live in the present," Birgit said, still not looking at him. "Children." She had the demeanour of someone fleeing a burning house while heavily sedated. "One foot goes in front of the other. They just keep walking. She's done it many times. Her chip was on her bracelet. She didn't mean to remove it?"

Not a real question. Birgit spoke English in an up-and-down staccato, resembling Swedish and Norwegian and making all her sentences sound like questions.

"Can you start from the beginning," he said. "Where were you, when the kid removed her citizen-chip?"

Birgit didn't answer. She just stared ahead, unseeing, transfixed. A low whistling noise arrived from the room where she was sitting. Unverified videos and photos popped up, showing her location. Wide lobby hall. Long wooden table. Colourful murals with trees, rainbows, and artsy-fartsy nature. People sprawling in a garden, smoking, red-glazed eyes. One of Fyr's famous communes. Maybe she was stoned. Not necessarily a bad thing. The quicker he got his hands on Mondo's research, the faster he could leave.

"She's free to roam," Birgit said. "She had a tracker. I always find her in the end?"

Not a question either.

"Was the kid alone?" he asked.

Birgit rocked back and forth.

"So many questions ... The other Finder didn't get anywhere either. I'm tired of questions. She's not a *void*. What a horrible word. She's only seven."

Carla hadn't mentioned another Finder.

Birgit lowered her head. Hair the colour of straw covered her eyes. Her shoulders started moving rhythmically, gently. She was crying. She stayed like this, head down, for a long time, a strange yellow orb on his tab.

"I can't look after her," Birgit said, sobbing quietly.

"I'm coming to meet you. Don't worry, we'll find her. I'm the best Finder in Uskania."

"Thank you."

"Hej dåu."

Goodbye.

Axel pulled his tab up.

He didn't like voids. If tracking technology interfered with their freedom, they should get the hell out of the islands. But a kid?

An old woman stared at him. She was sitting on the floor, long red earrings dangling below a bob of white hair, holding a half-eaten energy bar. No tech.

"Finder arsehole," the void said.

Loud chewing, teeth-sucking noises.

Axel adjusted his earphones, got up, and walked away. He fished his bottle of reclaimed water from his rucksack, refilling it by the fountain. Voids hated Finders. Crushing their bohemian dreams of a tech-free world, alright. Rules were for everyone. Why would they live among citizens, use their public services, eat their food? Deporting voids was the payoff for everyone following his channel, the reward for citizens depending on the AI. *Wear the chip and toe the line.* Resources were limited, and fairness didn't owe anything to the human species.

But a kid?

Outside the port, the sun stood midway in a sea of pink, velvety stillness. Too hot for wits. A map on his tab showed the route to Birgit's commune. Against the grey tarmac, another tab paraded digested news of Mondo Foods. More vertical food labs. Crop enhancements. Gene editing. The contract to provide New Food to Uskania. Why did people get so worked up about lab food? Mondo creations may have been vile, but better New Food than No Food. He couldn't find any information about Dr Birgit Olsen and her research. Made sense, if it was secret. Articles referred to the building in Svalbard as the Doomsday Vault. *Dated name, folks.* Doomsday was here.

A familiar sight hit him in the face, like bad breath. Fyr's old town. Where he used to play with the other kids, queue for the soup kitchen, steal from well-off sellers. Nothing looked the same. On the pavement, tall metal racks held three-wheeled titanium skeletons with paint peeling off. E-bikes. The wasteland behind the town hall had been partitioned into narrow square roads and lined with brightly coloured prefabricated houses in corrugated iron. This ghastly architectural style featured in every video about Fyr. Above the doors of the colourful houses, quaint wooden tablets with cryptic names. *The Mullets. The Firefighters. Queer Company. Mari's Friends.* The famous Fyr communes. The names were hand-painted in delicate fonts, adorned with fancy drawings of leaves, flowers, and twirling twigs. Suited the neo-hippies living in the slum.

A crowd of voids gathered along the road, loitering by a compost bin. On Fyr, voids weren't scuttling away and hiding, as they did on the other islands. They were being helped by citizens and walking around without a care. Axel activated a filter on his tab. The group by the composting bin spiralled into a throbbing mass of yellow-tinged pixels, squeezing into vertical lines, and virtually disappearing from his tab. Everyone without a citizen-chip was gone. Only thin vertical stripes in mustard yellow remained. The street looked much better now.

After a long steep stretch, Axel turned into a secondary road. The commune where the food scientist lived was at the edge of town, next to the dark slopes of the Beranger. Further up the hill, as the slope peaked, three people queued up across the road. A woman wearing a long, white dress, and two middle-aged twins standing in front of her, next to a white "X" on the pavement. Drone collection point. The woman stared at Axel with a weird Mona Lisa smile, squinting. Something was off.

Axel gasped for air.

A blow bent him in half.

Thin, mustard-coloured lines whirled around him, pulling at his rucksack. More blows. He fell to his knees. A yellow line ripped the rucksack's strap off his shoulder, kicking him on the side of his ribs. Rolling on the ground, Axel shielded his face.

When he finally removed the filter, it was too late. The voids were gone.

The woman in white crossed the short steps separating them, kneeling next to him. Her public ID beamed on his tab.

Jen, twenty-eight years old, artist, Fyr.

"Are you okay?" she said. "Don't worry, they just wanted your bag."

Food, water, stun gun, a set of extra tech, clothes. Everything he had brought with him for the trip was in that rucksack.

Axel sat up, rubbing his back, sore. "Did you see where they went?"

"No," she said. "They target citizens from other islands."

He felt his face getting hot. Only USK citizens could see his public ID, including the fact that he was from another island. Had she given him away?

There was a buzzing noise from above. Whirring at speed, a drone flew over their heads. The twins jumped up and down, doing mock-claps with their hands. Descending towards the "X" on the pavement, the drone tilted left and right, rotor blades creating a whirlwind. The woman gathered the fabric of her white dress, holding it tightly between her legs. The plastic box dropped on the cross with a dry thud. Lunging forward, the twins cut the cable ties, opened the zig-zag flaps. They passed around four parcels and a piece of paper. The woman took two of the packages and held out the paper towards Axel.

"This is not mine," she said.

"It's not mine either," Axel replied.

She touched his stomach with the paper and slid her eyes in quick sideway movements, like a deranged chameleon. "Should I drop it on the floor, or are you going to take it? I don't want any trouble."

He looked down at the small card. A familiar symbol. Red circle and pitchfork. The farmers' logo, with the words "JOIN US" underneath. The woman shoved the paper against his midriff and rushed down the slope. The twins had also started walking away, one slightly ahead of the other. Axel collected the paper from the ground. An actual https:// link was handwritten on the back. Was this the farmers' idea of analogue advertising? He didn't like the look of it. First, the robbery. Now, an advert. He wondered if someone was watching him, besides the AI. A couple of e-bikes went past on the road below. Axel pushed the card inside his back pocket and continued uphill.

The last house at the top was painted in blue and yellow stripes. The wooden panel above the door announced *Our Blue Boat Home* and included a childish drawing of a sail-boat within an oval frame.

Birgit Olsen lived here.

Winds from the north sent a chill down his spine.

He knocked at the door.

Through the corner of his eye, he saw a shadow shifting against the mountain.

The forest for the wheat: Interview with Dr Zhang, Tree Lovers Radio

Tree Lovers Radio (TLR): Dr Zhang, can you explain the New Food switch and how China is doing with our land use targets?

Dr Nina Zhang (NZ): The New Food switch is a set of international land use measures and food production guidelines to reverse global temperature rises. The measures include phasing out livestock, building more New Food labs, and converting 75% of agricultural land into forests. In China, we're about halfway to meeting our land use targets.

TLR: Do you agree with those who say we can capture carbon from the atmosphere?

NZ: No, not really. How many Chinese carbon-capture unicorns must fail before people understand that forests are our only hope? Trees absorb sunlight, allowing the planet to reflect less incoming light. Without forests, feedback loops will keep getting worse, greenhouse gases will keep increasing, and temperatures will continue rising. Farms must go. We need trees instead.

Chapter Five

(Hildr) Rain

Clouds grew darker and thicker, a low ceiling over their heads. The wind crept in, an insidious guest. First disguised as cool breeze; then whipping and hindering their steps, making their padded capes flap, like sails pushed in the wrong direction. Against the clouds, prodding the sky, an uncanny object rose from a cliff. A wooden cross. Human artefact, in the absolute wilderness.

"I bet it was someone's last will," Bas said. "We used to have a cemetery. My grandmother was buried there after the purge."

The purge. Hildr wondered if that was how locals referred to the dramatic events from eighteen years before. She remembered the quaint communes, the volcano rising behind Birgit's greenhouse, the passage between neighbours' houses leading to the beach. And now, what was left? An island purged of its citizens, just a handful of voids and new migrants waiting to be deported.

Hildr stopped in front of the wooden cross, with its core of rusty wire firmly stuck into a pile of rocks, overlooking the Arctic Ocean.

"I'm sorry to hear about your grandmother," she said.

"The cemetery is gone. Thawed permafrost caused a landslide. Bones from old corpses surfaced on the road."

"You have a fascination with corpses."

"Are you not fascinated by these old bags of flesh and bones? People with technology can pretend to be disembodied. Not us." He turned to Hildr, eyes sharp as swords. "Why are you here? Don't lie to me. Don't fret, and don't postpone again. I'm tired of waiting for your story. *Who* are you? I'm helping you find your way to the farmers, aren't I? You can trust me. I won't tell a soul."

The moment she'd been dreading had arrived. Bas had told her so much. He had shared his food. She had to give him something. But how much?

"Have you ever met a Dev?" Hildr asked.

His livid face wasn't a good sign.

"What? No. I think most of them live in Reykjavik?"

Hildr spoke slowly, as if soothing an animal, diffusing the focus from the words themselves. "I've ... I've lived at one of the Devs' boarding schools for a while. I've learned a lot about the USK software and the AI model."

"You lived with the Devs?"

His eyes were scary now. Wide, stern, accusing. His body language had changed, signalling huge tension and doubt.

"They ... they took me in, when I was a little girl."

"Why?"

"I ran away from home, and USK looked after me for a while."

"I've never heard of Devs looking after anyone. They care only for their own interests."

"That's not true. They are kind people, dedicated to looking after citizens."

"Are you out of your mind? Genetically enhanced humans created by an AI model? They're closer to machines than to us."

This was not going well. She couldn't disprove so much misinformation in a casual chat.

"Think about it," she started. "USK gives citizens everything they need to survive. There are no jobs left, no money to be earned. This makes citizens feel like children. Who do children rebel against first? Parents. The very people who are trying to protect them. It's human nature, don't you see? You strive for independence, you can't have it, you rebel. That's why people hate Devs, technology, and the model."

She realised the double meaning of her words too late. He had also rebelled against his father.

"I can't believe it. You're helping the Devs, aren't you?" Bas said. "You're here to catch the farmers."

He was pacing back and forth. Angry.

"No," she said.

"How come you have no tech? Where were you before? How did you travel to Fyr?"

"I'm not sure," she said. "I'm having trouble ... remembering things."

Bas squinted. "What do you mean? What do you remember?"

Hildr examined the ground under her feet, yellow moss erupting from crevices on the rock. She saw the prison guard with the language of a bureaucrat and the minutiae of a taxidermist, collecting her citizen-chip, headphones, cameras, health nodes, laying them on a square metal tray, a pool of blood forming around the small, sharp pin that had just been removed from her head.

The clothes too. Take them off. They're going to generate unwanted attention. I'll get you new clothes, from one of the migrants. Don't worry about the tattoo. Ula will see it and know you're telling the truth. Are you okay? I know it's not easy. Let's repeat it together. USK looked after you. You became a Dev. You turned against the AI and were kicked out. While you were waiting for deportation, you managed to run away to the beach. Tell Ula how you escaped from Fyr eighteen years ago. She will be excited to finally meet you.

Hildr closed her eyes, focusing inside herself.

"I remember going into a tiled room. Water pouring over my head. I remember a woman squatting next to me, urinating. Lots of women around us. Naked."

She would never forget them. Sullen, silent, resigned.

"A communal shower?" Bas sounded expectant. "They have communal showers in the removal centre. What happened afterwards?"

She opened her eyes. Bas was looking at her, listening attentively, brown eyes wider than ever.

"The water stops, and someone touches my arm. A different woman, fully dressed, in a grey uniform."

Bas's eyes shone. "Yes. A light grey jumper with a blue logo on the chest. That was my parents' uniform."

He believed her.

She continued. "I follow the woman in uniform, into a room filled with buckets and mops. She hands me a pair of trousers and a vest. I put them on." She looked down at her clothes. This part was true. "The woman points at a wheelchair, in the corner. I'm not sick, I tell her. I don't need a wheelchair. She insists. The wheelchair seat is too small for me. I feel trapped. My knees stick out at an awkward angle."

"I can see that happening."

Her story was convincing.

"The woman opens the door," Hildr continued, more confidently, "goes behind the wheelchair, and pushes me out of the storage area. I hold my breath. She starts running, accelerating down a corridor. We do a sudden U-turn. We almost smash against a wall. She brings me through a side door, out of the building. A van is parked in a walled precinct outdoors, with the back doors open. The woman wheels me into the van. There's a strong, chemical smell of heavy-duty laundry. The doors slam shut, the tyres screech. Someone had held the clutch for too long. I can't see who's driving. A flattened cardboard box has been wedged in, hiding the driver's cabin. After a few minutes, the van stops. I see daylight and a group of people in the distance, by the shore, dancing."

"That's us!" Bas was nodding along, like an excited child. "You ran away from the detention and removal centre yesterday, before you met us at the beach?"

"Yes, I think so." Sprinkling bits of truth was easy, and they made her story feel authentic.

"And before the removal centre, you remember the Devs' boarding school?"

She slumped down on the rock, next to the wooden cross, looking out to the sea.

"Somewhere in Iceland. It's all a haze, memories jumbled together, timelines blurring."

She saw the square metal tray again and the metal pin covered in blood. It was safer for her not to remember more details about what she had seen at the Devs' school.

"Your memory problems sound more serious than the typical hangover of the first days without tech," Bas said.

Hildr raised a hand to her scalp, where the pin had gone in.

Bas squatted next to her.

His eyes refocused.

"What's this?" He leaned on her shoulder, fumbling between her cornrow braids. "Can you stay still, please?" His fingers tickled behind her ear. "Here," Bas announced. "Can you feel this bump?" Her skin crawled. "It's a scar," he said. "And you have dried blood on your hair, around it. Do you remember hitting your head during your wheelchair escape? Wait ... I know *exactly* what happened."

"Do you?"

"They did a procedure on you." He spoke deliberately, as if explaining something important. "USK doesn't want you to remember."

Hildr was dumbfounded.

"Why would they do that?"

"You've committed a crime, obviously. A serious one. My father told me about criminals who've had procedures. USK deported them and they couldn't even remember why. What do you actually remember?" Hildr kneeled on the ground, hands on her head. "Do you remember what day is your birthday? Do you remember what you had for lunch before yesterday?"

A criminal. Kicked out by the model. That was the story she was supposed to tell Ula. The amnesia was the emptiness bringing everything together.

"I remember the boarding school in Iceland," she started. "Tall windows, stained-glass murals." Her voice was soft, with a tinge of hope. "Children everywhere. I can't see their faces, but I remember the sea at the end of the road, and the mountains behind Reykjavík, near the old airport." She was looking right through Bas, as if he were made of air. "I remember Fyr too, from many years ago. Steep streets, colourful houses."

"The old town?" Bas said. "Are you from here? Do you remember family or friends? Are you related to Ula?"

Hildr gazed at the cross, the promontory, the ancient fjords.

"They're not real memories ... they're more like dreams, hints, scraps of emotion. I close my eyes and I perceive sights, tastes, places, and these memories affect me; they make me happy and excited, or sad and apprehensive, but I don't know where the emotions are coming from." She closed her eyes and visualised the greenhouse, Fyr's mountains, like tall banners hanging from the sky, impenetrable. Further away, the volcano emerged as a white after-world.

Bas touched her hand. "Don't worry about the past. You can start again now."

Hildr scowled. "I don't want to start again."

"You're a criminal kicked out from the model and dumped on a remote island to be deported. Why wouldn't you want to start again?"

Thunder growled against the sky.

No time to answer.

The clouds opened, releasing a curtain of rain so cold and merciless, it made her question the whole journey. They ran down the hill, breathless. Thick droplets opened craters on the sand. Nowhere to take cover. They leaned against the mountain, side-by-side, panting against the drumming of rain. Hildr threw her wet cape over their heads.

"It'll make a roof," she said.

"We should have brought a tent. I told you the tents were waterproof. But no, you didn't listen, you never do. You just keep rushing forward, like a headless chicken."

Hildr bent her legs and lowered herself to his level, smoothing out the cape above their heads. The rain was unforgiving. Their fabric-cum-roof was soon drenched. Icy water ran down her neck, creeping inside her clothes.

"Great time to berate me." She lifted her heels inside the trainers, pressed them down with a slosh. "Perhaps if you hadn't stopped so many times to rest or to dance, we'd be somewhere up the mountain by now, taking cover."

Bas's mouth was ajar.

"Do you know a place to take cover? Go ahead, run all the way up and take cover, be my guest! I've never been welcome in your little trip anyway. If you don't appreciate my company, I'm going back to the camp."

Hildr gave him a scornful glance. "That's perfect. You're leaving now?" He was being dramatic on purpose.

"Of course not. When the rain stops."

"The sky always clears after the storm." She was calling his bluff.

"I guess you don't need my food either?" He removed an energy bar from his bag and held it right in front of her nose. *Strawberry Delight.*

"I'm not hungry," she said.

She was starving.

"Here." He snapped it in two, handing her half.

She smiled.

They stayed under the cape, teeth chattering, shoulders shaking, munching. Their roof was pointless. A cold, wet bog. A small waterfall gushed down the mountain.

Slowly, the light went from cool blue to the deep red tinge of dawn.

The thunderstorm moved farther, behind the gorge.

"We need to get our clothes off," Bas said.

His voice was croaky. He might be catching a cold.

"How d...d...do we go up...p...p?" Hildr's jaws rattled away at the consonants.

She didn't want to remove her clothes, even though she was freezing. They had to keep going.

"I have a rope but no harness," he said. He had changed his mind about coming. A bluff. She knew it. "Shall we get some rest first? The rain is easing off."

"Rest?" she said. "Again?"

"People rest every day, you know."

"We slept just a while ago."

"No, that was like ... sixteen hours ago," he said.

She shuffled away from the rock, keeping the cape above their heads.

"We're drenched," she said. "How are we going to rest like this?"

Bas shifted closer to her, touching her arm. "Perhaps you could hug me, like last night. Or we could do something more fun to pass the time ..."

A twinkle in his eyes.

Hildr jumped back.

"How old are you?" she said.

The padded cape fell on his face.

"None of your business," she heard Bas saying from under the sodden cape. She hadn't expected this either. "One of the perks of becoming a void is getting rid of pointless labels," Bas's muffled voice continued. "What you see is what you get, do you know what I mean? How exactly does my date of birth define my suitability for sex? Age is a pointless construct in our circumstances, you have to admit. We have no duties, no rights, no social constraints. You're a convict. You should enjoy yourself while you can."

Was he serious?

"I don't think sex is a good idea right now," she said.

He pushed the cape aside, hair all over his face. "I'll be right here. Just tell me if you change your mind." His eyebrows moved up and down.

"Okay, I'll do that."

Water rolled down her temples.

She felt like smiling but forced herself to keep a straight face.

The rain was relentless, and he was impossible.

Also funny, kind, and generous.

They were much closer to the Beranger now. She could see the white peak clearly. When the rain stopped, they would share another energy bar and head up the mountain together. That sounded like a plan. She couldn't believe a void was helping her.

USK 2.0 launch conference, Keynote speech

This year, the model is better than ever. Food for all, a safe place to live, and the ability to live your own dreams. That's what we voted for when we got rid of the last politician. And that's what the Devs focus on, day in and day out, to achieve our vision. Today, we unveil USK 2.0, our second major iteration. We followed our three core principles: collect data, focus on citizens, do the right thing for the planet. Remember how it used to be? In the dark ages. People got sick, and doctors drained out the bad blood. The world got warmer, and businessmen sold more air con units. Nowadays, we have ubiquitous sensors, artificial intelligence, and fermion computing. We can measure, record, predict, improve, ad infinitum. *Our data model will eventually become flawless. Do the right thing for the planet, and our future is bright.*

Chapter Six

(Axel) The commune

T he man who opened the door had greasy hair and dark rings under his eyes. His public ID announced *Bil, twenty-five years old, musician, Fyr.* Behind him, a flash of white cupboards, cooking paraphernalia lining the walls, a large aluminium sink. A kitchen. What's a commune without a kitchen? Even when there's no need to cook any more.

Bil looked expectantly at him.

Axel, thirty-two years old, freelancer, Iceland.

"Dr Birgit Olsen asked me to come," Axel said, hoping this would be the golden ticket.

"Jah, man," Bil said. "We have a rule. Guests wearing technology must turn their cameras off inside our house."

Guests wearing technology. It was the Wild West.

"Okay." He would play cowboy.

Bil took a step back, letting him in.

Axel's eyes adjusted to the darkness. A foam mattress stood upright against the window, its dense padding dimming the light from outside. A long wooden table had been pushed to the corner, with broken benches stacked on top. Next to the table, a grimy sofa, innards exploding. From behind the table, mattress and sofa, a dozen scraggy people emerged. Axel felt the hairs on the back of his neck rise. No public IDs. He noticed their bare ears, wrists, necks. Voids. Wearing long dresses in bright patterns, holding glasses and bottles.

"These are our guests," Bil said. "One bad word and you're out, jah?" Axel held his tongue. The voids dispersed into the kitchen, settling back into what had probably been their positions before he'd knocked at the door. "Grab a beer, man." Bil pointed to a fridge at the end of the kitchen counter.

Alcohol wasn't his thing, but he felt the urge to be polite. *Blend in.* The dishwasher was ajar. Axel grabbed a glass from the top rack and brought it to his nose. He could smell whisky. A woman wearing a yellow tracksuit with a matching beanie leaned against the fridge. She looked like a bloody cartoon. *Pat, thirty years old, idle, Fyr.* Besides Bil, she was the only other USK citizen in the room. She looked nice, despite the dreadful clothes. Small and compact, big grey eyes, nice round boobs. No other citizen on Fyr had left their occupation as the default 'idle' under the pretence of doing *art*, so he immediately warmed to her honesty.

Pat moved over, making space for him to open the fridge. Unbelievable.

He had never seen this much food before, except in an industrial storage facility. More than a hundred New Food cartons were neatly stacked on shelves, divided according to their coloured labels. A handful of high energy meals (red), two special medical diets (yellow), and plenty of low-energy (blue) and ethical meals (green). He was a red. Shunning bugs on ethical grounds was ludicrous, when everything was fake meat anyway. He'd give unicorns a go if they tasted as good as narwhals.

Pat pulled her tab up and gave him a broad smile.

"What's your question, stranger?"

She was looking straight into his eyes. Creepy.

"I have many," Axel said.

How could they host illegals without any consequence? They were obviously over-ordering food and leaking it to the voids. Messing with the model.

"Are you not here for the oracle?" Pat asked.

Axel pulled out a can of beer and flicked it open.

"I'm here to speak to Birgit."

"She's in her bedroom," Pat said, upbeat. "I knew you weren't from Fyr as soon as you came through the door. Dressing in black in this heat is quite the fashion statement. Is that a Viking symbol on your beard? So picturesque. You have a curious accent too." She squeezed the puppy fat on his arm, below the short sleeve. "And you're well fed, clearly. What sort of freelancing do you do?"

"Gig work, odd jobs," he said.

"What kind of jobs?"

"Painting, electrics, plumbing."

"A plumber all the way from Iceland. Cool."

He didn't understand her excitement. In other islands they had regular ship lines. On Fyr, they may have had more connections between people, but in everything else they were outliers. A glitch on the map. If the island was sucked back into the volcano, Uskania would be all the better for it. The voids around him seemed to be waiting for something. Their whispers got louder, like buzzing mosquitoes. What were they waiting for?

"Did you mention an *oracle*?" Axel said.

"Art foretelling," Pat replied. As if the words made any sense. Her yellow beanie was pushed down to just above her big, grey eyes. Her whole face was a cheerful circle.

"How does that work?" he asked, unsure if he wanted to know.

"We prepare an art installation and open it to visitors on Midsummer's Day. People ask questions. The art answers. It's the tradition. I thought you were here to see it." The happier she looked, the wider the octaves in her musical accent.

"Fascinating." Axel cocked his head sideways, concealing his thoughts. "And what kind of questions do you ask this *oracle*?"

Pat's smile showed him a full line of front teeth. "Anything you want. Do you have any burning questions, stranger?" She was doing that intense look again.

Maybe she was flirting with him.

Honesty required voice-free communication.

"Hosting illegals is a terrible idea. You don't need an oracle to tell you that."

Pat dropped her enthusiastic grin.

"I'm sorry?" she said, with her mouth.

She seemed a nice person, if slightly dim.

"The more you give to them, the less is left for citizens. USK needs to account for every person in the island."

"There's no room for you here," Pat said. "You're a proper dickhead, aren't you? I should have trusted my instincts when I saw you come through the door with those stupid clothes and tattoos."

She pulled her tab down, cutting off their thread.

"Everything alright, Pat?" Bil asked from across the room, noticing her body language.

Pat raised her chin and put her hands on each side of her mouth, like a megaphone. "We need to ask Birgit to stop bringing thugs into our house!"

Hypocrites. People-huggers. He loathed them all. *Find the kid, film Mondo's stuff, get the hell out.* A migraine was flaring up, pain dulling between his eyes.

Axel stumbled into a corridor leading to the entrails of the commune.

Across the corridor, he saw it.

The oracle.

A crowd had assembled in a bedroom, staring at a double mattress, surrounded by bunk beds. Hovering above the mattress, four wooden pillars held a sheet of a translucid, soap-like material. Above it, a web of intricate threads soaked in red paint waved with the wind from fans positioned in each corner. He felt the gentle breeze from the fan facing him. Plastic pipes hung from the ceiling, like a musical instrument. Everyone was mesmerised by the paint dripping from the pipes, then onto the soap layer, enlarging and twisting into spirals as if pulled by an invisible centrifugal force, and sliding down the pillars until a clean, translucid area remained floating above the mattress.

Fourteen people without technology in this room, adding to those in the kitchen. Street cameras must have spotted the voids coming into the house, and yet the software wasn't cracking down on the commune. It was exactly as Carla had said.

The crowd gasped. A line of red paint had pierced through the soap, falling on the bed. The double mattress was already covered in similar lines, like an abstract canvas. *Art foretelling*. What a bunch of lunatics. Axel endured the circus, shifting his weight from foot to foot. An old woman stood next to the mattress, wiry white hair, head tilted backwards, hands gathered at her chest. Bringing her head forward, she opened her eyes.

White corneas, like a zombie.

"The oracle spoke again," the woman started, a mere scratch of a voice, "answering your question about the … floating devices. Did you call them buoys? They're not buoys. Buoys are beacons of hope. The devices they're putting around our beaches are weapons. They kill."

Another woman came forward, in boots and overalls, shaved head contrasting with neatly arched brown eyebrows. "Fyr is the only island putting up a fight."

It took Axel a few seconds to recognise the face without the hair framing.

Ula Svenson, the farmers' leader. What a special den this was.

"When USK installed buoys around the other islands, there was no objection," Ula continued. Blue eyes, wide jaw, the same steely look she had in the videos. "We're the only ones who understand what they're doing." She left theatrical silences between her sentences. The crowd was in thrall to her. "First, they split us into citizens and voids, trying to control us through technology. They will not stop there." Solemn, addressing the whole room. Her voice became louder. "Uskania made a deal with the corporate elites. New Food will bring a further split. The elites are hiding our old food in secret farms and pushing New Food to those who can't afford anything else. Those who eat New Food will have no minds of their own. It will spread through your blood, your heart, your brain. You'll be under their control, following their commands like puppets."

Interesting. She believed New Food did something to people's brains. He usually just got a bad gut.

"How can we fight them?" A man asked.

Ula's eyes sharpened, her thin lips pressed more tightly together. "Remove your citizen-chip and join us. We're building a farm on Fyr. Old food will sustain us. Everyone is welcome, if you're willing to work hard."

Another blob of red paint fell on the mattress in two long streaks. The woman with cataracts lifted her hands and waved them in the air. "The oracle spoke! It's true! See how the paint fell in two halves? There's going to be a further split among us."

Axel felt sick.

Beer rumbled in his stomach.

Enough.

Stepping back into the corridor, he saw a closed door, leading deeper into the commune. He knocked briefly, and let himself in.

Dr Birgit Olsen sat cross-legged on a beige sofa, white tunic hanging in folds around her lap, blonde hair damp and scraped back. Behind her, plant drawings covered a big sketching wall, the same one he had seen during their call. The number 37,243 had been circled with incandescent chalk, surrounded by strange patterns and formulas. To his left, a cabinet with white drawers and a low table covered in empty New Food cartons. To his right, a kid's bed draped with soft toys. Heavy curtains drowned the pink light from outside, projecting warm undertones onto piles of mattresses, cushions and boxes scattered on the floor. There were cardboard boxes stacked in every corner. Dozens and dozens of boxes.

"I'm glad you found us," Birgit said. Her skin was pale and dry, with a roughness to it. "Did you visit the oracle?"

Clues to Mondo's research might be all over her bedroom. Perhaps even the boxes were important. They looked like junk.

"Yeah, saw it," Axel said, releasing his bee camera and taking a step forward to hide it behind his back.

"Don't mind our foolish ways. The oracle is an excuse to gather, drink, express our fears. I see you have a beer already. Have a seat."

Have a seat. Where exactly? He looked at the glass tubes inside the cardboard box by his feet. Seeds. Rice and cassava. Crop history and DNA sequences appeared on his tab, leaf and root morphology, places where rice and cassava still grew, best time for the harvest. He stepped over the box, careful to keep the bee camera behind his back, kicking a cushion out of the way, prodding a pile of mattresses with his other foot, allowing the camera to capture everything.

Birgit looked at him through half-closed eyes. "Are you okay?" she said.

"How many people live here?"

"More than the mattresses ... As many as in a whole street in the place where you come from." Lethargic, slow, sedated. Definitely on drugs. She didn't seem to notice a thing.

Axel became bolder, sending the bee camera to peek above his head, filming the wall behind the sofa.

"We have voids in Iceland, but we don't keep them at home."

"We don't segregate on Fyr," she said. "Everyone is welcome. Your national programme is too harsh on people without a citizen-chip."

"You work for Mondo Foods, right? What do you do, exactly?"

A low whistle sounded in the room, the same as he'd heard during their call. It was coming from the wall behind her. Birgit unfolded her legs and placed her bare feet on the floor, head level with his waist. A new tab fired up. Before he could dismiss it, a video of a blonde sucking his dick started playing.

Terrible time for predictive porn.

As if she knew, Birgit shook her head.

"I can't wait for her." Her voice broke.

Axel sat at the other end of the sofa.

Not again.

Birgit was crying.

"Were the voids here, when the kid disappeared? They might have something to do with it," he said.

"She left on her own."

"Why would a kid do that?"

"It was my fault," Birgit said. She pulled her feet up to the sofa, pressed her forehead against her knees. "I never wanted children. I was sterilised in the first wave. Never had the urge to become a *mother*."

Axel winced at the word. "How did you get custody?"

"We found her as a baby, me and the others, those who lived at the Blue Boat at the time. On Fyr, people move often between communes. *Shaking up the water,* they call it. I stay because of my plants. It was hard enough building the greenhouse, let alone carrying it from home to home.

"One evening, we went for a midnight walk. None of us could sleep with the heat. When we got to the beach, someone noticed a bundle on a dune. A blanket from a rough sleeper? A carrier bag? We got closer. And there she was. Wrapped in a handknitted blanket. No citizen-chip. She just lay there, staring at the sky, eyes full of hope. Four months old, the others reckoned. I only know growth stages for plants. We sat down for a long time, next to her, looking at the mountains, the sea, expecting someone to come back. No one came. Had she been abandoned? She couldn't have been there for a long time and look so contented? Why would anyone leave their baby behind like this?

"We brought her back to the commune and took turns looking after her. We applied for a USK citizen-chip. We made the decision together. *It takes a village to raise a child.* Hildr would have food, home, a future. The software asked questions, did a full medical check-up, analysed her mitochondrial DNA. They told us she'd come from Rwanda and East Africa. Meaningless. We all came from elsewhere. There are over ten nationalities in this house alone. My family is from Sweden. What about yours?"

"I'm from Iceland."

Birgit didn't flinch. "Icelanders would find you too dark for their history. Your family probably emigrated here recently, like many others. Fyr used to be deserted. Now babies grow on the beach." Birgit's pupils contracted to reveal more of her icy blue irises. "Today she probably wouldn't have been allowed into the model. Too many have arrived."

The kid's story was not too different from his own. Except his DNA had come from Scandinavia and the Middle East, and he had been unfortunate enough to meet his real mother. Kids never asked to be born, did they? Frankly, it was a bad choice.

"Since we found her," Birgit continued, "the other flatmates moved out, one by one. I'm the only one left from that time. I kept looking after the baby. Force of habit. Make someone do the hardest thing day after day, week after week, and it becomes second nature, as natural as breathing. I bathed her, fed her, read her bedtime stories. After the first few months, it became something else. Beyond habit, beyond need. Accepting my fate as a mother was ... redeeming. Hildr became the reason for finding a way out of the crisis. A personification of the future. If this child went hungry, it meant everyone was doomed. Does this make any sense?"

Birgit's eyes were red, glazed, as if pleading for forgiveness.

"Maybe," he said.

No fucking clue.

"But in the end, she is her own person," Birgit continued. "I cannot control her, protect her, keep her inside a jar. It's my fault. Our fault." Her guilt had morphed into anger. "Do you understand? Children have no responsibility for the mess we created."

Birgit lowered her head and covered her face with her hands. Her shoulders trembled, her breath became deep and uneven. She was clearly disturbed, but there was something strange about the scientist. She seemed too sorry for herself, and more worried about the food crisis than her daughter. It was as if she'd fallen into a rabbit hole and couldn't climb out of it. Natural or adopted, she was supposed to look after the kid. Whose fault was it when kids ended up on the streets, when they stole and begged for food, when they had nothing to eat at night?

After many rounds of the room, the bee camera slipped back inside Axel's watch.

"Where were you, when she left?" he asked, trying to get her to focus.

"In the lab," Birgit said.

"Can I see it?"

Birgit rubbed her face, lifted her head, stared through him with blood-shot, glassy eyes.

"She's not there," she said, flatly.

"I need to collect more data about the case."

"Data?" Birgit opened a shared tab and retrieved a video. A black, willowy girl, with long bony legs and thick, braided cornrows, played outside the commune, hiding behind a rubbish bin, peeking and smiling at the camera. Cute. "I let her wander in the summer. She likes exploring, visiting other communes, looking at the big ships by the port. I worry only when she heads to the beach. I'm afraid she'll try to join her family, wherever they are."

"What tech did she have on?" Axel said.

"The chip was in a bracelet, which she left behind. She rarely wears the rest. Maybe someone found her, gave her food and a roof. Without the chip, they wouldn't know where she lives."

"You said you hired another Finder. How far did he get?"

Birgit pressed her eyes shut. "What time is it?" Her gaze darted to the wall, then back to Axel. "I need to go." She got up from the sofa and rushed past him, leaving a trail of musky soap. "I can't lose another one." She opened a drawer, rummaging inside.

"Lose another what?"

She pulled out a rucksack and gave it a good shake. Glass vials fell on the floor. Seeds. Tomato. Corn. Black-eyed beans. Grass peas. She emptied the bag onto the kid's bed. High entropy warning on his tab, also known as *a mess*. Cataloguing failed. She walked to the white cabinet, collecting clothes, bits and bobs, stuffing them into the bag she'd just emptied. Axel followed her frenzied ritual from the sofa.

"Are you going somewhere?" he tried again.

She collected a pair of socks from the floor and squeezed them in with the rest.

"Spitsbergen."

The seed vault was in Spitsbergen.

"Are you leaving the kid behind?" He couldn't believe it.

"You don't understand," Birgit said, eyes glazed. "I don't have a choice. This is our last hope. If I don't go now, we're doomed. Billions will die of hunger."

A mad scientist with a messiah complex. Just what he needed.

"And the kid?"

"I have fifty thousand kroner in my savings account," Birgit said. "The money's all yours, if you bring her back here." She slid her feet into a pair of trainers.

She grabbed her rucksack from the floor, flung it on her shoulder and opened the door.

"That's it?" he said. "What about the data?"

"Ask Pat. She has a copy of the central logs."

Birgit closed the door, leaving him alone in the bedroom. Pat. The woman with the yellow beanie, the one he had met by the fridge. The woman who had called him a thug. Pat was supposed to help him. Time to reset their relationship.

Voice-free communication: a small revolution with the new V2105 device, article on TechMonk

CommsQuant today announced the release of the long-awaited Bluetooth Voice-Free Kit V2105. The V2105 comes with a node attaching to the lower eyelid for stye-resistant, durable application. The patented technology relies on users' eye movements to communicate digitally, hands-free and voice-free. The device has 99.89% accuracy in reading eye movements and retrofitting the verbal messages originating them. The new AI engine requires one week of voice communication to establish the personalised eye-to-speech recognition. After initial setup, another week per year is enough to ensure ongoing accuracy in voice-free communications.

Chapter Seven

(Birgit) Rice

I'm on my way. The Finder is in charge. If you're hearing these messages, it's a good sign. It means you're back. I'm sorry I couldn't wait for you. What would you have done, in my position?

You came into the lab and asked for a story. *Play on your own for a while,* I said. The skill to entertain ourselves should not be underestimated. I thought not giving in would make you resilient, and stories are not my strong point anyway. I've always been grounded, like my seedlings. Now you've done a runner, the biggest in your running career. How else can I explain what we found, where I'm going, why I can't wait for you?

Let me tell you a story.

A grain of rice has 37,243 genes. That's twelve thousand more genes than humans. Did you think humans were complicated? Not compared with rice. Can you distinguish the subtle differences in their shape, from the elegant ovals of long-grain rice, to the shorter, plumper Bomba and Arborio varieties? Can you spot the exquisite colour palette available in the rice genome, from black rice to golden rice, from translucid jasmine to snow-white basmati? An artist would take a lifetime to capture the colours of rice. Have you ever felt the hardness of rice's gemstone structure, its resistance to incremental degrees of heat, the way it softens under high steam? Can you imagine starch slowly melting into the soft, delicious texture of boiled rice?

Over two hundred thousand rice varieties once existed on Earth. A catastrophic history led to the handful we have today. Climate breakdown, pests, diseases, wars. Rice used to feed two-thirds of the world. When rice died, people died too. Heads of state met once a year for the rice convention. I read their lips in muted livestreams. *Climate changed too fast ... too little arable land ...* At the end of the conference, the heads of state covered their ears, eyes and hearts, and went back to their corner of the world, carrying fewer bags of rice.

I'm sorry.

That's not a good story, is it?

Let me start again.

Once upon a time, there was a blue-and-yellow dragon-fly who lived in a hot, muggy paddy by the Danube. Rice grows in rice paddies, which are shallow ponds filled with water. The water in the paddies absorbs heat from the sun, keeping rice warm during the night. Besides providing the ideal habitat for rice, paddies are also fantastic homes for many bugs and critters. Close your eyes and imagine this dragonfly with his two pairs of thin, clear wings, doing pirouettes on long swishy leaves, sipping mosquitoes and midges from thick bushes along the riverbanks, dancing punch-drunk in a thick sunset of moths and butterflies. Unfortunately, on a dark and stormy night, the dragonfly was blown away, twisting and rolling in the air, flapping his laced paper wings, swept along by gale-force winds that whooshed him towards the North. Over the Baltic, the dragonfly got stuck in a cloud of rain; above Barents, he caught a lift on a flying carpet; on top of the Arctic, our friend rode on the back of a seagull.

Exactly two days after the storm had struck over the Danube, I was in my lab, here on Fyr, studying a gene controlling gelatinisation and causing starch in rice to break down, when I heard a noise.

Thump, thump, thump.

It was coming from outside.

Blue and yellow shone against the wood.

The dragonfly had landed inside a puddle, on my windowsill.

I opened the window.

"It's cold," the dragonfly said. "Where are your wetlands?"

"We have no wetlands on Fyr," I told him.

"What about rivers?"

"No rivers either." I thought this was obvious, even for a new visitor. "The only freshwater comes from the melting snow in the summer."

"I've been rolling in the wind for a long time. I'm cold and hungry. Please help me."

I had been thinking about rice, so my idea was bound to be rice-shaped. I remembered that a certain breed in my lab, a short Japanese variety, can grow in northern climates. With the dragonfly watching, I dug a ditch inside my greenhouse, filled it with water from the reservoir, and threw in a couple of special Japanese rice seeds. Soon, we encountered a problem. The temperature was fine during the day but got near freezing during the night. A wider basin would have absorbed more heat during the day, but our reservoir didn't hold enough water.

"Can we fill it with sea water?" the dragonfly said.

I laughed at first, but realised he was serious. I explained that rice is extremely sensitive to salt. Saltwater would destroy our paddy.

The blue-and-yellow critter grew desperate.

"I have an idea," I said. "One of the genes in rice controls salt tolerance. If we can tweak that gene, our rice might survive."

I spent hours in the lab. When I had finished, we pumped sea water into the basin. Sunlight warmed the water. The water soaked the soil and warmed the rice. Days passed, and our seeds finally germinated.

Our rice paddy bloomed.

When summer arrived, the miniature wetland was brimming with mosquitoes, water striders and moths. While I tended to my plants, the dragonfly buzzed around, joyful, bumping into my head.

"Thank you," he said.

At the end of summer, when dragonflies have almost finished their lifespan, my blue-and-yellow friend, who had flown from the Danube in the cusp of a storm, a cloud, a flying carpet, on the back of a seagull, grabbed a grain of my special Japanese rice, and flew away with it, over the Arctic Ocean, all the way to the island of Spitsbergen. He found a big vault under a mountain and lay down to rest in front of the gates.

His grain of rice is now one of the seeds in the Svalbard vault, waiting to become a wetland filled with dragonflies.

Important changes to your USK 2.0 user agreement

We're letting you know about important changes we're making to your USK 2.0 User Agreement, including your Citizen-chip Rights and Terms & Conditions. Like most countries signing up to the New Food switch, we did our best to tackle the food crisis following the repurposing of land and the gaps in lab food provision. We've enriched old food crops, planted fruit trees, and reduced food waste. Despite our best efforts, our data model shows that, at current levels of consumption, Uskania has less than two generations before we experience severe food shortages. To mitigate this risk, we have come up with a new set of food allocation and behaviour rules, prioritising children and those who need better nutrition. The alerts you'll see in your USK tabs reflect these new rules. Please do the right thing for the planet and help us make the new changes a success.

Chapter Eight

(Hildr) Tattoo

Hildr and Bas lay side-by-side on the sand, clothes soaked in rain, cold and uncomfortable, drifting between sleep and alertness.

The heavy rain became a drizzle in the early hours.

The sky became brighter, the clouds thinned.

Hildr got up and stretched her back. Something went *click*, slotting into place. Bas was still sleeping. She rubbed the base of her neck and ambled along the beach, removing her socks, trousers, her long tunic, the woollen thermal layer underneath. Dripping wet. She inspected the white tattoo on her leg. *Do the right thing for the planet.* The familiar message. Stooping in her undies, she spread her soaked garments over an upright slab, the drag of the water making the fabric cling to the rock. Then she sat down and waited. After the rain, the sand and the sea had drained of colour. She was surrounded by shades of dark grey.

When Bas stirred awake, Hildr wrapped her wet woollen top around her leg, tying the sleeves over the white tattoo with a knot. He grabbed their capes and his rucksack, making his way to where she was sitting.

She crossed her arms in front of her bare chest.

"Morning," he said. "I'll remove my clothes too, so you won't feel bad."

"I don't feel bad at all."

Her statement contradicted all the evidence. Her teeth chattered, her arms shook with the cold.

"What's that?" Bas was pointing at the woollen top wrapped around her leg.

"I scraped myself on a rock."

"Ouch. Not good news. Let me disinfect it." He lowered the backpack from his shoulder and dropped it on the ground.

"No," Hildr said. The word came out louder than necessary. "Don't worry." She patched up her abruptness. "It doesn't hurt."

Bas searched inside his bag.

"I've been living without health sensors for long enough," he said. "Trust me. Better safe than sorry. You won't immediately know when something is wrong. Even a small scrape can get infected."

"I said *no*."

She didn't want to explain the tattoo.

Bas stared at her, seemingly unable to make sense of the refusal.

"Would it help if I looked the other way?"

"It's okay," she said. "It doesn't hurt."

"I'll look the other way. I promise."

"It's not even a scratch," she said.

Bas looked mystified. "What is it, then?"

"It's ... it's ... a bruise."

"A bruise?"

"Yes. A very small one," she said.

"What colour?"

"I don't know."

Why did it matter?

"And it doesn't hurt?" he repeated.

Hildr nodded vigorously, keeping her arms wrapped around her chest. Perhaps she was being unreasonable. Perhaps she shouldn't worry. She could tell him the whole story. What was she afraid of?

"I think you're lying," he said.

He suspected.

Hildr's cheeks got warmer. "Why would I lie?"

"I know exactly what's happening here."

Bas had that worldly grimace again.

"What's happening here?" she said, rubbing her upper arms up and down, anxiously.

"You're embarrassed," he said. "Because of what I said last night. Don't worry, I won't ask you again. You know what? Now, you'll have to convince *me*."

"Convince you of what?"

"You know what."

Bas shrugged and turned away, strolling in measured steps, head down, as if looking for something that had dropped from his pocket.

Hildr realised why she didn't want to tell him about the tattoo. If Bas found out about her affiliation, he would hate her.

She liked Bas. She didn't want him to hate her.

Her throat tingled.

"Is there any water left in your bottle?" she said.

With his back to Hildr, Bas rolled his jumper over his head and undid his belt. His trousers fell on the ground. Her jaw dropped. His legs. Thin as sticks. His back. Each individual rib visible beneath the skin. Bas loosened the elastic band from his long dark-brown hair and turned towards her. She looked away. Quiet footsteps. Jingling. Sloshing.

He placed the container next to her naked thighs.

They sat together, naked, taking turns to drink from the same water bottle.

Wind swept the clouds aside.

Through the gaps, sunlight reached them.

From the sun's position, Hildr guessed it was near midday.

"I can't wait any longer." She got up from the rock, touched her clothes. Still damp. "How long will it take us to get to the top?"

"A couple of days, I reckon," he said. "I know a footpath, but it doesn't go all the way."

Hildr put her trousers on, removing the woollen top from her leg before pulling them up to her waist. She slid inside her tunic and turned around to face him again.

A flicker of emotions crossed Bas's eyes.

Bewilderment. Confusion. Anger.

He'd said he'd look the other way.

He plunged at her feet, lifting the hem of her trousers.

"What's this?" Her white tattoo was on full display. "What's this?" he asked again. "What's the *right thing for the planet*?" She hesitated between fight and flight modes. Neither was adequate. "Are you a Dev?" No place to hide, no alternative tab. "Are you a developer working for the USK software? Is that why you were at their boarding school?"

She was trapped in her own silence, missing the chance to react fast.

Bas rushed to collect his clothes from the sand.

"You're a bloody informer." Fuming, he hooked his jumper around his neck and thrust his legs inside his trousers. "An undercover Dev trying to catch the last farmers." He seized both capes and the backpack.

Hildr stood in his way, opening and closing her mouth, like a fish out of water.

"I'm not an informer," she said.

Too little, too late.

"It's on your skin! Why would you tattoo their mission statement if you didn't believe in it? It makes me sick. Was it the right thing for the planet to leave almost three thousand citizens on Fyr to starve?"

She didn't understand.

"That's not true. The model was built for citizens. It wouldn't do any harm to them."

"Some of the dancers were here, when the purge happened. USK blew up the old town and left everyone to starve. Hundreds of people panicked, jumped into the water, and never made it to another island. The rest wasted away and died of hunger. I've heard about families committing suicide together ... People scavenged for the dead!"

He had been lied to.

"Who told you that? Ula Svenson? It's not true. USK evacuated all citizens, before cutting off the island."

"First you were silent, then you claimed amnesia, and now you lie. You can't look me in the eye and admit the truth."

Her worst fears had been confirmed. Bas had swallowed their lies. Did he really believe USK would kill citizens? Looking after citizens was the AI model's sole purpose, why it had been created in the first place. Stubborn, pig-headed void.

Hildr clasped her big hands around his shoulders.

"Look at me. My mother was a scientist working at the Svalbard seed vault. Eighteen years ago, she helped Mondo Foods with a secret research project."

She was painfully aware of his cynical glare.

"Are you changing your version of events again?"

"It's the truth."

"This is ridiculous."

"I swear it's the truth. Mondo keeps their research confidential to control global food prices. If we find what they're hiding inside the vault, USK will be able to feed more people."

"Oh yeah? Let me get this right – so now you're saving us from starving? Why didn't you tell me from the beginning? I would have carried you on my shoulders all the way up the mountain." His voice crackled with sarcasm.

"I wasn't supposed to tell you anything, but I can't keep quiet any longer. I'm looking for a bracelet I lost on Fyr. My mother sent me several messages. They are kept in my old chip, in the bracelet. Ula hid it up in the mountain. That's why I must find Ula, why I need to make sure she believes me. I desperately need to get the messages back. Do you understand? If we find Mondo's secret, we can help more migrants."

She was blurting out her arguments as fast as she could.

Bas wasn't in the mood to listen.

"Let me go," he said, pulling away.

She pushed down on his shoulders.

"Please ..."

His feet sank further into the wet sand.

"Stop pinning me to the ground!" His face twisted with anger. "Do you enjoy stepping over the little people?" His messy hair spewed sand. "You've been defending the model since we first met."

He thrashed, kicked, a pipe bursting with too much pressure.

"Why do you see everything in black and white?" she said. "There are no easy answers. The model isn't perfect, but it's the best option we have. By removing your tech, you've disengaged from the world."

"*Disengaged?* Did you say *disengaged?* What was I supposed to do? No schools, no jobs, nothing left to buy. Live lightly and spare the planet! Eat New Food, travel by foot, have no kids! Nothing for me to do, except eat like a bird and dance my head off!"

The screams died in his throat.

"No one can hear you now," Hildr said, still hoping to win the argument. "You disengaged from the world when you removed your chip. You said you wanted to make a difference, but you turned your back on the only solution we know. If every person behaved as selfishly as you, we would still be wrecking the planet."

"*This* is the real world," he shouted, raising his arms. "Do you hear me? This beach, the migrants arriving in their terrifying submarines, this massive wall of rock in front of me. I don't need technology to *engage!*"

He had lost, and he knew it. Only raw anger left.

Bas tried to go around her tall frame. She stood her ground, blocking him. He placed his hands on her chest and pushed hard. How could he not see it? Technology wasn't evil. It was simply a means to an end. Developers had a say over how the data was used. The AI model was the way out of the crisis. She wondered how to steer him back into the argument, how to achieve maximum impact.

"You're just running away, like your father."

Bas pressed his forehead against her sternum and let out a cavernous howl.

And then, it dawned on her – what was she doing?

He controlled nothing except his body.

She couldn't take his freedom away.

Hildr stepped aside. Bas fell on the black sand, on his hands and knees. He got up, grabbed the padded capes, the rucksack, running back to where they had come from, not pausing to look back. She watched him stagger along the shore, until he looked like a thin mirage drifting on the horizon. When she couldn't see him any more, she turned towards the Beranger. The volcano stood proud against the clouded sky. Hidden at the top, the bracelet, and Mondo's secret. She would have to convince Ula and the farmers to give it to her. She could not fail. Too many people depended on Birgit's messages, and the doors they would open.

PART TWO: IT'S ALL ABOUT DATA

On the supremacy of data models: excerpt from lecture at Reykjavik University, by Professor Emeritus Lynda Wiranata

Data models can find patterns, make predictions, estimate hidden factors and enable better decisions. Models have existed for centuries, but their use has exploded with the advent of artificial intelligence, fermion computing, and ultra-fast computer processing speeds. AI models are used in climate projections, finance, linguistics, the military, and many other fields. In our islands, the explosion of sensors and data sources sped up the accuracy of the USK model, allowing us to adjust rules and regulations and achieve the best outcome for citizens. Our success relies on playing with people's heuristics, biases and limitations. People are not machines, and they are not rational. The more we can calibrate our models to the real world, the better they get at helping overwhelmed citizens left behind by a fast-changing world.

Chapter Nine

(Axel) Logs

Axel sat on Birgit's sofa and cleared his throat. "Alright everyone. If you've followed me for a while, you should know there are five steps for finding voids.

"Step one. Find the tech. Did the subject remove every device from their body? The citizen-chip is often the only thing they remove. They see it as a symbol of control. If they still have other tech on, your job is half-done. Cameras, earphones, mics and health nodes all emit online fingerprints and can be traced back to a location. I often come across several unregistered devices in the same area. Voids tend to gather at the edges of cities, like hairs on plugholes. Finding the chip on a cliff could mean suicide, but it could also mean the void wanted it to *look* like suicide. Don't fall for it.

"Step two. Get the central logs. Watch the last videos, the movements, the tabs they browsed. Analyse the themes, the keywords, the concerns. Not the upfront facts, but the details least likely to raise suspicion. Those are the things the void hasn't bothered to cover up.

"Step three. Speak to their acquaintances, neighbours, friends. In that order. Find out the exact time they went void. The time stamp will give you access to reliable data.

You can't trust their friends. Satellites, urban furniture, passers-by are better sources.

"Step four. Put all the data together and use a suitable app to come up with hypotheses. Finder's Glass is rubbish. Skip that one. It wouldn't find a void's knickers even if they were hanging on the clothesline. There are many data platforms available, and you'll find (excuse the pun) Finders swearing by each. Try them out for yourself and decide.

"Step five. Run the hypotheses, follow their leads, go places. Check if the void is hiding in any of them. If they are, congrats. If they're not, try again. Got all that? The job would be easy if you could follow steps. The bad news? It's not. Fuck off if you thought it was easy. A rule book won't make you a good Finder. It will make you mediocre to average, at best. Voids will outwit your formulas. I've caught enough of them to know. Watch and learn. But be quick. Our movements are feeding more data into the model. As we speak, drones are being trained to find voids. USK got rid of the police, law courts, schools. One day this job will go too."

The bee camera flew back into his watch.

This case wasn't going to be straightforward.

He pushed Birgit's sofa aside, revealing the full extent of the chalk drawings. The strange geometric shapes and equations turned out to be genetic annotations about rice. Axel put his ear against the wall. That strange whistle again, like an old steam train trapped inside. He knocked at the plaster. Hollow. A number pad gleamed from the wall. He keyed in Birgit's corporate ID number. Long shot. The pad returned a sad two-note tune.

He inspected the empty New Food cartons on the table. Rice pudding. Loads of rice pudding. If Birgit had been in the model, she would have been nudged to improve her diet. Fifty thousand kroner. How much chocolate cake would that buy him? He could stop the videos, relax for a while.

Axel opened the bedroom door.

Data collection mode.

To the left, the oracle room and the kitchen. Across the corridor, two more doors. A bathroom to his right. At the end of the corridor, opposite the main entrance, a glass door leading to the back garden. The scent of earth was more intense there. Musty. Smudging the glass with his breath, Axel made out a paved stone path running from the back garden door to an outdoor building. Birgit's greenhouse.

He strode across the garden, put his hand on the handle. Locked. Inside, a blur of green. Next to the greenhouse, plants sprouted along the wooden fence and on brass shelves lining the corrugated walls of the commune. Between two shrubs, next to a hanging plant pot, an empty hook.

Dead-end.

He strolled back inside the house, returning to the oracle room. Ula was there, with the rest of the *art foretelling* lunatics. Pat was sitting on one of the bunk beds, arms and chin resting on its metal rails.

Axel sent her a direct message. *"Can I ask the lottery numbers?"*

She jumped off the bunk bed, eyes of a scaredy cat.

"What are you still doing here?"

"Can we speak somewhere private?" he said, voice-free.

"I thought I had asked you to leave." She was cute even when hissing.

Behind her, Ula Svenson droned on about corporate elites and old food hidden in secret farms.

"*I could broadcast this circus. There's a good price on your friend's head.*"

Pat's eyes opened wide, panic on her face.

She attached to Axel's back like a limpet and pushed him inside Birgit's bedroom, closing the door behind them.

"*Who* are you?" she said.

"Birgit asked me to speak to you. I'm looking for her kid."

"Another Finder? That's why you're so weird."

"I kick criminals out of our islands," he said. "You should be thankful for people like me."

"I didn't agree with Birgit's decision to call a Finder, but I respect her wishes. My help is conditional. You'll need to stop referring to voids as criminals."

Woke warrior. Never had to fight in her life.

"Understood," he said. "Where is the other Finder?"

"He quit," Pat said.

"Why?"

"No idea. The case was too difficult, I suppose."

He still wondered why Carla hadn't mentioned this. No amount of data revealed by the algorithm, too much or too little, was casually dispensed.

"How many voids were here, when the kid disappeared?" he asked.

"A few came for the oracle. Several live here."

He had figured that out. Mattresses everywhere, the extra food in the fridge.

"Everyone is a suspect," he said.

Pat took a deep breath. "Did Birgit really ask you to speak to *me*? She must be secretly blaming me for Hildr's disappearance. I was the last one to see her."

"You're not a suspect," Axel said.

"No one in this house would harm her." She scratched under her yellow beanie. "On the day Hildr disappeared, we were playing hide and seek. I counted to ten and she hid, then she counted to ten and it was my turn to hide."

"I know how hide and seek is played."

She rolled her eyes. "I bet you do. Let me finish. While we were playing, someone called me from inside. They were setting up the oracle and needed my help. Hildr's tech had a proximity chime enabled, did Birgit explain that? A sound she heard when Hildr was nearby. We were playing outside, so Birgit didn't pay attention when the chime slipped away."

"Where was Birgit?"

"In her lab."

"Where is her lab?"

Pat looked at him in disbelief. "Right there." She pointed at the chalk board behind the sofa.

"On the wall?" Axel said.

She scoffed. "*In* the wall. Do you have a problem with English prepositions?"

"Birgit said the kid wore the citizen-chip on a bracelet. Where is it?"

"I don't know," Pat said. "We couldn't find it."

"Did you check the logs? Where did the tracker show it last?"

"The last known location was inside the composting bin, on the road outside. We looked in the bin, around it, couldn't find a trace of the bracelet. Someone must have turned off the tracker." She fiddled with her beanie, twisting and patting it around the edges. "Birgit managed to look after the child for seven years without any major incidents. And when I'm with her, *this* happens. Maybe it *was* my fault."

"Did the kid's central logs show anything unusual?"

"Her health signs were stable," Pat said. "No fast breathing, no raised heartbeat, no sign she was unwell."

A professional job. Except she was seven years old.

"Someone must have helped her," Axel said. "The tech wouldn't disappear from the map unless someone knew exactly what they were doing."

Pat shook her head softly, eyes fixed on the ground, then slipped her hand inside the beanie and scratched. No relief from the itchiness.

"I have ... an idea," Pat said.

"An idea?" He repeated.

Pat stared at him.

She snatched the yellow beanie from her head.

A shaved head.

Like Ula.

"Maybe the tech was faulty?" she said.

She desperately wanted to believe the illegals were innocent.

"USK logs all faults," he said. "If there was a problem with the kid's tech, they would tell the mother and provide a new citizen-chip. Without a working chip, the kid has no access to food. She's out of the model."

"Well, that's precisely why USK would hide it, right? It's their responsibility. If citizens found out that innocent kids were being kicked out willy-nilly, they wouldn't trust the system."

What a load of nonsense. Who was she trying to protect?

"When is Birgit coming back from Spitsbergen?" he asked.

"I don't know. She goes to the seed vault a couple of times a year. Trying to save humanity from starving, you know? We make fun of her. A little. There aren't many scientists on Fyr. She's been under a lot of pressure. When Hildr disappeared, she went mental. I mean, even if something bad had happened to the kid, we would still have found a clue somewhere, wouldn't we? Birgit hasn't slept since she left. She paces around the house all night long, from the lab to the greenhouse and back again. She eats nothing but those." She pointed at the pile of rice pudding cartons on the table.

"Do you have a key?" he asked.

"I'm sorry?"

"To the greenhouse."

A shadow of doubt crossed Pat's face. "Yes."

"What about the lab?"

She was holding the door behind her back, as if she were ready to storm out.

"Let me be honest with you," she said. "No offence, but I don't see the need for Finders. I respect adults to decide for themselves when they've had enough. The endless tracking, the nudges, the sanctions ... It's enough to drive anyone nuts. I have many friends who removed their ..."

She looked up at him, unsure if she should be sharing this information.

"I don't work for the algorithm," Axel said. Mostly true. "My assignments come from friends, family, lovers left hanging. Unless there is a personal score to settle and someone willing to pay for it, I couldn't care less about people going void."

"How do you find them?" she asked.

"Data. It's all about data. Birgit said you had a copy of the kid's central logs."

"Is that all you need? You should have said before."

With two swipes, Pat sent him the link to a file.

"What about the lab, can you open it?" He pointed at the keypad next to the sofa.

Pat didn't look convinced.

"I'll come back later," she said. "Please stay out of sight. Don't push your luck." She lifted one finger, touching the Vegvísir tattoo on his arm. "I wouldn't want anything bad to happen to you ..."

She slid out of the bedroom, closing the door gently behind her.

He cursed himself.

Not only was Pat hiding something, but she was definitely flirting with him as well. This combination irritated him more than either fact in isolation. Her allegiances were not in the right place, yet he had to play nice.

He worked on Hildr's logs all afternoon, hearing people coming in and out of the room next door. Where was Pat? She'd said she'd come back. By dinnertime, he couldn't think any more. He needed fuel. Rucksack gone, a full fridge nearby. Scavenging it would have to be. Axel opened the bedroom door. A middle-aged couple in sandals and white socks were crossing into the oracle. He nodded at them. "Got your questions ready?"

Sliding into the kitchen, he assessed the group. No Pat. Seven voids and a big citizen in a red dress. *Gef, fifty-three years old, artist, Fyr.* Blond, taller than him, large square chin, engaged in lively discussion. Maybe he was the other red label. Gef eyed Axel with suspicion as he opened the fridge.

"Have we met?" Gef asked.

"I'm a friend of Birgit's," Axel said. "Crashing on her couch for a couple of days." Risky, but best to claim his territory.

Another group had finished visiting the oracle, and they were about to leave. While Gef distributed handshakes and high-fives, Axel saw his chance to run back to the bedroom. He put a New Food carton under his arm.

Fake meatballs and cheesy pasta. Unimaginative, but kept you going. No cutlery so he ate with his bare hands. Rummaging for a tissue, Axel found a card in his back pocket. The paper ad delivered by drone. He had forgotten all about it. He opened the URL in a new tab, browsing a video gallery with thumbnails. Quaint. Videos posted by Ula Svenson and her supporters, including the one he'd seen at the port. Mostly appeals for plant seeds, farming tools, and an "open invitation" to join their farm at the top of the Beranger. How whimsical. One video drew his attention, the setting looked surprisingly familiar. A bed with four posts and a small crowd gathered around. It was the oracle room.

Axel pressed play.

On the video, a man was being stripped naked. A group of people laid him on the mattress, forcing his limbs apart, and tying them to the four wooden posts. Red liquid swirled above his face, floating and spiralling like the throbbing eye of a storm. The thick, red droplets fell on his forehead, face, eyes. The man howled. Several hands kept him from turning his head away. They emptied buckets of red ink on his chest, dabbing little arabesques on his skin with sticks, forks and brushes. Barbarians. It looked like the crowd of voids he had met in the house. Why were they attacking this man? After they were done with the paint, they removed the man's earphones, life sensors, nodes. Fumbling and scraping, they pulled something bloody from behind his ear. A chip.

They were disconnecting him.

The group dragged the man to the back garden and tied him to a metal hook on the wall, the one he had seen earlier, next to the hanging plant pot. More people came out of the commune, watching the man's miserable state. Rowdy groups emerging between ivy, shrubs and ceramic planters, pointing, laughing, strolling back inside, their long dresses floating with the breeze. One of the voids looked straight into the bee camera capturing this dismal scene.

"This is how we handle Finders on Fyr," Gef said.

The video ended.

Axel felt a wave bursting in his chest. He got up off Birgit's sofa, pulled drawers out of the cabinet, kicked himself for making a noise, growled, punched the sofa cushions in silent rage. This was why Carla hadn't told him about the previous Finder. Skinned alive, tortured, and disconnected from the algorithm.

Did Pat know?

Where was Pat?

Where was Carla?

He didn't have a number to call back.

A fucking trap.

Voids were targeting Finders. An eye for an eye. He was locked in a madhouse with dozens of them. If they figured out his real job, he might not get out alive. He was in at the deep end, but fifty thousand kroner could pull him to the surface. He had to watch his step, find his way to the kid. He was the best at the job. He just needed data. He needed zettabytes of data.

Chirrups in the void: launch of New Food in Uskania

@Wonderwoman5: Does anyone know what they put in New Food?

@Snoozzzz: It's just crap created in a lab. Synthetic nutrients, starch, toadstools and bugs mixed into sausages.

@HanselBigBoy: The name New Food is meant to drive a "positive shift in consumer mentality", because who wants to eat cockroaches? Real food is for rich people.

@Wonderwoman5: [Face palm] That's what I thought. Eat and shut up.

Chapter Ten

(Hildr) Climbing

She'd been climbing for hours. Five hours? Six hours? Without tech, she wasn't sure how fast time ticked. When she'd been with Bas, a rocket-strong optimism had propelled her forward. Now, such optimism seemed foolish. If he hadn't believed her, why would Ula? She knew Ula had her old bracelet with Birgit's messages, containing more information about Mondo's research, and what they were hiding inside the vault. And she remembered Fy's old town better than her home in Iceland. Gaps remained in her memory, holes that couldn't be plugged with anything but guesswork.

Hildr fooled her growing hunger by focusing on the practicalities of climbing. A steep path criss-crossed the mountain. She stepped on improvised holds, pushing against shallow dents of rock never meant to be climbed. Her movements struck her as learned, smooth, infallible. She progressed to the height of a five-storey building, mainly using her strong legs to gain traction. Without food and water, time ticked slower than ever. Eight hours? Twelve hours? Her legs shook with tiredness. She latched onto protruding slates, relying on the lesser strength of her hands and arms, shielding her face from falling rocks. She thought she saw someone watching from above. She must be hallucinating.

A bad grip made her lose an hour's worth of climbing. She cursed herself, pressing a scratch on her shoulder. She looked at her hand. Bright red. With no tech, her vital signs wouldn't be sent to USK. No medicine would be dropped by drone. Another fall and she could die here, on the mountain, alone. Against the dread, an upbeat melody played in her head. Where had she heard it before? Rubbing off the dried blood, Hildr hummed the melody out loud.

One level up, the next challenge awaited. A massive wall of gravel and barely a single piece of solid rock to hold onto. She walked at a slant, dragging herself upwards, pressing down on moving ground. Dust soared up her nostrils and burned her eyes. She looked up. If a larger rock got loosened, it could cause an avalanche. No wooden cross would mark her grave. She pushed these thoughts away, coordinating the rhythm of her steps with the melody in her head.

Every time she lifted her foot, her tattoo became visible. *Do the right thing for the planet.* The Dev's pledge. She would keep her promise. She looked down at the beach. The height was dizzying. A day must have passed now, since Bas had left. She was hungry. Why had she not eaten more of his energy bars? She was cold. At this altitude, the Arctic wind pierced through her bones. Why had she been dropped on the beach without a jacket? She was thirsty. The dust rising from her steps made her throat burn. She would kill for a sip of Bas's water.

Higher up, a soiled white blanket had been draped along gravel. Hildr scratched her eyes with her knuckles. The blanket didn't go away. She climbed, getting closer. All solid substance had leaked from inside, but she could still feel the power of the animal it had belonged to. Only skin, bones and fur remained, plus the large teeth at the front, a permanent snarl fixed in what remained of the polar bear's snout. Hildr tugged at the bear's fur, releasing it from its shrivelled bones. She found a large stone, drew it above her head with both hands, and hit the bear's ribcage, over and over, until each rib loosened from its mantle, chinking against the gravel. She pulled the limbs out, yanking the skull against the ground, and ripping the pelt from the spine with a mighty roar.

After some time, it was done.

Hildr dragged the polar bear's pelt and wrapped it around her shoulders.

Cold was no longer a problem.

Hunger and thirst remained.

The higher the climb, the higher the fall, but after days of climbing, she couldn't afford to drop. Time didn't matter. Pain was irrelevant. Clinging to sharp-edged recesses, hanging from the smallest flaws on the mountain wall, her limbs gained magnetic traction. The effort needed to pull away became greater than the strength needed to cling onto the rock. Fierce winds swept the mountain and dissipated as they moved near Hildr's spidery figure. An emotional elevation accompanied her physical ascent. She felt she was winning a game, reaching the next level. A veil of mist and prowess hung around her. She didn't need anything, or anyone.

She was Hildr, the giant.

Hundreds of metres above sea level, speckles of white appeared within deep fissures. Ice. She scraped it with her fingernails. The coveted substance disintegrated into infinitely smaller pieces, before reaching her mouth. Her head rose above a natural ledge, a recess protected from wind and the straight downward slope. Hildr crawled in, wriggling her limbs inside, licking the icy rock for moisture. She lay in a foetal position, arms crossed over her chest, pulling the polar bear's skin over her head. How comfortable. To curl up on herself, instead of sprawling on the wall.

Endless twilight.

Clouds rushing past.

White cliffs, cracking.

Eyes half-closed, mind half-dead.

The whole Earth trembled. Large chunks of stone, ice and snow broke loose and rumbled down the mountain. A white cloud of dust formed above the debris, collecting itself in a wave, rolling towards her. How many minutes until the snow covered her eyes, her nose, her mouth? How many seconds? How long until she could no longer breathe?

A voice.

Bas stood next to her with his water bottle, pouring its precious contents into her mouth. *I'm sorry for leaving you. Without technology, I don't know what is right or wrong.*

"We'll get to the truth," she said.

The truth, the chorus of Devs repeated.

Data leads to the truth.

Hildr opened her eyes.

She was curled up on the mountain ledge. Alone. Water was falling on her face. She put her tongue out, collecting dribble from her chin, licking her fingers.

Rain.

Rain at last.

A man bent over Hildr, moving his lips. Light-brown skin, olive-green eyes. The sounds coming out of his mouth meant nothing. She had crossed the threshold of thirst, hunger and tiredness where all emotional integrity collapses. Her identity was a crumbling house built on unsteady foundations. The man spoke in riddles, fretting over her folded limbs, pulling at the white polar bear pelt, pouring more water into her mouth, carrying her on his shoulders.

Did she dream it?

Others came. Men and women, grabbing her by her limbs, bearing her weight, carrying her up the mountain. They removed her wet clothes, wrapped her in blankets, and laid her on a worn-out mat which barely softened the basalt underneath. They fed her white, sweet granules.

"What's your name?"

"Can you hear us?"

Through this and more, Hildr slept, fitfully, turning, dreaming of snow-covered mountains and granulated sugar.

When she woke again, a different person was bending over her. A young, pretty woman, brown freckles on rosy cheeks, blue eyes, long auburn hair. Hildr was lying in a cave, surrounded by rows of domed tents in faded colours. Her head was pounding, her lips chapped. She licked them. An iron taste. Outside, grey clouds and howling winds announced a storm.

She tried to sit up.

"Is this the farmers' camp? Is Ula Svenson here?"

The young woman patted her on the arm, as if to discourage the effort.

"I'm Liz." She pointed at her own chest, like a child greeting another. "Please don't get up. You're too weak. We found you unconscious. When was the last time you ate? You *must* try our famous soup." Her lively blue eyes were beaming.

Hildr looked down and noticed the tattered robe they had put on her, a terrycloth towel with loops sheared off on one side, wide shapeless sleeves sewn in and embroidered letters on a small breast pocket. She pressed her chin down, grazing the tight shiny threads, reading the word upside-down: "*PAT*".

Liz smiled. "Sorry, it's probably the wrong name. The clothes used to belong to another person. She's gone now." Her eyes rolled upwards, towards the ceiling of the cave, like a swooping bird taking off and crashing to earth again. "People always come and go, don't they? Moving is good.

When people stay still for a long time, it's usually a bad sign. Will you stay with us for a while? You'll meet Ula soon."

At least she was in the right place.

Hildr felt needles pricking the tips of her fingers. She lifted her hand to her face.

"Where are my clothes?" The white sleeve dropped to her elbow, revealing her dark, lustrous arm. She looked down at the tattoo on her leg. "Did you see me naked?"

"Don't worry." Liz closed her eyes. "*Do the right thing for the planet*. We saw it." A firm voice, eyes beaming open again. "You don't need to explain yourself to me. The important thing is that you've removed your technology. That's the first step. They cannot brainwash you with their silly videos." A benign, idiotic smile lingered on her lips. "We can talk about it, if you want? Maybe talking will help you get closure." Liz's thick eyebrows jumped up and down, like sticks thrown to a happy puppy. "Yes, let's talk about it. Then we can move on and talk about something else."

Closure? Everything was opening.

"I'd rather wait for Ula," Hildr said.

Liz's smile widened. "Excellent. Mama will be back soon. First, rest. Later, I'll show you around the camp."

Polar bears' extinction in the wild off by twenty years, Science Weekly

Polar bears have been wiped out by climate change just twenty years later than we predicted 100 years ago. By modelling the energy use of polar bears in 2020 and back-tracing the amount of food and Arctic ice required to sustain them, researchers calculated polar bears would disappear from wild settings by 2100. Today, polar bear populations have officially been declared extinct. Specimens survive in zoos across the world, and lack of food continues to be an existential threat to many other species.

Chapter Eleven

(Axel) E-bikes

At night-time, the commune grew quiet. Pat hadn't returned. Axel moved the pile of mattresses from Birgit's bedroom into the corridor and locked the door. He would give freeloaders no reason to disturb him. Birgit's couch was uncomfortable, but beyond that, the night was uneventful. At five in the morning, Axel cleaned Birgit's drawings off the blackboard and scribbled his notes on the kids' logs. At seven-thirty, he couldn't pretend to work any more.

Breakfast time.

Watch your step.

Loud snoring noises could be heard from the oracle room. No one in sight. Probably because they *oracled* until two in the morning. He washed his face and emptied his bladder in the toilet across the corridor. In the open-plan kitchen, two double mattresses had been laid on the floor, a small crowd of voids snoring on top of them. A woman had slipped through the gap, onto the floor tiles. Bad luck. Axel opened the fridge and helped himself to a red carton. Smoked lamb rib with mashed potato. *Like fucking Christmas.* At 7.38am, someone stumbled into the kitchen. *Well, well.* No need to comb the other rooms. Pat had gunk in the corner of her eyes and a creased T-shirt with a drawing of planet Earth smiling from side to side, or breast to breast.

Axel gave a mock bow.

"Morning, roomy," he said, without opening his mouth.

Pat jumped back. "Jeez, you scared the hell out of me. What are you doing up so early?"

"I waited for you," he said.

She opened the fridge and removed a blue carton from the top shelf.

"Sorry, I got held up last night." She didn't try to disguise the lie, didn't bother to look apologetic, or offer the help she had promised. Removing two chopsticks from a drawer, Pat started wolfing down chunks of fried bread with onion, the disturbing meal inside her New Food carton. "Shouldn't you be working on the case? How are you going to find Hildr if you're always hanging around our fridge?"

Funny pants.

"I know what you did to the other Finder."

Pat stared at him, chewing.

"I warned your friend to be careful," she whispered. "When Gef found out he was a Finder, it didn't go down well. The whisky did the rest. So stupid."

"Not my friend. Who was he?"

She eyed him up and down.

"Gunnar," she said. "Gunnar Grimson." Meal resting on the counter, she moved her hand slowly over the short, blonde stumps on her scalp, like a nervous tic.

"Where is Gunnar right now?"

She shrugged. "I managed to get him out of here alive. Are you here for Hildr or for your friend?"

"I told you he's not my friend. But he might have important information."

"I found your channel. Maybe he's taking lessons from you."

"The public videos are for the extra ad credits. If finding voids was easy, Finders would be out of work."

One of the voids groaned from the mattress on the floor.

Pat bounced another mouthful of greasy onion into her mouth.

"Let's go to the garden," she said. "We can speak there without bothering anyone."

Axel followed her down the corridor, past the oracle room with the snoring chorus, through the glass door leading to the back. Outside, the remains of a fire. Plants and shrubs sprouted around the limestone path and in pots hanging from the walls and fence. Through the steamy walls of the greenhouse, the jungle of green. Pat walked to the side alley and leaned against the wall of the house. When she saw that Axel wasn't following, she shuffled back, closer to him.

"Can we go in there?" He pointed at the greenhouse.

"I left the key in my bedroom. Did you look at Hildr's central logs?"

Annoying.

"There wasn't much I could use," he said. "I need to triangulate."

Pat licked her lips. "Triangle-*what*?"

"My method for finding voids requires three data sources. The central logs, external devices, and interviews with witnesses. I clean and process the three sources and run the data through my probabilistic model."

"Seriously? You have a model? A data model? I thought people operated in a different way."

"People are highly fallible. This job requires data. A mix of science and dirty work, like old medicine. Having my own model is critical. Ready-made Finder apps are rubbish. I thought you had watched my videos?"

"I didn't pay much attention, if I'm honest. So Hildr's central logs are no good?"

"That's what I just said." She was wasting his time. "Her geo-tracker was compromised." Pat either had no idea what he was talking about or pretended she didn't. "A professional voiding job uses a hack that jumbles the chip's location for the twenty-four hours prior to the log-off request. In the kid's case, the log-off request was sent from inside the compost bin, on the street outside the commune. The twenty-four hours before log-off are blank in her geo-tracker. Can you get the key to the greenhouse?"

His lamb rib and mash was gone, but Pat was still poking at her fried onion with greasy chopsticks.

"And what are you going to do, without the geo-tracker?"

She hadn't acknowledged his question. Being difficult. On purpose. Axel felt like grabbing her by the scruff of the neck and shaking her into compliance.

Be nice. You need her.

"We usually look at the void's history in the central logs," he said. "The tabs they used, what they browsed. Unfortunately, kids don't follow the same logic. Her last tabs included only games and cartoons."

"No geo-tracker, and you can't use her browsing history. Does that mean you don't have a clue?"

Testing what he knew.

"We have the chime," Axel said. "You mentioned the kid's chime was always on, because Birgit wanted to hear her playing nearby. The chime has a unique frequency which can be captured by urban furniture. We need to pick the best data sources and look for the chime's signature. Cast the net too wide, and the data will take too long to process. Go too narrow, and you won't find anything meaningful."

Pat had a weird smile on her face. "You lost me there. I was looking at the drawing on your beard."

Was she flirting or poking fun?

He indulged her again. "The e-bike network on Fyr has cameras and sensors to track vehicle use, charging levels, acts of vandalism. As the kid ran around the island, the cameras and sensors from the e-bike network will have picked up her chime. That's our second data source. There are docking stations in almost every street."

Pat's mouth opened as if she was going to say something. A smell of onion wafted towards his face. She did a rolling movement with her finger, swallowing the last mouthful.

He was running out of patience.

"Are you going to help me or not? I need to go inside Birgit's greenhouse."

"Why?" she said.

A head interrupted them.

Bil, the tall musician, was peeking through the glass door. He came out to the garden, dishevelled hair still bearing the shape of a pillow.

"You guys are up early," Bil said. He planted himself by Axel's side, eating from a blue carton. "I gather Birgit's away, if you're sleeping in her bedroom? Don't think she likes men that way. Are you watering her plants too?"

Axel spotted a long, fat shape with brownish granules in Bil's carton. Cricket sausage, from the looks of it. Pat had finally finished her breakfast, a gloss of saliva dotting the corners of her mouth. She looked concerned.

"Leave before he asks too many questions," Pat said. *"He'll tell the others you're a Finder. Remember what happened to Gunnar."*

"I thought we had an agreement," he answered. *"You were supposed to help me."*

"I'll come and find you later," she said.

He had heard that one before.

"A polar bear ate your tongue?" Bil was chewing with his mouth open. "Hey, you're using voice-free behind my back, aren't you? We still speak with our mouths around here."

Pat gave Axel the *go* look again, gesturing with her head.

"Not efficient," Axel said. *"You could use your mouth to eat."*

Axel opened the glass door and stepped back into the house, grabbing the last sausage from Bil's carton to prove his point.

Ugh. Tasted like soap.

He spat it out.

"What's wrong with you, man?" Bil said.

"Don't go in the kitchen," Pat said. "There are people sleeping in there. It's not even eight o'clock."

Pat and Bil stared at him from the outside.

Bil lifted his empty blue carton and licked it, like a dog.

He couldn't shake off the feeling that something was wrong. What was Pat hiding? Back in Birgit's bedroom, Axel researched the only e-bike network in the island. Old models, no thrust to lift off the ground; wheels were literally what you got if you picked up a two-seater on Fyr. He spoke to the office in Reykjavik and asked for the e-bike logs. The office replied with an invoice. Birgit had promised a load of dosh, hadn't she? Maybe he could get an advance. He called Birgit. It went straight into her mailbox. Twice. Thrice. Four times. By lunchtime, he was getting edgy. If Birgit disappeared from the map as well, he needed a new plan.

A new tab opened. Not Birgit. A man. Round face and droopy eyes. The name and job title rolled over the bottom of his tab. *Oscar Frias, Head of Human Resources for European Research and Low Latency Projects, Mondo Foods International.*

"What business do you have with Dr Olsen?" the Mondo Foods manager asked.

He sat on a pristine white beach, wearing a sombrero. It looked like the fucking Caribbean. Wasn't the Caribbean roasting by now? Even so, it was still a tax haven.

"Freelance job," Axel said.

Companies received frequent reports from their citizens. Location, productivity levels, calls made and received. Almost as snoopy as the model. This guy had probably seen Axel's attempts to reach Birgit and decided he was a person of interest.

"Why is she going to Spitsbergen?" Sweat ran down Oscar's forehead.

"She's going to the seed vault," Axel said.

The big round man wiped his sweat with the back of his hand, bee camera revealing a shimmering turquoise sea behind him. If the Mondo manager told him what their research was about, Carla would be a happy bot.

"The vault doesn't open in the middle of summer," Oscar said. "It would flood the tunnels with warm air."

Your job, man. Not mine.

"I don't know about that. I'm only telling you what I heard."

"Her trip hasn't been cleared with line management. I was hoping you could tell me more about her intentions."

Sounded as if Axel wasn't the only person Birgit had left hanging.

"I'm not acquainted with Dr Olsen's plans."

"That's disappointing." The Mondo manager got up from his deck chair and started panting along a beach, puffed-up chest heaving with the effort. In the middle of the walk, his camera cut off, stranding Axel with funny cat videos. *FFS.* "You're searching for her kid, right?" He was back again, looking like he was having a heart attack, but somehow managing to keep speaking. "I checked your bio and your reviews. You're some kind of private detective like the other what's-his-face ... Gunther something. Listen. Dr Olsen is not authorised to go into the vault, and she's not responding to our messages. We think she's having a ... mental health crisis. I have no idea what's going on in your little island at the North Pole, but we believe she's about to do something stupid. Whatever happens, she mustn't go underground."

"That's not my problem. Aren't you tracking her?"

"Yes, Sherlock. She's on the ferry heading to Spitsbergen. Our staff in Longyearbyen will attempt to intercept her at the port. There's another problem though. She has been sending DNA-protected messages to someone called Hildr Olsen. That's her daughter, right? The messages are decrypted at the receiver's end when the right DNA is present. Only the kid can listen. Dr Olsen sent two messages yesterday. She's sending a third message right now."

DNA encryption protocols had been created by corporates to protect confidential information. Why would Birgit use it with the kid?

Axel sensed an opportunity.

"I can let you know when I find the daughter. Would that help?"

"That would be a step in the right direction. We'll pay you for exclusive access to the messages. No one else can get their hands on them, do you understand? If you tamper with the messages, you won't get a penny."

Triple-booked.

His price tag was increasing.

"I'm only accepting advance payments."

Oscar grumbled, waving the bee camera away from his face.

"Half now, half later."

They agreed the amounts.

Blue seas again.

The data from the e-bike company included video logs and transactions for every vehicle and docking station on Fyr. Three exabytes. This kid was worth gold.

Lying on Birgit's couch, Axel pivoted the data by trip category and removed known anomalies. The parameters added up to more than two million columns. Readings from safety sensors, weather trackers, air-quality filters, geodesic navigation, and data from the e-bikes' sound, video and GPS logs. He ran a Fourier transform of the sound's binary capture into Hertz. The child's chime sequence threw back dozens of potential matches. Sound waves were continuous, and the sampling rate from the recordings low-quality.

Axel aggregated the list of Fyr postcodes and homed in on the Blue Boat commune. A neat map view of the evidence. Filtering by the day of Hildr's disappearance, he projected the map onto Birgit's blackboard and circled four spots where the e-bike network had picked up her chime. One circle was right outside the commune. The girl had probably played near the charging dock before going void. Two minutes later, the chime was recognised by a passing e-bike further down the street. He located the e-bike occupant. A neighbour living in the commune next door. From there, the sound jumped to a hairdressers' salon, about twenty minutes' walk away. The fourth and final place was a street downtown, in the opposite direction. After that, nothing. The chime had disappeared from the map. Three clues to follow up. Maybe data anomalies, maybe significant.

A new tab opened in his field of vision.

Carla.

She hadn't uttered a word about the other Finder, but as soon as they heard the call with Mondo, she was back on his case.

"I see you're making progress, Mr Jóhannsson."

"What happened to Gunnar? Why didn't you tell me?"

"The estimated wait times for a new citizen-chip are available on the USK website."

Bastards. That would be him too, if the mob got their hands on his tech.

"What about the kid, will she get her chip back?" USK didn't like to upset corporate citizens.

"I'm pleased to report we can offer a replacement and look after Hildr Olsen until her mother returns."

"You heard her boss calling. She's not picking up the phone to any of us."

"Dr Olsen contacted us. She needs permission from the Trust to go inside the vault. She didn't give us as many details as we were hoping. What are you waiting for to get inside her lab?"

"Taking the wall down? Too risky."

Carla didn't care if he was impaled by a group of savages, as long as USK got what they wanted.

"Your risk levels depend on many other factors, Mr Jóhannsson. I called to inform you that you have less than twenty-four hours to complete the job."

He didn't like ultimatums.

"I have a method."

"I almost forgot," she said in a cheery tone. "Your first order of grass-fed sirloin beef is ready. The delivery will be booked once we get the video footage from Birgit's lab."

"When I'm ready."

"And the greenhouse."

"My collaborator has been misbehaving, but I'll bring her back to the right path."

Being a triple agent didn't mean he was being greedy, did it? He was simply hedging his bets. If he could convince Pat to help, it would be doable. Carla stared at him in silence.

Reading his pulse. Assessing his stress levels. Deciding if she could trust a triple agent.

"I strongly recommend you leave Fyr before this evening," she said.

She clearly didn't trust him, but this wasn't a job for a drone.

How does the DNA of old crops help us improve New Food? Mondo Foods Q&A

Rest assured there aren't any harmful components in New Food. Plants, like most living organisms, use DNA to pass on traits to their offspring. By understanding which genes affect plants' taste, consistency, resilience and nutritional value, our award-winning scientists can apply the same rules and principles in the lab. Lab cultures are different from farmed plants, but by tweaking their chemistry we can arrive at similar flavours and textures. Sometimes the results taste even better than the real thing. That's how we created bestsellers like Maca-cheese-pop© *and* Mondo's Indian Flavour Collection©. *Lab-based, DNA-improved goodness.*

Chapter Twelve

(Birgit) Potatoes

The ferry is packed with citizens and tourists. Locals wear thick hand-knitted woollen beanies bearing the names of old Arctic missions; outsiders have cheap synthetic beanies covered in corporate logos. A crest of foam trails behind the stern. I admire those who see shapes and meanings in sea foam, clouds, tea leaves. I see nothing. Nature is fact. Nature changes. We blame the climate, but it was us, humans, who broke the balance. New Food became a necessity, not only because we need forests. Farming was doomed. High temperatures arrived when plants were flowering and most vulnerable. Periods of scorching weather started lasting longer. Rainfall became unpredictable. Crops fell out of sync with weather patterns. Bees and pollinators were the first casualties.

Do you know what the irony is? Ten thousand years ago, climate change gave us farming. Long, dry seasons arrived after the last glacial period. Humans settled in villages, growing rice, potatoes, corn, the staple crops that went on to feed us for the next millennia. Farming allowed modern civilisations to flourish.

Now, the world is changing again.

You're too young to understand. For now, you need only a roof, New Food, and the loving presence of a responsible adult. Sometimes, I wanted you to stop being a child, to grow up as fast as possible. Plant by spring and harvest by autumn. Was it too much to ask? The efficiency of plants? Instead of the complex, selfish, slow-maturing human genome.

I'm sorry.

I was supposed to tell you a story.

The Svalbard seed vault holds more than two million seeds, including crops from every country in the world. While climate played havoc with our planet, scientists shipped copies of old crops to Spitsbergen, keeping them in the ice, protecting the Earth's genetic legacy. Without genetic diversity, we can't produce New Food, and we can't save farming. We use plant DNA, evolved over millions of years, to find the right traits, and genes capable of surviving the challenges ahead.

For the humble potato, the worst enemy was not the heat, but a small fungus-like organism. *Phytophthora infestans.* Late blight, mutating and migrating like the flu virus, and constantly changing to overcome plant resistance. The Great Irish Famine had been a warning. Gene diversity was our main weapon against late blight, but the Irish relied on a single potato variety with no defences against it. When warmer temperatures brought late blight to new regions, potatoes were in trouble. The remarkable tuber became a treat for the wealthy. For the rest of us, potato flavours were extracted and synthesised in lab-produced starch.

Isn't it amazing, how fast humans adapt? Lab food is probably all your generation will ever know. Cooking is a thing of the past. When I was a child, many took to the streets to protest against New Food. They held banners with pictures of raw potatoes, dirty and coarse, scattered across fields. Ever since the Spanish had brought them to Europe, potatoes were part of our tradition, our history, our identity. The government was heavy-handed against the protests. When there are no bargaining chips, things can quickly descend into chaos.

They say we are what we eat.

When the food we eat changes, does it change who we are?

A story.

Years ago, before you were born, a man washed up on the beach, near our home. We were gathered by a campfire. Most housemates excused themselves, packed their things, went back to the commune. No point in succouring the dead. But by the time the rest of us got to the man, he'd rolled over and opened his eyes. Not dead. His nose was long and slanted like a ski slope, his lips swollen above a protruding jaw, his skin stretched over his cheekbones. He was wearing shapeless brown rags. A manikin made of mud. He didn't speak any English. Through much gesturing and moaning, we gathered he'd arrived in a dinghy. His travelling companions (he held up both hands, many fingers adding up) had died during the crossing (his elbows shook and trembled, copying the waves, his arms stretched out to the sea).

We carried him inside the commune, gave him blankets, water, New Food cartons. We poured warm Scotch into mugs. Sitting around the table, we asked him questions. Absent eyes, no soul behind them. The man was holding a fork, poking cubes of potato starch. Someone said the word "potato" and a spark of recognition lit his face. PO-TA-TO, we repeated, like demented children, wondering if he understood he was alive, that we were his rescuers and not just ghosts in the underworld. The man put a hand inside his pocket and pulled out a black sphere, ugly and rough. At first, I thought it was an animal's stool – why had he carried a lump of faeces all the way here? Then his grip on the sphere loosened, and it rolled over the wooden tabletop. I lowered my nose, scratched its skin with my nail. Not a stool. A potato. A rare and extravagant wild purple variety, never seen in our islands before.

Using my best head-nodding skills, I asked the man's permission to take the specimen to my lab. The sheer scale of the coincidence was baffling. The potato contained the Rpi2, a single gene giving the highest broad-spectrum resistance to late blight. The man looked at me with a puzzled expression. I was laughing out loud. "A true survivor," I told him, patting the black gem. "Can I borrow it?"

The spring frost had just gone, and a growing bag lay empty in our garden. I filled the bag with composting mix, cut the potato in two halves and dug them into the soil. Buds started coming through in less than a day. Every night, we would sit with the man around our long kitchen table, poking yellow mush with forks. The potato eaters. Not real potatoes yet, but their processed New Food replacement. Housemates covered their cameras before coming into the kitchen. With no English, the man's prospects weren't bright. If he was caught, he would be deported back to continental Europe. When he spoke, guttural sounds came out of his throat. I think he was Dutch.

One night, the man walked down the corridor and looked at the growing bag in our back garden.

"Late-harvesting," I said. "One hundred and twenty days before we can eat new potatoes. Will you stick around until then?"

We were used to hosting illegals, but two housemates had had recent warnings from the algorithm and grew edgy around him. A week later, an argument blew up.

"Why does he have to eat at the table with us? Why doesn't he stay out of sight?"

The next day, the man was gone.

Maybe he *did* understand English.

Exactly one hundred and eighteen days later, in the middle of the night, someone raided our back garden and took the wild potatoes out of the soil.

Nothing was left for us to harvest.

Somehow there was a sense of justice in the crime.

They weren't *our* potatoes, after all.

I wish there was a happy ending to this story.

The following week, videos emerged from the north of the island, documenting a strange occurrence. Black spheres were rolling down the mountain. The university contacted me, due to the organic nature of the finding. They sent me a specimen for analysis. I cut it in half. Dark blue and purple, white twisting lines. The same wild potato variety the Dutchman had carried in his pocket. I planted it, letting the flowers bloom and dry, and sent a box of seeds to Ms Holm, the clerk responsible for logging samples in and out of the seed vault.

The Dutchman's potatoes are now under the mountain, waiting to be planted, watered, pulled filthy from the ground.

Coleslaw is good for you: a gastroenterologist's advice

A patient arrived at my clinic last week. His previous diet consisted of bread, a bit of meat and dairy, a lot of coleslaw. One month ago, government officials visited his family farm in Pittsburgh. They told him they would tell others. People would come and destroy his family's crops, free their cows and chickens, spit on their ruthless selfishness, for ignoring the environmental consequences of farming. The officials brought blue and green cartons, blurting out the words my patient knew from the adverts. "New Food is produced in bioreactors, combined with yummy flavours and vitamins, and shaped into mouth-pleasing meals." He flipped through the cartons. Sausages. Just sausages, with different flavours. He came to the clinic too late to avoid surgery. I've heard many stories like this. Whatever officials say, I recommend a gradual switch to New Food, combined with laxatives and double the normal intake of water. Sausage in, sausage out.

Chapter Thirteen

(Hildr) The farm

The farmers' camp at the top of the mountain lacked technology and the most basic conveniences. No internet or electricity. No plumbing or running water. No double glazing, air conditioning, beds, mattresses, cushions. Yet tools and arrangements seemed reasonable and appropriate, and life flowed with the precision of a production line. As soon as Hildr was able to stand, Liz linked arms with her and showed her around the camp. She was much shorter than Hildr and moved with the springiness of a sapling.

"There are thirty-two farmers in the camp." Liz's voice croaked. "Soon to be thirty-three, if everything goes well." She patted her belly, smiling. "Each person has a job to perform. Feeders, cleaners, runners, improvers, entertainers, idlers. At the beginning of the day, each person draws one of the jobs." She showed Hildr a fabric bag with small beads tinkling inside. "Check the drawings." Hildr inspected the faded icons. Lettuce, broomstick, shoe, magnifying glass, mask. "Do you want to count them?" Liz asked. Hildr shook her head, dropping the beads back inside the bag. "Don't worry." Liz brushed away her disappointment. "I'm sure they're thirty-two. No one left recently. Most of the beads have brooms and lettuces. Cleaners and feeders. Runners and improvers are twice as many as entertainers and idlers. Even Ula is part of the rota."

"Interesting."

There was no work left in Uskania, but in the mountain they had *jobs*. She contemplated Liz's descriptions with the curiosity of someone learning an alien culture. Liz explained shifts were observed for a full day, until it was time to rotate to the next job. During winter months, it fell to the entertainers to keep an eye on the spinning constellations and announce daybreak.

Liz giggled as she copied them.

"They are so funny. Squatting and bouncing like frogs, flapping and crowing like roosters. Can you imagine, waking up like that? Some have beautiful voices and prefer the opera. *Die Meistersinger von Nürnberg* is my favourite aria. I know the endless chattering from the singers in Nuremberg by heart. Others shout plain nonsense. *Pancakes with honey drizzle! Crocodiles and strawberry jam!* Oh, I hope you can stay with us. If you heard the entertainers in the morning, I'm sure you wouldn't want to leave any more."

Hildr grimaced.

When would Ula return?

Liz made her follow the farmers as they did their chores around the camp. Ten cleaners scrubbed the sleeping quarters and storage area, a shallow cave where they kept their old tents, connected to a dome supported by an aluminium structure. Inside the cave, blankets hung from the ceiling to act like partitions, creating separate 'rooms'. Tents were left unzipped, aired, washed with rags soaked in water, homemade vinegar, and hydrogen peroxide.

"Cleaning products are so expensive," Liz said.

The cleaners then moved on like a bee swarm into the living quarters, which during the summer was outside. Five feeders crushed earthworms into flour and prepared the bread and protein-meal for the day. Another five trekked down the mountain. Hildr held her breath as she followed them, approaching a new area.

"Here's the farm," Liz said, observing Hildr's reaction.

The *farm* consisted of two rows of black manure inside thick jute sacks, raised from the ground by rocks and sticks, emanating an intense and penetrating smell of excrement, mould and organic material. One of the composting sacks had a mass of purple and red earthworms. The small critters squiggled and twisted inside the manure, making the soil look alive. The other row had an assortment of leafy plants – collard greens, kale – in pale colours and varied shapes. Liz was looking at Hildr, mistaking her shock for admiration.

"Amazing, isn't it?" Liz said. "This is where our famous vegetable soup comes from."

Hildr had never heard about their soup. She hadn't heard about the jobs, the tasks, the logistics. Everything was new, and at the same time incredibly old. Medieval. All she knew was that the farmers were a group of voids who had stood up against the algorithm and launched a terrorist attack on Fyr eighteen years before. What had happened? Liz probably wasn't the best person to explain the history. She seemed too young, despite her pregnancy.

They walked between the rows of manure.

"Can you believe it?" Liz said, smiling. "Some people think we're starving. But, as you can see, we have plenty of food."

"Is this all you eat?" Hildr asked.

Liz looked confused. "Why, yes. It's enough for soup, bread, and protein bars. We get everything we need from the farm. A few years ago, an Arctic seaworm washed up on the shore. A huge one. We feasted on it for weeks."

"And in the winter?"

"In the winter, we eat the protein bars we prepare during summer. Please don't worry. The worst that can happen is a bout of scurvy, or low-calorie lock. No one has died from hunger in a long time." Her smile seemed an odd accompaniment to this statement.

Hildr frowned. "Do you know there is New Food down at the beach? The guards from the detention centre give away spare cartons."

Liz scraped the soles of her frayed trainers against the rock. "Please don't say that in front of Mama ... New Food is not allowed in the camp. Greedy corporations make us believe New Food is the only alternative. It's not true. Did you know in France they grow courgettes without soil? Low-calorie lock isn't even that bad, it just makes you sleepy. You lie down for a little longer than usual, and by summertime, the crops are back. Some animals hibernate during winter. That's worse, isn't it? We make sure people move for at least one hour per day. And scurvy is bad for your teeth, but it won't kill you. Shall we go back up?"

Hildr was lost for words.

How could Liz bring a baby into this?

She followed the runners, who were carrying out tasks between the camp's two main levels, holding buckets of earthworms and leaves to prepare food, and water from the rain and melting snow to refill water bottles. They lugged stools from the toilets, a ditch under a throne of rocks, and added them to the composting mix in the jute sacks. Hildr's stomach twisted and rumbled, hunger and nausea combining in disturbing ways. Walking back to the living quarters, they sat on the ground, filling copper mugs with bouquets of worn-out cutlery, in preparation for lunch.

"Where did Ula go?" Hildr asked.

"She'll be back before you know it," Liz said. "She's up at the volcano. We're expecting a donation of cornflour. Runners used to climb to the volcano's mouth to check for deliveries. One day a parcel blew up." Liz pointed at a woman with a flowery scarf, the shape of her skull visible under the thin fabric. "Nowadays, only Mama goes up. She doesn't want anyone else to get hurt. We have many benefactors who send donations, but also many haters. Unfortunately, USK spreads lies about us ..." Liz stopped mid-sentence, fidgeting with a spoon, following the rounded edge with her finger. "I'm sure you've heard some of the terrible things they say?" She kept fitting spoons in the copper mug between her legs, each one making it drum with a sharp metallic clang.

"I'm not sure," Hildr said, lying.

If Liz was Ula's daughter, she must have been born on the mountain. She didn't know anything beyond what the farmers had told her.

"The worst lie of all," Liz started, "is that we were responsible for what happened on Fyr." A spoon tipped her mug.

Clang. "Oh no." Liz rushed to pick the spoons up. "We'll have to wash them again."

"And you weren't?" Hildr asked.

Bas had a different version too.

"What?" Liz said.

"You weren't responsible?"

"Of course we weren't responsible."

For the first time, she looked serious.

"What happened, then?"

"The USK software disconnected innocent citizens and left them to die of hunger," Liz said.

"Why did they do that? Do you know?"

"No. Maybe they wanted to get rid of us? They didn't have enough food for everyone and wanted an excuse to kick more citizens out of the software."

So naive. Like Bas.

"Why would the algorithm turn against citizens, when it was created to protect them?" Hildr asked.

"I don't know ... but the Devs did nothing to stop it." Liz leaned in, touching Hildr's hand. "The outside world is full of bad people ..."

As she leaned back, the copper mug tipped again. The spoons spread on the ground with a clattering ruckus.

"What are those for?" Hildr said, suddenly exasperated.

"Hygiene. Until I have the baby, I'm only supposed to be an improver, an entertainer, or an idler. My job today is to improve things. The ground is full of germs. Not a good place to keep our cutlery."

"Surely it's not that bad."

Liz shook her head, solemnly. "We used to collect rainwater and drink it straight away. People died, until we figured it out. Improvers had the idea of boiling the water. We also sew tents and mend holes in old clothes."

Improvers, feeders, runners, cleaners.

What a cast.

"What about the entertainers, where are they?" Hildr asked.

"You'll see them later. They prepare a play every night. Comedies are our favourite."

"Don't I need a job too?"

"You're an idler today. Idlers take turns at having a rest from the duties. Everyone needs a rest. You were so weak."

The routine gave structure and meaning to their days. Everyone needed a purpose. Was it any worse than Bas's dancing? Disconnecting from the algorithm had made their lives empty, forcing them to find comfort in these tasks. Liz had been born here. She didn't know any better.

At lunchtime, the farmers came into the living quarters and sat in a circle. Liz brought the soup, a watery mixture smelling of garlic and cabbage, and helped to ladle it from buckets into crockery bowls. Fragrant odours rose in the cool, dry air. Hildr held her chipped bowl with both hands. Everyone made slurping noises, in a weird sort of communion. Striking, to see all the farmers in one place, thin, dry, wrinkled, with stained nails and ragged clothes. Most had long, white hair, and missing teeth. Many wore patched parkas and fleeces, a few robes like hers. The youngest members had cotton vests and trousers. June was mild enough, if you were young and kept busy. A smell of stale sweat lingered in the group. Hildr didn't recall being shown a place to shower, but she might have missed it. Time would tell.

At the end of the meal, one of the older women addressed her.

"Are you going to tell us why you came?"

She didn't want to say too much before Ula's arrival.

"I've had a procedure. My memories are jumbled."

"Convenient," the woman said.

"I ran away from the detention centre. The dancers at the beach helped me."

"You're a Dev," another woman said.

"No. I lived with Devs for a while, but I was kicked out."

"Why?"

"I tried to sabotage the algorithm," Hildr said.

Liz had the face of a scarecrow. She looked around the group, pleading with the interrogators. "Mama will know what to do. She's not the first to come up. You all inspected her body. She has no tech. What if she's the girl?"

The girl.

Did they suspect who she was already? Which girl were they referring to? A murmur rose from the group. Some farmers agreed with Liz, trying to pacify those who protested. The older woman got up and left the circle. Others followed. Cleaners collected bowls from the ground. Feeders went back to their jute sacks. Runners and improvers resumed their tasks. Hildr offered to rinse her empty bowl. A man took the chipped crockery from her hands, shaking his head.

"I can help you," Hildr said to another cleaner.

Her attempts to perform a job, any job, were silently pushed aside, as if she had broken their unspoken rules of hospitality.

At night, they slept in pairs. Hildr paced the cave under the midnight sun, peeking inside tents as the farmers prepared to sleep, nursing a vague hope of spotting what she had come for. Ula must have hidden the bracelet within the rock.

Hildr was handed a sleeping bag with a sour smell and told to curl up on one side of a two-person tent. She was relieved when Liz took the other side. The first person to greet her and the last to say goodnight. Liz looked at her with her big, shining eyes and the same enigmatic smile she had worn all day.

"Is it true, the amnesia?" Liz whispered. Hildr had hoped to avoid any more talking. Her eyelids were drooping. "Oh no, you're so tired. Poor you. Don't worry. Only the present is important. Both of us. Here." Liz placed her hand over hers.

Hildr bit her lip.

"Did you ever go to the old town?" Hildr asked.

"No. I've lived here all my life."

She looked at Liz's face in the twilight, noticing the brown freckles dotting her cheeks, the orange from the tent's fabric projected on her eyes.

"I heard you ask the others if I'm *the girl*," Hildr said. "What girl were you talking about?"

Liz rested her chin on her hand, stroking her face like a cat grooming itself.

"Mama asked me not to talk about it. For years, we were looking for a girl who disappeared during the purge. A tall, black girl, like you. When we couldn't find her, Mama said the girl would come to us instead and show us the way to the underground farms."

"Underground farms?"

"The ones planted by the Goddess. I thought it was a story for children. Until yesterday, when we found you down the mountain. Mama couldn't hide her excitement. She went straight to the volcano to send a message."

"She went to the volcano to send a message about me?"

"Please don't tell Mama I told you."

"Does Ula think I'm the girl?"

"Every girl grows into a woman. Some become tall, like they've had their feet dipped in manure." Liz stifled a giggle so it wouldn't be heard above the camp's quietness.

Underground farms. The old conspiracy theory. Did they know anything about Mondo's research in the vault?

"How can plants grow without sun?" Hildr asked.

"I don't know, but Mama says the Goddess lives in a place with endless food. Bigger than our farm."

"Don't you think that's too good to be true?"

"The girl climbing all the way here sounded unbelievable as well."

Hildr blew raspberries with her mouth.

At least Liz trusted her. None of the others did.

"Endless food ..." Hildr repeated, half-asleep. "I must find the way to this magical place." At that moment, she was too tired to dream.

The light got crisper at the crack of dawn. Hildr was lying awake in the tent, listening to her own thoughts and the wind murmuring outside the cave, when someone opened her tent's outer zip. She leaned forward, hesitating near the threshold. Two steps away, under the domed cave, a white woman sat cross-legged. Lean and dry, probably in her sixties, light-blue eyes. She had grey hair in a bun at the top of her head and deep crevices under her cheekbones. Hildr crawled out of the tent.

"I came to speak to you," Hildr said.

Ula's features became animated.

"It's a long way to come." Her voice was coarse and snappy. "Why don't you speak?"

It was as if she knew what Hildr was going to say.

"I need your help."

"You're a Dev." The same speed of thought, a spring reaction.

"I was kicked out," Hildr said.

"Cut the fluff. What do you want?"

Liz's head popped through the tent's opening. "Maybe breakfast?"

Ula's eyes wandered to Liz, then back to Hildr.

"Shall we go for a walk?"

More awards for Inverness wine, The Scottish Wine Connoisseur

Inverness keeps winning prizes. We spoke to Giovanni Moretti, winemaker at Bogbain Farm Vineyard, during this year's Decanter World Wine Award ceremony, where his Bogbain Silver Muscat won the gold medal. "The secret to our success includes special land permission and steady investment from corporations," Mr Moretti said. "And weather, of course. The weather in Inverness has become perfect for wine. We have temperatures like those in France two hundred years ago. It won't necessarily give us lots of big fruity flavours, but we get lovely light red and sparkling varieties, with honey, acacia and peach notes. This is one of the great virtues of the situation, really, for those who thought climate change was all gloom and doom."

Chapter Fourteen

(Axel) Clues

N eighbour, hairdressers, downtown. Three clues to investigate, places where the chime on the kid's bracelet had been recorded by the e-bikes. He would start at the end. Distant voices floated in from the garden. Axel peeked through the glass. Gef, Pat and Bil sat outside with a dozen voids, laughing, passing around a smoking pipe. A pang of disappointment grew inside him. Another broken promise. Pat was not on his side. She was on theirs.

Going through the kitchen, he grabbed a red carton smudged with blotches of fat. *Tchi-ken curry,* Mondo's Indian Flavour Collection. Nasty stuff, but better than going hungry. He grabbed an e-bike and headed downtown. Prefabricated houses lined the dusty road, a faint hubbub of traffic above. Parking on the docking bay where the kid's chime had been captured, he looked at the house across the road, two storeys of offensive green. Discarded boxes of Inverness wine were piled up outside the entrance. Loud dance music blasted from upstairs. He read the little handwritten plaque above the door. *The Haunted Shipwreck.*

A bald man appeared at the window of a crooked loft.

"You missed the party," the man shouted, above the music.

"I'm looking for a seven-year-old girl."

"No kids in the house, but there's a lot of them around."

He made his way to the hairdressers. Customers sat around a central podium waiting for their turn, legs disappearing into long footmuffs surrounding the base. People in white coats rushed around their swivel chairs. He had never understood the hairdressing ritual. It was like asking strangers to wipe your ass because you couldn't see the hole eye-to-eye. He could cut his own hair. The first hairdresser shrugged when he showed him a photo of Hildr. The second ignored him. The third cocked his head, taking a good look at her face.

"Fyr is full of children," he said. "I hope she's okay. So many wanting a chip, I bet no one will bat an eye if this one vanishes. Tell you what. I can't give you a copy of the salon's data, but I'll give you temporary access to my personal logs. You have until midnight. Don't get your hopes up. Spotting the kid in the videos will be like finding a hairpin in that trolley there."

Axel biked back home, annoyed by his slow progress. At the commune next door, he stopped for the neighbour. He wasn't home but messaged to ask if he'd join him at the beach. Axel opened a new tab, placing a fisheye at the top of the mountain. Coming down to his real position, he went down a passage between two houses, an uneven dirt path veering right and down towards a wasteland of old furniture. Within a courtyard, a pile of aluminium carcasses stuck out from under a tarpaulin. Ovens, blenders, food-processing combos, remnants of old routines. Reeds, growing from a swamp with broken stalks, stood between him and the beach. He wasn't keen on dirtying his only change of clothes. The alternative was to reverse into the path, follow Birgit's street to the crossroad, and access the seafront from the main road. What would the kid have done if she'd been standing where he was? She would probably have crossed the swamp.

Axel climbed over a fence, landing in the yard with the kitchen appliances. He pulled the loose end of the tarpaulin. Objects rolled over. Rusty toaster. Broken juicer.

"You're damaging them. You're damaging them." Two messages, in unison.

The twins he had met at the drone collection point were watching him from a window. Axel wrapped the tarpaulin around his feet and paddled through the swamp, mud creeping up his heels. When he got to the other side, he scrubbed his shoes on dry ground.

The Arctic Ocean.

Black sea. Black sand. Black sky.

He had slept many nights on the beach. He steadied the impact of the memory, letting the darkness drain from his mind, walking along the coast. By the water, moss drew lines on the lower layers of rock. A man with dark-rimmed glasses knelt near the waterline, patting a pile of volcanic sand into what looked like an oversized erection.

Raj, sixty-five years old, sand sculptor.

"I saw her the day she went missing," Raj said. "I told the scientist many times. Keep an eye out for yer child. Dangerous, ain't it?"

"Was she alone?"

"No. I don't know the chap."

"Citizen or void?" Axel asked, although he knew the answer already.

"Void."

"Can you identify him from street logs?"

Raj stopped patting the sand and placed his hands on his thighs, staring into the distance. "There was something different about him. A pointy beard. Like a devil. I thought he was wicked."

His initial hunch had been right. The voids had something to do with it. They had no tech, no cameras, no tracking. Pat and the others in the commune were playing with fire. What did they expect?

Axel headed back to the Blue Boat commune. In the kitchen, Gef sat at the wooden table, nursing a cup of brown liquid. Axel knew it wasn't coffee because coffee was too fucking expensive. Not part of Uskania's welfare package. A new pile of red-labelled cartons was tucked away in a corner. Delivery day. He grabbed a fake pork knuckle with sauerkraut.

"Hey," Gef said, getting up from the table. "The *blue* cartons are for guests."

Axel looked at his pork knuckle. "Gotcha," he said. "I'll keep this one. Nasty virus." He coughed on top of the food, for good measure, and slipped into the corridor.

At the opposite end, Pat was coming in from the back garden.

No escape route.

"You're hurting me," she said, pulling away.

"*You said you would help.*"

He dragged her by the arm, towards Birgit's bedroom.

Pat put her foot between the door and the doorframe.

"I watched your videos," she said. "I know you're from Fyr. Your mother arrived here as an illegal. How can you be so hostile to people in the same position as you once were? Don't you understand that USK is using people like you as their mouthpieces?"

"*You can't have your cake and eat it,*" he said, still voice-free. "*Where is Birgit's kid?*"

Pat's grey eyes shone with disdain.

"You're a murderer."

"*Who are you trying to protect?*"

"Bil knows you're a Finder," Pat said. "He's threatening to tell the others."

"*The blood will be on your hands, not mine.*"

Axel banged the door on her.

Fuck.

Their friendship had soured, and he still didn't have footage from the lab. *You have less than twenty-four hours.* Why had Carla said that? He opened the hairdressers' videos. If the chime picked up by the e-bikes was a technology blip, the sound was unlikely to feature again. If it wasn't a blip, then he was on to something. Maybe he would watch the kid being snatched away. Axel fast-forwarded the video to the right spot. From then on, he processed it in real time, minute by minute, keeping his eyes peeled for the match in Hz frequencies. A white spike appeared on his tab. He replayed the moment, compared it with the e-bike logs, went back to the beginning. No doubt about it. It was the girl's chime, bright and clear. On a second dataset.

Only one problem.

The kid was not in the video.

He replayed the file, squinting at the frozen frames. Customers scowled mid-way through the trimming and combing. He zoomed in and out of each face, playing the video frame by frame. The same adrenaline kick, each time the sound frequency matched. Still no kid. He went into a separate folder with the payment transactions log. The name of one customer leapt out. He checked the ID, made sure it was the same person. Pat. He looked at the time stamps. Pat had been at the hairdressers *at exactly the same time* as the kid's chime. He restarted the video. That's why he hadn't noticed before. Pat's hair was only shaved at the end. In the rest of the video, she had long, blonde hair.

He heard a drumming noise.

Not from the video.

"Can you open the door?"

Pat was outside the bedroom, whispering through the keyhole.

Why the lies, the deceit, the delays?

He unlocked the door.

"I'm sorry for calling you a murderer." She opened her hand, revealing a silver key. "As an apology, I'll show you the greenhouse."

Birgit's greenhouse was about ten metres long by five metres wide, with a skeleton of aluminium beams rising to about three metres high in the middle. The light was a high-intensity blue, as if a white giant had replaced the sun, the air moist and balmy, cut off from the rest of the garden. The earth's nutty scent crept up on him and settled under his nails, although he hadn't touched anything.

Next to the glass walls, pots lined the ground, with more pots and planters on shelves above. His tab duly listed the different species. Cucumber. Lettuce. Broad beans. Peas. Thin wooden planks separated potatoes, peppers, tomatoes, squashes, and pumpkins. More plants sprouted in pallets and composting bags. Onion, leeks, carrots. At the back, a wild patch of scrambled earth contrasted with the neatness elsewhere.

Pat had disappeared briefly. Now in she came, holding a New Food carton. Fake beans and chickpeas. Vegetarian burger.

"Amazing, isn't it?" she said. "We can feel Birgit's love for these plants."

Axel's bee camera buzzed around, collecting its pollen. Carla would be pleased.

"Do you know anything about her research in the vault?" he asked.

"No. Something to do with plants, I suppose. Why do you ask?"

He didn't believe her.

"When did you shave your hair?" He said. Pat stopped chewing her burger. "Did you shave it yourself?" She shook her head. "Did you do it at the local hairdressers, perhaps?" She nodded. Still silent. "Did you see Birgit's girl wandering around there?"

"No," she said.

"What about *The Haunted Shipwreck*, do you know the house?"

Pat shook her head in slow motion. "I didn't see her there either."

She had a nerve.

A familiar odour hit him. He looked towards the far end of the greenhouse, spotting the spiky-leafed plant under a pyramid structure. *Cannabis sativa.*

"Why are you lying to me?" He said. "She wasn't alone. Who was the man playing outside with her?"

"I'm telling the truth." She had a pained expression. "I swear I don't know where Hildr is. What did the data show?"

"I'm still missing one source. Can you help me?"

"How?"

"I need to speak to everyone who was here."

"Everyone?"

"Including voids," he said. "If you want to find the kid, you need to get them to speak."

Pat nodded, solemnly. "When?"

"Now," he said.

Axel turned an empty pallet upside down and slapped a bag of compost on top.

Pat sat beside him, on a separate pallet.

She shared her tab with a soft blip and pressed 'call'.

His interviews typically included three questions: icebreaker, core, and speculation. The important thing wasn't what people said, but *how* they said it. Facts and events degenerated into fantasies in the workings of the most imperfect machine – the human brain. The icebreaker was food. People loved talking about food.

"That's a weird question." The woman on their tab had a round, freckled face. "My favourite meal is Milanesa steak.

Why have carbs separate from your protein, when you can have them together?" She spoke as if she was teaching an aerobics class, loud and over-excited.

"Did you see a little girl playing outside?" Axel said.

"At the Midsummer's oracle? Yes, I remember the girl. She was with Pat."

Pat jumped, as if death had tapped her on the shoulder. Under her beanie, her scalp shone with perspiration.

Icebreaker and core were done. Time for speculation.

"If you were a kid running away from home, where would you go?"

The woman took a while to consider this. "I'd hide in the port. New Food arrives every week. Empty containers from the previous week's delivery return in the cargo. I would catch a ride out of Fyr in one of those."

Pat's eyes darted across the glass ceiling.

"Call the next one," Axel said.

"Rabbit," the old man said. "We used to breed rabbits, before the ... uh ... ban. Oh yes, the little girl, I remember her ... she ran around like a ... uh ... hurricane ..."

Speech cluttering. Lucky finding. Good correlation models for speech cluttering had been published by academic sources. At the end of the interviews, he could run a full cluster and regression analysis with word frequency and speech oddities, such as cluttering.

Speculative question.

"When I was her age, we had freedom," the old man said. "I would convince the fishermen to take me in their boats and get the sea breeze running through my hair. All gone now. The freedom, fishermen, my hair. We thought the AI model was a good thing. Now they keep changing the rules without asking anyone. They're even tying a string of buoys around the island. No one can get in or out. Who would have thought it would come to this madness?"

One hour later, Axel had recorded seven interviews. All the accounts corroborated Pat's story. Hildr had gone to play outside and vanished faster than a leg of Serrano ham.

The heat increased inside the greenhouse.

"Can you ask your housemates?" he said.

Time to prove her good intentions.

"To come … in here?" Pat said.

"Yes."

"For an interview?"

"Yep."

She looked resigned. "I'll do my best."

With a rustle of leaves, she walked out of the green-house. An aura spread in her wake, the sun poking holes of warmth in the cool, blue brightness. Axel counted the minutes. Prodding the cannabis plant. Squeezing the pea pods. Smelling the sweet peppers. At thirteen minutes and twelve seconds, the door finally opened. Pat came in, followed by Bil. He took a seat on the ground, crossing his legs like a yogi.

Axel joined his hands at the chest, making a bow.

"Don't," Pat said. "Hindu greetings are for those who mean it."

Through patches of green and foggy glass, Axel saw the rest of the flatmates assembling outside. Shadows. Dark moving blots.

"Cricket omelette," Bil said. "My favourite food is cricket omelette. As long as the crickets are chopped, not crushed into flour. Man, you look stressed. Have you tried food yoga?"

Axel bit his tongue.

Had they told the others he was a Finder?

"I'm the one asking questions," Axel said.

"The show you're running here is nonsense, jah?"

One of the blots approached the glass. The door screeched open. A woman came in, wearing jeans and an oversized jumper. Long black hair, and strikingly sad dark eyes. No tech. She looked up at the glass ceiling in awe, taking in their private microcosmos.

She offered a smile.

"I'm Coraline," she said.

Without planning to, Axel smiled back.

"What's your favourite meal, Coraline?" he asked.

"Any food my stomach can digest." A soft voice, with a tinge of French. She kept her face at an angle, long hair parted, fringe hanging to one side. "I know you're trying to find Birgit's daughter. I spoke to her a few times. Loneliest kid I ever met. She asked me about Africa. We had that in common. She said her family was from Rwanda. I told her mine was from Algeria. It's tough. Not having a connection to our roots, not knowing the place we came from."

"Who was she playing with, on the day she disappeared?"

Her eyes meet his.

"He did nothing wrong," Coraline said.

"Who are you talking about?" Axel snapped. "Is everyone trying to protect a void?"

Pat and Bil stepped forward at the same time.

Coraline dismissed them with a wave of her hand.

"I spoke to the other Finder, before you," Coraline said. "He also thought everyone without a citizen-chip was a criminal." She ran her hand through her hair, pulling it behind her ear, revealing a smooth jawbone. "We're not criminals. We helped Birgit look for her girl. One of our friends spoke to Hildr, before she ran away. Her tech had stopped working. That's why she got rid of it."

"Does your friend have a pointy beard?" Axel asked.

Gef burst into the greenhouse.

Shorts, large military boots, and red lipstick on his lips.

He stepped forward with a menacing look.

"Pack your stiff arse and get the hell out of here. We know who you are. The fascist shit you say on your videos! The number of people you've deported! You have some guts coming in here. We eat people like you *alive*." He opened and closed his mandibles like a shark.

"I'll leave," Axel said. "Can I just have a word with Pat?"

"He's our last hope," Pat said, looking at Gef.

"We want him out," Gef said.

Gef and Bil escorted Coraline out of the greenhouse. As soon as they were gone, Axel sent his pallet flying towards the pumpkins.

"What the fuck have you done?"

"What?" Pat looked surprised. "I thought you were going to thank me."

"You told them, didn't you?"

"How else would I convince them to speak to you?"

"Why did you have the kid's bracelet at the hairdressers? Why didn't you tell me about the man with the pointy beard?"

"I explained everything. Her citizen-chip wasn't working. The chime was still active, but the chip was dead. I gave you her logs. I convinced people to speak to you. What else do you need from me? Why can't you find her?"

"I need more data!"

"Why don't you admit it? You haven't got a clue. Did you come up with this by yourself? The triangulation, the three sources, the data modelling? It's like you're trying to copy the algorithm by counting pebbles and drawing on the sand with a stick. You can't compete with artificial intelligence powered by gazillions of data points. It's futile. You're making their predictions more accurate every day, don't you get it?"

"Why did you lie? Why are you still lying?"

"Speak to me properly and I will tell you."

"Say that again?"

"Don't speak to me like I'm a variable in your data set. I'm sick of being treated like data. Connect with me like a real person."

He saw figures moving outside.

"Why would I do that?" Voice-free.

Pat walked towards him. "Speak with your mouth and look into my eyes. You don't know me that well, do you? You don't have access to this." She lifted her wrists. Her health measurements lit up. Sugar, hydration, stress, exercise, sleep, heart rate. "The only way to get to the truth is by speaking to me and caring about what I have to say."

She was hallucinating. He had to strip out her lies, the social conventions, check how her speech patterns fitted the models, look for the truth beneath the drivel.

"I need data," he said, still voice-free.

Pat let out a hollow laugh. "You can't even make an effort to speak to me?"

She was so close now. He could see her pupils contracting with the light.

A loud bang pierced through their ears.

They both winced, looking up. The glass ceiling of the greenhouse was shattering over their heads. They ducked under the cucumber shelf and braced for the shock.

Food yoga: a mindfulness routine cultivating calm and clarity

Grab your meal, sit on the floor and close your eyes. Take your first bite. Notice the textures, flavours, temperature. Let your teeth and tongue explore the shapes inside your mouth; let them tingle, tease, melt. Another bite. All animals eat. Think about the physics and metaphysics of being a creature who needs food, who craves nutrition, every day. Think about how food crosses cultures and languages. Think of ingredients. Recipes. Preservation and processing methods. Culinary traditions. Have you finished your meal? Congratulations. You've just become more human.

Chapter Fifteen

(Hildr) The farmer

Hildr followed Ula down the same route she had followed with Liz, a fifteen-minute trek dotted with narrow paths and wide cliffs. They were heading towards the jute sacks where the farmers grew their food, but before they reached the farm, Ula stopped next to a precipice. The abrupt wall below their feet was sickening, a breath-taking expanse of dark water opening below. No room for error. A misstep and they would fall. Below them, the meandering outline of Fyr's coast, with a steep dark hill neighbouring their own, and a black strip of sand on a remote beach. Floating ice platforms speckled the Arctic Ocean. The sun hovered above a low, thick mist. They leaned with their backs against the rock, facing the precipice, side by side, not daring to approach the edge.

Ula broke the silence.

"I come to this place often. It's a cleansing ritual, like sweeping the soul." Her accent was unlike any other on Fyr. "When I'm here, I don't regret my decision to come to the mountain." No guessing tone in her stream of words, only certainty.

Hildr was taken aback. "And the other times, you regret it?"

Ula's lips twitched. The skin around her mouth was knitted in ridges, like the mountain.

"Did you ever wonder why folks without technology are called voids, when we were around long before the digital age? People living in their tabs should be the *voids*, so we can become humans again. We're not the ones hiding behind entertainment, social filters, virtual lives. We're the ones facing the real world." Each sentence had the speed and certainty of a prophecy. Ula may have looked frail but her voice was full of strength and determination.

"My question is," Ula continued, "why did *you* remove your tech? We've had other people coming to us, but never someone like you. It's unheard of. How could it happen? They breed Devs in their halls like a piece of code, to maintain the cogs of the AI. You're a glitch. What happened?"

There it was. The moment Hildr had been preparing for. The words she chose now would be more important than ever.

"I'm not a Dev. I used to live here, on Fyr. My parents were migrants. I ran away from home. But I always kept a dream, deep in my heart, about changing the algorithm."

"Changing it?" Ula cut in.

Hildr recalled her discussions with Bas, the arguments he had raised. "You know, I always wondered ... why me? Why was I lucky enough to get a chip, but not those who stayed behind? It doesn't make any sense. Last week, an opportunity came. I was caught. They removed my tech, erased my memory, sent me away to be deported. I would be on a ship by now, if someone hadn't helped me."

"Quite a far-fetched story, don't you think?"

Ula didn't say this with shock, or bitterness. She sounded almost mocking.

Hildr kept her composure. "I have no logs I can show you, if that's what you want. I can't prove what I'm saying. But innocent until proven guilty – wasn't that how it was, before technology settled disputes? My word must be worth something."

Ula laughed. "Do you think I expected you to show me *logs*? Logs are worth nothing. Words are worth nothing either. I need actions. That's why I brought you here." Ula stepped towards the edge and turned her back to the precipice.

Hildr gasped.

Ula was too close to the edge.

Was she going to jump?

"Tell me," Ula started, "what do you know about the farmers?" Her voice echoed against the mountain wall. "What reaches the amazing USK software and the likes of you?" The breeze released strands of her white hair. She pulled them into the plaited bun at the nape of her neck. "Did you think we wouldn't make it without the algorithm, and without food corporations feeding us their horrible crap? This was how humanity survived for thousands of years. Sowing seeds with our own hands, tending the land, reaping the fruits."

"It's admirable," Hildr said, keeping her doubts to herself. "And I'm sure your ideas would be adopted by the algorithm, if they could feed everyone."

"USK went from an innocuous logistics platform to the most powerful brainwashing machine in existence. What a fantastic creation. People feel so lucky to have data models, instead of corrupted politicians. They marvel at how well the software copes with increasing amounts of data. How lucky they are to live in such an advanced society, instead of dealing with hunger, drought, uncertainty. Citizens didn't even notice when they stopped mattering. When they became data fodder for the machine. It's disgusting."

She was too animated for someone standing so close to a precipice. Hildr's thoughts raced. If Ula was mad enough to believe technology would bring about the apocalypse, she might be crazy enough to pull her in with her. They'd both hurtle down the mountain.

"There were good reasons," Hildr said in a measured voice, "why citizens trusted the model. You asked me what I knew about the farmers. Not much, but what news do you receive from the outside? In Asia, autocrats make decisions on behalf of millions. In mainland Europe, city-states can't cope with the influx of people from the south. In the Americas, extremes of poverty, and gated communities hosting millionaires. It's easy to rule in times of plenty. But how do you decide who gets the last piece of bread? At least USK is ruled by data, and the model can be continuously improved."

Ula's eyes turned manic under the pale light of the sun.

"The chip has taken over your brain, like a cancer." Her voice had become harsher, a rumbling thunder. "You can't see the truth when it's right in front of you. Elites created and perfected technology to maintain power." Her mantra was entrancing.

"Please be careful," Hildr said.

"They're hiding our food in underground farms."

"You're too close to the edge."

"They're tagging people with chips, like cattle. They're feeding people their horrendous lab junk."

Her monologue was reaching a crescendo of madness.

Hildr's eyes wandered beyond the cliff, towards the fluttering waves. The sun reflected on a chunk of floating ice. This was the conversation with Bas, all over again. No standing on the edge.

"Does it have to be black or white?" Hildr asked.

Ula's face muscles tensed up. "You said you wanted to change the algorithm."

"I tried to."

"How?"

"I can't explain the exact details … because of a forced amnesia … but I remember we planted a … a bug in the software."

"A *bug*?"

"My role was to suspend the disentanglement field and build a … a back door to the production environment."

"And what would this bug do?" Ula asked, as if she knew the answer already and this was merely a pantomime she had to endure.

"It would … delete records from USK data centres. Thousands of citizens would vanish from the model overnight. Resource calculations would fail. The software would kick into emergency mode. In emergency mode, we could rewrite substantial parts of the code."

"And what would happen to the deleted records?"

"They would … they would be restored from a backup."

Ula sighed a long, pained moan. "And you thought you were doing the right thing, by planting this *bug* in the software?"

Did she not believe her?

"Yes."

"Our collective memory is short," Ula said. "It doesn't go beyond a couple of generations. Climate breakdown, democracy's collapse, New Food ... these changes have little bearing on us. People who lived through war will do anything to avoid another war. Once they die, we're thrown into war again. People forget. Corporations have longer memories."

She stood silhouetted against the Arctic sky.

"I'm sorry," Hildr said. "How does this relate to what we were talking about?"

"Can't you see? Everyone expects the end of the world. If we grow more plants and breed more animals, we'll kill the planet. That's what Mondo and the elites want us to believe. If we don't, civilization as we know it will die too." Ula's stray grey hairs floated around her translucent hairline, like a Medusa. "Our downfall was on the cards for a long time. We'll be remembered as the farmer-people who choked their own fields. Our lot will be pruned from the evolutionary tree." She closed her eyes.

Ula was in a trance. She didn't make any sense.

Behind her, the abyss.

If Liz had been right, Ula suspected she was *the girl*. Why hadn't she mentioned this yet?

"I grew up on Fyr," Hildr said. "I wish I remembered more from those days. I left my citizen-chip behind, in an old bracelet."

Ula turned aside and spat on the ground.

"You're a bigger fool than I thought. But not dangerous. The proof is that you haven't tried to push me. Enough of this. The day is rising."

Ula stepped away from the edge and started climbing, back to the living quarters. The lump of sticky saliva stood shining in the sun, at the edge of the precipice.

Hildr noticed her legs were bouncier, her joints relaxing.

Had she convinced the legendary Ula Svenson?

When they got back to the camp, Liz was waiting outside the tent.

"Is she staying with us, Mama?"

Ula's reply was out of earshot, but Liz's smile said it all.

Your favourite encyclopaedia explains: Disentanglement field

A disentanglement field *is the popular term for the scalar field method deployed by fermion computing to excite physical tachyons until they spontaneously decay. The technique emerged from CERN's Large Hadron Collider experiments with the Higgs boson [1] [2], allowing fermion computing to be developed to its full potential and becoming the basis for widespread industrial use [3] [4] [5]. By using a disentanglement field, technology companies can ward off unauthorised use of ferbits, including attempts to bypass quantum encryption and gain access to financial and healthcare data [6]. Before disentanglement fields, advanced fermion applications such as voice-free communication, digital IDs and digital health tracking were widely distrusted by consumers [7] [8] [9].*

Chapter Sixteen

(Birgit) Wheat

I was tired, but I couldn't sleep. The old man sitting next to me on the ferry kept me company. We got talking. I discovered my grandparents had lived five hours from his native Kiruna, in Tromsø. The ferry approached the barren field of Longyearbyen's harbour. Among the people awaiting their loved ones and dockers busying themselves with the mooring, I spotted two sullen-looking men in blue fleeces. The man from Kiruna linked his arm in mine, and we disembarked together. His granddaughter was waiting with her pickup van. *Do you want a ride into town?* I gave her Ms Holm's address. Looking back through the rear windshield, I saw the two men in blue fleeces, frantically searching for someone.

Ms Holm received me at her flat after a two-minute wait. Late visit. Her eyes hinted at fatigue, but her voice remained warm and welcoming. She didn't expect to see me at this time of year. She had worked at the seed vault for thirty years, winter in and winter out, opening the gates to committees from all over the world. I told her I had to go inside the vault without delay. I lied about the reason, of course. To protect the secret, and because people are not ready for such a change yet. I wonder if my decision will still seem shocking when you receive these messages. I wonder how many will have died by then, mourning our old crops. Ms Holm convinced me to wait. She said she would take me to the vault first thing in the morning. We shared a carton of New Food, and a slice of real sourdough for tea. Exquisite. My last normal meal.

How about another story?

About wheat.

From its origins in the Fertile Crescent, wheat reached countries across all latitudes. Wheat led the Green Revolution in India, winning Norman Borlaug the Nobel Peace Prize. Bread, pasta, flour, cake, pizza – wheat was everywhere. Then summers became hotter, and winds blew harder. Wheat stem rust, a fungus responsible for plagues and famines mentioned in the Bible, spread to new, dry areas. The only way to mitigate the fungus was to engineer resistant species; to build resistance, we needed access to different genes. The seeds in the vault saved wheat from extinction. How can you make up a story like that? Stories are a distortion of facts, someone's fight against the world. Facts are the world fighting back.

My grandparents left mainland Europe at the end of the last century. They had nothing to eat. In Old Europe, countries didn't agree on the best way forward. Some nations signed an agreement welcoming displaced migrants. Others closed their borders and became isolated. The Nordic islands had a vision. They decided they would organise resources, provide food and a minimum income for all citizens. The need to limit resident numbers was the price they paid for having food in the fridge.

Meanwhile, rocketing temperatures and sea level rises had brought an anxiety people were keen to escape, no matter what, even if it meant subjecting themselves to surveillance. Thousands came to Fyr, an island where they had to quarantine for three months before they could be admitted as permanent residents. Like many others, my grandparents were tagged, and every aspect of their behaviour was scrutinised.

This was before New Food. I remember walking through a shantytown of prefabricated houses, up to the school, where they distributed jobs for the season. The town needed helpers to prune and collect vegetables from the big greenhouse, a job machines hadn't yet mastered. Kids learning about biology and food production were best suited to the job.

On my second summer volunteering among the dark-green leaves of carrots and swedes, I met a girl with beautiful olive skin and a headscarf. Her name was Tahmeena, or Tah for short. She told us it was the name of a Persian princess. She acted like a princess too, with such straight posture, and a voice that sounded so entitled, we almost felt obliged to offer her our loyal service. Tah told us stories of bazaars with exotic fruits: dushanbee, dragon fruit, melons, rambutans. Her hair smelled of apricots; her skin was as soft as ripe peaches.

At noon, we would sit on the ground and unpack our lunch on our laps, eating with the appetite of real farmers. My lunch was usually tinned food. Tah always brought a bundle wrapped in fabric, holding a wholesome flatbread shaped in a circle, thicker around the edges and poked with holes in the middle, like a flower drawn on pale clay. She would open her homemade bread, and the wheat fragrance would drift and blossom, as rich and vivid as her stories of bazaars and forbidden fruits. Tah told us her mother made the bread with wheat from Tajikistan. *You always carry homemade bread with you,* she said, *even if there is food where you're going. You take a flatbread just in case, as you would take a bottle of water on a long journey.*

Tah went on a different journey that summer. I can still hear her desperate cries, see her proud princess figure breaking under the blow. Her family was being deported. Tah's older brother had committed a crime, the caretakers explained, keen for the lesson to filter through to the rest of the kids. He'd been caught at the port stealing coal, a fossil fuel used to make cement in the old town, and heavily rationed. Later, I found out that Tah's brother had stolen the coal for their cast-iron stove, where they baked the homemade bread.

I never smelled fresh bread again.

A week after the incident, grandmother and I were walking in front of a low house, heading to the seamstress who mended our clothes. Grandma spoke to me in her soft voice – you could almost miss it if you weren't paying attention. *Your friend Tahmeena used to live here.* The door was open. A trolley with cleaning products stood outside. I sneaked into the house with a vague hope of saying goodbye. Tah was not there, of course. An L-shaped sofa, a wooden table, a cabinet, a first-aid box, a whiff of disinfectant. Nothing left of Tah. No smell of bread or faraway fruits.

I heard Grandma shouting my name outside. In my rush to leave, I knocked a ceramic pot, making it dance on the polished wooden surface of the cabinet, until it came crashing down. A mass of beads rolled out on the floor, raining over the feet of a man who appeared out of nowhere, casting his shadow over me.

"What are you doing in here?"

Pink rubber gloves. Mean face. Grandma rescued me just in time, pulling me out of the house, beads crunching under our feet. *She is looking for her friend.* As we retreated, I grabbed a handful from the floor and put them in my pocket. At home, before dropping my trousers in the laundry basket, I emptied the pocket into a tin box embossed with a sun and moon, a present from my father. The beads were golden kernels of wheat. Twenty-one of them. Years later, I discovered the seeds I had collected from Tah's floor belonged to a wild strain from Central Asia, containing genes resistant to wheat stem rust.

Isn't it a fantastic story?

I wish none of it was true.

Before leaving for Svalbard, I put the tin box in my rucksack. The moon and the sun, with twenty-one golden seeds inside. I couldn't leave it behind. Tah's fragrant wheat is going into the vault with me.

The tale of Hildr, the giant – the part at the beginning

"Please promise you won't run away again."

"I promise, Mama. What about the story?"

"I will get to it. I'm still shaking."

"I'm sorry, Mama."

"Once upon a time, the Earth was covered in glass domes brimming with fruits and vegetables ..."

"Why were the domes made of glass?"

"Glass is see-through. Farmers used glass because they wanted to admire the world outside, stare at the forests, the snow-covered mountains, the beautiful glaciers sliding across the sea."

"But it was too hot."

"Only in the summer. For most of the year, it was manageable. Farmers tended their crops, planting cereals and leafy vegetables. Our old food laced the planet with beautiful green ribbons seen from the sky."

"Were all crops green, Mama?"

"Most of them. Let me continue the story. Among the farmers, lived a little girl called Hildr, heir to all humans, daughter of none."

(Axel) The lab

The greenhouse ceiling fell on their heads with a shattering noise. Glass projectiles hacked into Axel's thigh. When the shards stopped raining down, he walked out from under the shelf and assessed the damage. Two of the glass sections had been reduced to their metal skeletons. Half the building's roof had been destroyed. The alternative universe inside was exposed, open to the elements and the blue sky. Everything looked brighter, but also less intense. Birgit's plants, pots and flowers lay crushed under pieces of broken glass.

"Look." He pointed at a large chunk of limestone. Someone had thrown it in. "Are you going to defend your friends now?" Through the gaping hole above, they heard voices and laughter.

Pat looked around at the damage, taking shallow breaths, as if her lungs had been punctured too.

"Your job is too toxic." Was she justifying their vandalism? She looked scared. She probably hadn't imagined they were capable of this. They had chopped off Gunnar Grimsson's ear. So they were definitely capable of this – and more.

"Why do you trust me, then?" Axel said.

Pat looked up at him with her big, grey eyes.

"Trust is tough," she said. Alliteration. An interesting occurrence, in natural speech. "I trust you because ... I don't know. I just do. Trust makes the world a better place." Concentric wrinkles spread around her eyes, like ripples in a pond. "I trust voids too. Everyone does stupid things. They deserve a chance as much as we do."

Her trust was even more admirable considering the size of the rock resting by her feet. It could have killed them both. Axel helped Pat onto solid ground, pushing the largest shards out of the way. Crushed glass tinkled under their shoes as they tiptoed out. Gef, Bil and a dozen voids sat a few steps away from the greenhouse, among an assortment of bottles and improvised ashtrays.

"I'll speak to them," Pat said.

Axel looked at her, puzzled. Was she serious? These people were dangerous, and they hated his guts. He headed inside, ignoring Gef's look of contempt. Pat stayed behind. Buying time, hopefully. The house was empty. Striding across the kitchen, Axel opened the fridge. Two red cartons. Lunch and dinner. Breakfast too. For the journey. The pile of red boxes wobbled in his hands as he raced back to Birgit's room. He locked himself in and chomped on pizza squares. He needed to get the hell out of this place. He would finish the triangulation on the way back to Iceland. Removing his trousers, Axel cleaned the wound on his thigh. It didn't look good. He sat on the sofa. Mondo's lab was right there. Maybe he should pull down the wall, as Carla had suggested. Pat was covering for him outside.

Axel stood up abruptly.

He trusted Pat.

How the hell had that happened?

A headache brewing. *The past is the past.* No painkillers. Axel ran to the kitchen, grabbed a bottle of whisky, and headed back to the room, drinking from the bottle. One last data source to go. The interviews. Text-clustering. Six people had mentioned the port. *Why are you always bitter and miserable?* The data shrank and oozed on his tab, millions of rows and columns. *Look around you.* Would the triangulation work on a kid? He looked up other kids who had disappeared. Accidents. Kidnap. Murder. *Do you know what happiness is, Axel?* He closed the tab, lay down on the sofa, shut his eyes. *Happiness is the ability to look around and be thankful for what you've got.*

Shouts.

Banging doors.

Steps in the corridor.

"It's me," a voice said, outside his door.

Pat.

She was wearing yellow pyjamas and carried a rolled-up blanket under her arm, like a bedtime cartoon.

"I need to tell you something," Pat said.

They locked the door.

"What's the shouting about?" He felt a surge of adrenaline. "Are they after me?"

He was in his boxer-shorts.

Pat shook her head. "Turn off your camera," she said.

"What for?" he shrugged. "USK is always listening."

"Turn it off *now*," she said.

She unrolled the blanket, draping it over the sofa. Then she grabbed Birgit's table lamp, plugged it into a different socket, and went on all fours under the blanket, pressing the switch. Finally, with a silent gesture, she invited Axel to join her.

"Brilliant," Axel said, stooping under the blanket. "What about the rest of the tech on our bodies?"

Pat raised a finger to her mouth, signalling him to keep quiet. Holding an old paper book on her lap, she removed a long, cylindrical stick from the spine, and started scribbling on a blank page with the sharp end. *Keep your hands behind your back and look the other way, towards the window. When your eyeballs become sore from reading this page at an angle, it's a sign that your eye nodes can't show what I'm writing.* Graphite. She was messaging him on paper with a piece of graphite. Cunning. *Now, raise your shoulders as high as you can. More. Raise them higher. You need to cover the health nodes behind your ears. Now put your hands behind your back. Make sure your wrist nodes and your bee camera are secured behind your back.* He wasn't good at following directions, especially when they were this uncomfortable. *One final thing,* Pat scribbled.

She pulled his chin towards his chest.

Cover your neck.

Two hunchbacks under a blanket, looking away from each other.

She turned a new page. *You're the first person I've seen with the chip on their neck. What are you trying to prove? Don't answer. Please read instead. I know who lives at the Haunted Shipwreck. Ula Svenson. Let me finish please, before you criticise me. I looked up your chip's registration date. You got it in the year they did the first big sweep. You were probably just a child. Is that why you're so messed up?*

Uncontrollable. That's the definition of a kneejerk reaction. Axel sent her little notebook flying across the floor. Pat looked at him in shock. She crawled slowly towards the book, like a startled cat. Axel started a new voice-free message, then stopped. He couldn't do it. USK would know. He signalled behind his back. Pat returned to the den under the blanket and handed him the graphite stick.

Keep your half-arsed Freudian analyses to yourself. His handwriting was too slow for his thoughts. *Do you want to leave the model? Be my guest. Get off the islands. Voids only survive because people like you cheat the system, stealing food meant for citizens. Where's the kid?*

Pat snatched the pencil from him.

I don't know where she is. I already told you. Why do you keep asking? What happened was a mistake. We couldn't let the fear of consequences paralyse us.

He strained his eyes to read under the faint light of Birgit's bedside lamp. What 'mistake' was she talking about?

Pat kept writing.

Did you ever want something so badly, with such overwhelming force, that the rest of the world vanishes around you?

Axel felt Pat's presence by his side, her warm breathing, how she dropped her own rules and turned to look straight at him.

They heard footsteps outside the bedroom.

Pat flipped the page on her notebook.

Her scribbles became jumbled.

We're preparing food and shelter in the mountains. We're starting a new way of living. We won't need USK, technology, or New Food.

We.

Was she planning to join the farmers?

A loud bang.

Someone was kicking Birgit's bedroom door.

"We know you're there."

Gef's voice.

The door shook on its hinges.

Axel rushed from under the blanket and opened the sash window. The evening breeze hit him like a cold shower. Pat ran after him, tugging at his top.

"Don't jump."

"They're too many," he said.

"They *want* you to run away. That's exactly how it started with Gunnar. It's a find-the-Finder, a twisted catch game." She rushed behind the sofa, typing on the keypad. "Here's a better hiding place. They don't have the code."

Birgit's lab. Aladdin's cave.

It looked like a cupboard.

"They'll pluck us out from that hole like worms."

"Keep the window open," she said. "They'll think you've left. They will give chase. The mood will fizzle out. They're too drunk and stoned. Please trust me."

More blows.

The door's lock wouldn't hold much longer.

Taking advantage of his indecision, Pat pulled Axel inside the lab, sliding it shut. Maybe he had misunderstood her plan. He thought she was going to tell the others that he had left through the window. Instead, Pat was inside Aladdin's cave with him, breasts jammed against his back.

Birgit's lab had been built for one person, and not a big guy like him. A narrow cupboard, one step wide, three steps long, with a large VR chair in the middle. Shelves and cabinets covered the wall at the back. Axel's watch cast a faint glow, creating moving shadows. Glassware. Machinery. The labels appeared on his tab. Cell culture machines. Freezers. Incubators. Shakers. Microscopes. The most impressive equipment was around them. The walls. Covered in high-definition, sensitive plasma nodes. He prodded them with his finger. With the right software, the room would become a professional immersion pod. The wall material alone was worth hundreds of thousands of kroners.

They heard Gef and the other flatmates breaking into the bedroom. Pat's ruse worked. They thought he had left through the window. Someone suggested going after him. Laughter. Someone started barking. More laughter. Someone threw themselves on Birgit's sofa, banging the wall on the other side. Inside the lab, absolute silence. The hostility didn't register in the same way. Axel was in a Zen state, wedged against Pat's breasts. A slight erection but no migraine, so all good.

The group camped in the bedroom, outside the lab, chanting.

Pat rested her head on Axel's back.

Not a squeak.

He could stay like this forever.

The voices subsided.

A low chorus of snoring took over.

Pat turned on the light inside the lab. A soft buzz, accompanied by a low whistle. The same sound he had heard when he met Birgit.

"Shit, the air vent," Pat whispered. "Let's hope no one wakes up. We need the oxygen."

With the light on, Axel took a better look at the walls, tapping the gel nodes. Pat sat on the rotating VR chair, with her legs folded up under her, and her feet on the seat, giving him space. They were breathing on each other's faces. He noticed a whiteboard. Birgit's notes. Not genetic annotations, like the chalkboard. A list of initials, followed by dates. *MExAI, USMES, MDA, SJLYR, SGSV.* Twenty-two entries in total, with dates, months and weeks in between, except for the last seven entries, showing consecutive days, in the previous week. Prompts on his tab provided possible meanings for the acronyms. MExAI. One of Mondo's pet projects. *Multi-Exoplanet Artificial Intelligence.* A space programme shooting AI probes into the sky, looking for life on other planets.

"*Do you know what these are?*" he asked.

Pat stared at the initials, mouthing them in silence. "No."

"*What mistake were you talking about earlier?*"

Pat hissed in his ear and wrapped her legs around his waist, pulling him closer, like a boa constrictor. A few gentle squeezes. Was it Morse code? He knew fuck-all about Morse code. She put her arms around his chest. Maybe she was doing a praying mantis. Next, she'd chop his head off. Pat reached for his hand and touched his palm. She was writing letters. On his hand. One by one, with her finger, drawing the letter's shape. *W,* followed by *E. We.* She touched his palm with her closed wrist to indicate the end of a word. It took a long time to decipher the full message.

We deleted people from the AI model.

Hildr was the mistake.

He thought he had misunderstood.

"*How many?*" he asked.

A thousand. Maybe more.

The farmers had deleted data from USK's servers? How incredibly irresponsible. Food and shelter cancelled for a thousand people, including kids. The algorithm had probably assumed they had gone void. On purpose. Pat's legs were wrapped around his torso. This was beyond people-hugging. He could barely move.

"Do you have her login details?"

Worth asking, if Birgit had given her the code to the lab.

Pat's heel dug into his waist.

"You can turn it on."

Axel started wi-fi casting. The world around them turned green, every gel node blazing, immersion pod giving them a sample of its power. They were surrounded by grass-like stalks, with silky threads stretching from long, supple leaves, and flowering tassels at the top. The green carried on beyond sight, everywhere they looked. Sunrays whirled through the field, as if a cloud had just cleared. Above their heads, a dash of blinding light. A flutter of swallows crossing the sky. They gazed, entranced, grasshoppers bewitched by the patchwork of nature.

"Is it corn?"

Pat's legs wrapped tighter around him.

Instantly, the walls went back to a dull off-white, plunging them into partial darkness.

No input.

The moment had lasted five seconds. A screensaver.

Axel's view turned yellow.

Not the immersion pod, or corn.

Hard to make head or tail of it.

His head was trapped inside Pat's pyjama top, stretching the flimsy yellow fabric. A nipple slotted into his mouth.

"I can't breathe," he said, sucking in her breasts.

He slipped out of her top, swallowing big gulps of air. Pat's clammy tongue got in the way. She pulled him closer. They both climbed on Birgit's chair. The chair didn't like it. The sturdy back support toppled over the counter at the rear of the lab, making their foreheads bump against each other like billiard balls. He sucked on her mouth breathlessly, pressing his hard-on against her pelvis.

The chair's wheels skidded.

The whole caravan crashed on to the floor.

Axel froze.

"Why did you stop?" she asked.

The gel nodes must have made a decent padding against the noise. Their cocoon was a self-contained world, a chrysalis. Pat pulled Axel's boxer-shorts down to his knees and banged him against the floor, the wall, the chair, the lab machines, as if he represented the very essence and struggle of the metamorphosis, the outer skin she needed to expel. After an orgasm, she became calmer, less demanding. They lay naked on the floor, heads under the VR chair, feet up against the wall. His stomach created a cup-shaped nest for Pat's shaved head, a hedgehog slipping into hibernation, intoxicated by the increasing amount of carbon dioxide. He felt her heartbeat returning to normal.

"Why do you hate voids?" she asked.

Her warm breath made his hair stand on end.

"I can't stand their sense of entitlement."

"Entitlement? Strange way to see it. What happened, when you lived here? You got your chip in the year USK deported thousands. The year when they tested those horrible drones ... What did they call them?"

"Pitbulls."

"That's it. I was young, but I remember the migrants being chased down the street by the pitbulls."

Why was she chattering so much?

"I don't want to talk about it," Axel said.

"Were your parents in the model?"

"Never met my father."

He had already said more than he wanted to.

"How did you get your citizen-chip?" she asked.

"I helped them."

"Who?"

"The dogs."

He would never forget them. Four metallic legs, oil dripping from exposed ligaments, cone-heads shooting bee cameras in every direction.

Pat looked alarmed. "You helped the algorithm hunt down illegal immigrants?"

"Yes," he said.

"You didn't have a choice?"

He kept quiet.

"It must have been traumatising?" Pat said.

Was she suggesting he had done it for fun?

"I enjoyed every single fucking moment," he said, revelling in her shock. "I found something I was good at, and I was rewarded for it. What's not to like? I was thirteen and hungry for more. If I hadn't helped them, I would have been deported. Do you know what was the most satisfying part? When I told the dogs where she was."

Pat's eyes were fixed on him, whites popping out in the darkness.

"Who?" she said.

"My mother. I took the Pitbulls to the house where she was hiding. She was lying on the bed, covered head-to-toe by a duvet. Playing dead. For the dogs. I could see her profile, her shape under the cover, quiet, still. A presence. Just a presence. That sums up her role in my whole fucking life. Void."

"You're scaring me," Pat said.

Axel got up abruptly, put on his underwear, sat on the VR chair, opened a shared tab.

She stared intently at the tab. Her eyes were wet. She was shaking.

He was shaking too.

How dare she judge him?

"Is this your triangulation?" she said.

"Have a look for yourself. The confidence interval is low. Not enough data."

"Can you find more data sources?" Pat asked.

Either she had recovered her faith in his method, or his other skills had made an impression.

"We can follow up on more clues to increase the confidence intervals," he said.

"What's this graph in the middle?"

"A stochastic model of the kid's disappearance, using a six-level analysis into consecutive hypotheses inferred from the triangulation. Assuming a normal probability distribution, we get this bell-shaped curve with the standard deviation."

The chair creaked and moaned as they leaned shoulder-to-shoulder.

"What's this?" she asked.

"What?" He moved his hand away.

"The photo you've just hovered over." The news must be handled with care. Pat wasn't going to like it. "The lines on this chart," she insisted. "What do they represent?"

"Each line is a guess for where the kid is likely to be now."

Pat was squinting at the central value and the vertical spikes next to it, getting progressively shorter towards the edges. *Winning hypothesis* was the title at the top of the chart. Cryptic enough.

Axel pulled a different graph into focus.

"These are the three main clues we can follow, to improve confidence intervals."

Pat slid back to the previous graph.

"Can you hover over this line again?" she said. "The one in the middle. What was the photo that popped up?" She wasn't letting go.

She touched the bars on the bell graph. The coordinates appeared, labels filling up with a map. Satellite photos. A set of bright, saturated green and brown pixels. Pat squinted and frowned, going from bar to bar, looking at the labels and the matching photos.

"Did you say this was where Hildr was likely to be now? This is a photo of the patch at the back of the greenhouse. And these are pictures of the mountain, random piles of scrambled dirt and bushes. How could Hildr be …"

Pat's confusion formed a dark cloak covering her face.

She shook her head, first a hesitant repudiation, then a full-blown denial of the *winning hypothesis*. She thought it out loud, eyes glazed, voice disappearing into a soft whine.

"Is Hildr dead and buried somewhere near our house?"

Try as he might, he could think of no other plausible conclusion.

Pancakes without eggs, article in the Part-time Scientist

I'm meeting the tall Frenchman outside Reims, near an abandoned motorway, a safe distance from an electrified fence. He is holding a wicker basket filled with real fruits and vegetables: apples, oranges, courgettes. A towering industrial facility roars in the background. The air is full of a lovely lavender aroma. "See that patch of soil over there?" the Frenchman asks me. "Too small and dry for trees. Everyone's obsessing about trees nowadays. We got planting consent for lavender. Lavender! Who's going to eat that? Maybe a pet cat." He hands me a beautiful red apple from his basket, saying "These are from inside." He proceeds to explain how hydroponics are used by astronauts to grow food in space, delivering nutrients to plants through a liquid solution. According to him, the method provides a rich, misty environment where plants can thrive. Combined with aeroponics, this avoids the need for large areas of soil. "But no one talks about hydroponics, do they? Putain. Companies just want to sell their ultra-processed food. If we can make pancakes without eggs, why can't we grow plants without soil?"

Chapter Eighteen

(Hildr) The play

In the farmers' camp, at the top of the Beranger mountain, Hildr drew a bead dictating her role for the day. She would be a feeder. She went down the path to the jute sacks and learned how to use a net to percolate earthworms from dirt. She helped the farmers crush the worms to make their protein bars, a dense mixture of boiled larvae flesh, beans and cornflour. They taught her to add scraps of nuts to some bars, and sugar, swede and fennel to others. Some bars were eaten on the day. The rest were stored in ice for the winter.

At mealtimes, Hildr sat with the thirty-strong group, in a wide, lively circle. Ula's presence had changed the mood. There were tales and anecdotes, chatter, songs and laughter. The extraordinary troupe had come alive, orchestrated by the great dame with frizzled grey hair. With Ula's blessing, the farmers showed Hildr their traditions: the giant shrouds embroidered with garish images of daisies, roses and tulips; the cows, pigs and goats sculpted on caves; the sacred dances and pagan lyrics to protect the harvest and ask for a bountiful year. Accounts of their lifestyle could be found all over Uskania. Their eccentricity had given them the status of unsung heroes, reviving a simple way of life, away from the comforts and downfalls of technology. The farmers' camp was the Ultima Thule of the Nordics, the happy land bearing the myths of fallen nations.

They kept her busy all day, and she didn't get a chance to spend a single minute alone with Ula. She wondered what was going on in the farmer's head, after their chat by the precipice. Did Ula think she was *the girl*? Why hadn't Ula mentioned this during their tense conversation? Hildr suspected the bracelet was hidden somewhere near the volcano, where Ula collected their drone deliveries. She needed an excuse to go up there.

By late afternoon, duties completed, Hildr finally spotted Ula on her own. The grey lady was sitting near the living quarters, making a slender piece of bamboo into a flute, under the faint light of the ever-setting sun. Using a Swiss army knife, Ula worked carefully and methodically, carving a mouthpiece, small circular holes, and delicate decorative patterns with spirals and lines. Hildr's height cast a long shadow as she approached.

"Have you thought about using candles?"

Ula looked up from her bamboo flute.

"Do you take us for Neanderthals? We have gas lamps. We take them out in the autumn. Plenty of light now. We can't afford to waste gas." Hildr was mildly vexed, but the old woman continued lightly. "Did you enjoy your work today? Should give you a good night's sleep. The entertainers are preparing the fire for the play."

Ula's tone was unrecognisable. She had apparently dropped the mad prophet act and become the caring host. Hildr did up the old red parka the farmers had lent her, protecting herself from the cool breeze.

"What about tomorrow, are you going back to the volcano?" She didn't understand why Ula hadn't yet joined the dots. She *must* suspect Hildr was Birgit's daughter. Yet she hadn't mentioned that or the bracelet.

"Getting itchy feet already?" Ula asked. "The mountain is not for everyone. You can be an idler tomorrow, if that suits you."

Perhaps Ula needed further proof she could trust her.

"Nothing to do with the jobs," Hildr said. "It's just … I have so many questions. I can't relax until I find the answers."

"You shouldn't stay idle then. That's why we have the rota, and keep ourselves busy. It greases the engine in our head until it makes no noise."

This conversation wasn't going anywhere.

"It's nice here." Hildr sketched a slow, sheepish smile.

Ula turned her face aside.

"I sent many messages to the outer world when we first came to the mountain. I wanted people to know it was possible to live without the algorithm." She continued her handiwork, carving the bamboo with her knife.

"I missed Fyr. I lived on the island until I was seven years old, before moving to Iceland."

Ula's eyes caught hers, like a sniper taking aim.

"What do you remember from Fyr? Can you speak our dialect?"

Hildr focused inside herself.

No words.

"I'm sorry. I was probably too young."

"What about Swedish, or Norwegian?" Ula asked.

Hildr shook her head. "A little Icelandic, but mainly English."

"Everything is in English nowadays," Ula said. "Fyr's dialect is gone. It was a mix of Norwegian, Icelandic, Gaelic and fifteen other languages, the lingua franca of the folk who first came to the island and wanted an inclusive language. Impossible ever to reproduce the recipe. The first generation even dropped their surnames and shortened the rest. A lot of us still have three-letter names. We are the descendants of those first settlers."

Ula. Liz. Bas.

A comforting quietness emerged from this exchange, a complicity. Language was an easy topic.

"I think I remember the dialect ..." Hildr lied, hoping to deepen their connection. Why was Ula not taking the bait? "I have an idea, but it's only a bud at this stage."

Ula frowned. "A bug?"

"A *bud*," Hildr said. "A bud that may flower one day."

The older woman let out a short howl.

"You make me laugh. First a bug, now a bud. What's your idea, then?"

She was back to shooting questions in a sarcastic tone.

"Liz told me you can send messages using drones from donations. Why don't we prepare lessons about Fyr's lost dialect and share them with other islands? I'll be your student. We could go up to the crater together."

Ula listened without protesting, her lips twitching slightly mockingly.

"What about what you told me yesterday?"

"What about it?" Hildr asked.

"You're not going to get in touch with your friends in Iceland? Are you saying you want to live on the mountain for the rest of your life?"

"I don't have anywhere else to go."

Ula dropped the bamboo flute and pointed the Swiss army knife at Hildr.

"Do you take me for a fool?" Her tone had changed.

Hildr trembled. The sharp blade was only a foot away from her face.

"Why are you saying that?"

"Stop this nonsense," Ula said. "Right now. Do you hear me? Stop. Your bug was our idea. Eighteen years ago, we prepared the plan, step by step. We suspended the disentanglement field. We deleted citizen-chips from the algorithm. Exactly as you described. We wanted citizens to be hit by the glitch, to revolt against technology, to demand answers from the Devs. It didn't happen. Instead, the algorithm cut off the island. We all know the rest."

A man in a woollen hat and grey overalls approached.

"The play is about to start," he said.

Ula put the knife in her pocket, collected her flute, and walked away.

Hildr stood with her hands in her pockets, legs apart, fighting a sense of vertigo.

Had she made up a true story?

The farmers had gathered outside the living area, shuffling together in concentric rows, positioning themselves in front of the area designated as a stage. A fire burned in a rusty steel barrel. A smell of stale sweat lingered. Ula sat at the front of the audience. Hildr chose the back row, lowering herself to the ground with a sense of impending doom. If Ula was speaking the truth, she had made a terrible mistake. Red flames flickered against the twilight. She let her mind empty itself, focusing on the tentacles of fire leaping out of the steel barrel.

Two men walked onto the improvised stage. Hildr recognised the farmers who had drawn the beads for entertainer jobs that morning. The man on the right was Liz's good friend, one of the youngest in the group, tall and lanky, with a stubble beard and dark circles under his eyes. The man on the left was older, with a stooped back and a protruding stomach. They were facing each other, profiles to the audience, waiting for the last murmurs to die away.

Silence took over.

The tall man feigned surprise, widening his eyes, and forming an "O" with his mouth, like a mime artist.

The older man copied him.

The younger man yanked his arms upwards, as if an invisible magnet was pulling him from the sky, shaking his body in dramatic convulsions.

The older man copied him.

They dropped their arms and raised them in the air again.

"Why are you copying me?" the younger man said.

"Because we look alike."

"I'm taller, fairer and younger than you. My eyes are blue, yours brown. Do you sleep in a prone or foetal position?"

"Neither. I prefer lying on my back. But I have two arms, two legs, and my nose sticks out from my face in a similar way." The older man crossed his eyes, pointing at his nose. "See? I'm definitely human."

The younger man looked nonplussed. He sighed and raised his hands in the air. The older man followed suit, yanking his arms with a slapstick spasm.

The audience laughed heartily.

"Stop copying me," the young man said, raising his voice to a falsetto. "The aliens will arrive soon, and I want to be the first to leave."

The older man squatted and put his hands on his head, whining softly. "Not again ..."

The tall man frowned. "Not *again*? Again what?"

"Travelling is all I've been doing for zillions of years ... Before the Milky Way, I was in Andromeda, Pinwheel, Tadpole, Avalanche, and galaxies with names I don't even know how to pronounce in your language. When a planet becomes uninhabitable, I move on to another one. It's almost impossible to find a good planet within a reasonable distance. Too hot or too cold. Not enough water, or not enough oxygen. The list goes on. I must travel for an eternity. I've just arrived on Earth. Please don't make me set off again." He was wailing, hands on his head.

"If you can travel anywhere, why would you stay here? The climate is changing."

"We have enough food on the farm ..."

"The Earth is full of pain and injustice."

"It's nice here, in the Beranger ..."

"There's too much uncertainty about the future."

The older man got to his feet, standing opposite the young one, like a mirror.

"Too much uncertainty about the *what*?"

"The future," he repeated.

"Time is just a way of measuring distance. I'm happy here, in the present."

The young man rolled his eyes.

They stared at each other, expressionless.

The young man threw his arms up in the air. The jerk made his whole body swing, like a diver ready to plunge. The older man hurried to copy him, wobbling on his feet.

"Is this the future now?" he asked.

Liz looked behind her, caught Hildr's eye and giggled.

Newfoundland meteorite carries alien protein, John H. Chapman Space Centre, Quebec

A team of scientists at the Centre for Astrophysics and Cosmology, University of Iceland, in collaboration with researchers at the John H. Chapman Space Centre in Quebec, generously sponsored by food multinational Mondo, has found compelling evidence for bacteria-like fossils and new chemical compounds in the Newfoundland meteorite. The core of igneous rock inside the 200kg meteorite dates from about 12 billion years ago, the period immediately after the Milky Way formed. The ancient rock is believed to have been part of a proto planet which was extensively fractured by the impact of celestial bodies in the bumpy early stages of our galaxy's formation. The finding strongly suggests primitive life forms exist in our galaxy beyond our solar system. Research team leader at Mondo Foods, Dr Birgit Olsen, said: "What we're looking at is potentially a new amino acid, a new type of protein alien to our planet. This is one of many avenues we're exploring and widens the scope of our research into organic forms of energy, contributing to the further development of New Food."

Chapter Nineteen

(Axel) The purge

Axel would have liked to have better news, but the results of his triangulation were clear. According to his data model, Hildr was dead and buried somewhere near the Blue Boat commune. That was the winning hypothesis. Most of the evidence pointed to a bad ending, and the few inconsistencies were unexplained as yet.

Pat shook her head, still in denial.

"Data models don't capture the truth … they're possibilities, estimations … Hildr was alive and well, until her tech stopped working."

"We're all alive and well, until we aren't," he said.

"You don't understand. It was our fault." She talked fast, syllables tumbling over each other. "It was all our doing. We interfered with the algorithm. Hildr's citizen-chip stopped working because we made it stop. It doesn't mean she's dead. She's not dead!" Optimism fighting against reality. That was Pat, in a nutshell.

Putting his arms around her waist, Axel tried to pull her back to Earth. "The reason why her tech stopped doesn't matter. It doesn't change the outcome of the triangulation."

Pat sat on his lap, burying her face on his neck. Her pulse drummed against his thyroid, blending with his own.

"It's not true ..."

Axel stroked her hair, softly. He desperately wanted her to be right. "Please don't cry. The confidence interval is low." A truth they could both believe. "Less than 70% across the nested hypotheses. There are clues we can follow to increase the confidence. If we feed the model more data, the results might change. Shall we look at the clues together?"

In theory, they should be digging for the body.

The practice was more complicated.

Pat lifted her head, pulling back from his chest.

"What clues?"

A photo of a dark-green composting bin appeared on their shared tab. On closer inspection, they confirmed it was outside the commune, where Pat had found the bracelet, by the path leading to the beach. She seemed more content with this plan, relieved they were not getting a shovel out. Distant voices arrived from outside their cocoon. Gef and the others had woken up. Axel touched his ear against the wall. Pat copied him. Their noses almost touched.

"How are we getting out of here?" he said.

She had got them in there. He was about to complain when a new notification arrived on his tab.

IMPORTANT.

The algorithm sent notifications all the time, but this one was so invasive it blocked him from using other tabs. Not a subtle way to get his attention. Pat was trying to open a new tab too, her hand floating in the same skyward gesture.

Axel clicked on the message.

Leave FYR as soon as possible. A salvage ship will depart at 21:00 local time. Do NOT bring local residents with you.

Eruption? Tsunami? Meteorite? Axel was ready to kick his way out of the wall, when his brain acknowledged they had a few hours to wait before the salvage ship left. He opened a new tab. Fyr's discussion channels were sputtering into life.

Pat touched his arm, sharing her version of the message:

IMPORTANT. If you know citizens on other islands who can host you, please complete this form. FYR is being removed from the model.

How could they remove a whole island from the model? Two hours of sleep and the kid's case still to close. Not a good turn of events. Outside the lab, Pat's housemates were talking louder. They had probably got the message too. Axel swung his shoulder against the door. The whole lab rumbled with the impact.

"What are you doing?" Pat said.

"Trying to get us the hell out of here."

Stepping around him, she pressed a button that was hidden from sight. The stink of weed was the first thing to hit him. He saw people running down the corridor. Two voids were still in Birgit's bedroom, next to the sofa, staring at him, speechless. He and Pat must look quite a sight, emerging out of the wall in their underwear.

Axel dashed to the window, pushing one of the voids out of the way. The man lost his balance and fell onto a pile of seed boxes.

"Jump." Axel instructed Pat.

The second man came to his friend's aid. "You're not going anywhere."

Axel grabbed him by the neck and held him up against the wall.

"Please don't hurt him," Pat said.

She sat on the windowsill, looking at them. What the hell was she waiting for? The illegal scratched Axel's hand with his dirty nails, struggling to breathe, feet dangling.

"Get out now," Axel shouted.

Bloodied skin peeled off his wrist.

Pat flicked both legs out of the window.

He let go of the man and jumped out after her. A group of flatmates stood by the greenhouse. Gef, Bil, Coraline, and others. Axel swerved in a cloud of dust and turned back, deeper into the side alley, away from the greenhouse, sprinting towards the fence which separated them from the main road. He lunged at the fence, fingers grasping the top, and hoisted himself up. Pat was shorter than him. She reached up but kept slipping, scraping her toes on the knotted wood of the fence. A warrior shout rang out from the back garden. From his vantage point at the top of the fence, Axel saw Gef and a crowd of voids sprinting towards them. He could make out their words as they drew closer.

"Finders keepers, losers weepers!"

The group repeated the chant, like football hooligans. *Finders keepers, losers weepers.*

Axel grabbed Pat's hand, pulling hard, all his muscles tensing. Her bare feet skidded on the fence, and they both tumbled to the other side, landing on the street. Spitting dust, they got to their feet. Their destination hadn't been spoken out loud, but they converged on the same path, behind the compost bin. They were running down to the beach.

Gef's shouts echoed behind them.

"Finders keepers, losers weepers!"

Axel looked back and saw the rabble leaping over the fence, jumping out of the windows, leaving through the front door, coming out of every hole in the commune, like maggots wriggling out of a corpse. He shot forward, down the path between houses. Pat couldn't match his head start. He hesitated, came back for her, grabbing her hand, dragging her along, veering between the back gardens full of old furniture, a drumbeat of footsteps behind them. They reached the swamp with tall reeds. Pat stepped onto the oozy ground, stumbled, tripped, sank onto her hands. Black mud smeared her face, and the legs of her bright yellow pyjamas. Axel grabbed her hand, pulling her up.

"Stop," she gasped, tripping again. Was she hurt? "We need to go that way," she said, pointing left. "If we go to the beach, we'll be easy prey. We need to hide on the mountain."

They pivoted, progressing in short jumps, avoiding getting stuck in the mud. At the edge of the swamp, Axel stepped forward and almost fell. The sand had given way under his feet. He stopped, open-mouthed. A vast area of *nothingness* stretched ahead, before the grey wall of the mountain. There was nowhere to hide. They wouldn't be able to reach the mountain before their pursuers were upon them.

"Switch off your navigation," Pat said, next to him, glued to the spot, arm outstretched.

"Why?"

"This area is not on the map. Switch off the map, turn off your filters, come out of your tab. NOW."

He followed her instructions.

Unbelievable.

He had never come across such a vast, uncharted territory. Where the nothingness had been, a whole valley emerged, a deep crevice meandering and coiling around solidified whirlpools of mud, like an old riverbed from a melting glacier. They were at the edge of the dried riverbank, bright and sharp as a computer-generated image. Countless voids were gathered in groups, along the valley floor. Axel and Pat stepped forward, falling down the steep bank, feet and legs dragging in a cloud of dust, reaching the bottom and gathering speed. Pat headed to the closest group of voids.

Four silent souls, dark eyes with rings underneath.

"Citizen," one of the voids said, acknowledging her tech with a blank expression. The others nodded, exchanging mute glances.

"Sorry to crash your party," she said. "If you help us hide, I will give you food."

Axel glanced over his shoulder. Gef and the others had stopped by the reeds, looking for them among the crowd.

"We don't have time to hide."

He pulled Pat towards the mountain, and they ran, passing more scattered groups. A hand reached up from the ground. A man. Waving at them. Long hair, brown jacket with fake sheepskin round the collar, and a dark beard outlining his jaw, longer at the chin.

When they reached him, the man was already on his feet.

"Are you in trouble?" The man said. "Come with me."

A pointy beard. *Like a devil.*

The Uskanian school for Devs, excerpt from award-winning documentary

After the graduation ceremony, new Devs choose their area of specialisation. Some become responsible for improving nutrition, healthcare or housing. Others dream about managing infrastructure, logistics or entertainment. Together, they look after everything required by USK citizens. No other nation in the world has achieved the same level of efficiency, unity and happiness. On the wall of the Planning Hall, a map with timelines shows human migration and mutation patterns over the last 200,000 years, since homo sapiens *came to dominate the planet. At the end of the sequence, a white tulip blossoms from the algorithm's code. A nova child, sleeping in her crib.*

Chapter Twenty

(Hildr) The jogger

U la walked over in the morning, before they drew beads. "You don't need a job today." Hildr set off behind the grey lady, carrying the rucksack she had thrown over her shoulders. She thought they were heading to the farm. Instead, they trekked along a rough path she had never taken before, crawling over loose rocks. They reached a wide plateau. Dried lava crumbled under her feet. Round the corner from the farmers' living quarters, a vision hit her. The ridges of the Beranger volcano, peak draped in snow. White flecks spotted the volcano's sides, like marble tears trickling down the Earth's cheeks.

"We're not going to the crater," Ula said. "We're going down."

The bracelet. Ula was finally taking her to the hidden bracelet. Where else could they be going? Hildr followed her along the plateau, barely containing her excitement. Ula's movements suggested a familiar route, but the long trek over dust and moss was a visible effort for the old woman. She was sweating and panting when they reached the edge of the cliff. No path led onwards, only a steep drop to much lower ground. Ula walked along the brink.

"Here," she said.

A large horn-shaped boulder hung at the edge of the cliff.

Ula removed a black harness from her rucksack and stepped into it, fitting the straps around her waist. She opened Hildr's rucksack and removed another harness, attaching carabiners, wrapping a thick sling around the horn-shaped rock, and bending a long rope through loops and hoops. Stopper knots. Ula's swift, confident movements didn't lessen Hildr's fear.

"Haven't rappelled before?" Ula asked. She kept looping and yanking at the rope. "You had a lift in your home in Iceland, perhaps?" They exchanged a subtle smile. "I need to prepare your knots in advance. I brought enough rope."

Ula repeated the process for the rope attached to Hildr's harness, tugging at the knots with stronger jerks. Flicking her rope over the edge, Ula pulled at the extension and was gone.

Hildr took a deep breath.

A leap.

Just a leap.

Their bounces alternated against the rocky wall of the mountain, like two fleas jumping down Goliath's back. Each time she gave in more rope, Hildr's heart leapt. She felt as if she was undoing her climbing achievement from days before. Ula reached the level below and Hildr landed a few seconds later. The older woman unhooked herself, wrapped the extension around her shoulder and carried on walking. Hildr ran to catch up.

"Are we going down to the beach?"

How ironic. Maybe the bracelet had been there the whole time.

"Not quite. I want you to meet a neighbour. He lives a few floors down."

Ula led the way, pointing at the best spots for them to keep descending. Around midday, sitting on a flat slab, they gobbled down a couple of protein bars. Two sleeping bags dangled from Hildr's rucksack, and she found a stack of bars inside, suggesting Ula had packed for an overnight stay. As if they were old travelling companions, the farmer opened up about her plans.

"We're paying a visit to an old friend. You must forgive him any impropriety. The older and lonelier one gets, the further one moves from the traditional demands of hospitality. He always refused to live on the farm with us."

Ula appeared to be mulling this over, eyes fixed on the overcast sky.

The journey had brought them closer.

"Liz told me about the girl," Hildr said.

Ula took a bite of her protein bar and coughed drily. "Liz is a child. She knows nothing beyond the rota."

She spoke with undisguised scorn.

"You discount everyone's opinions," Hildr said. "Why don't you live alone, like your friend?"

A derisory smile.

"The company has suited me so far. Keep your expectations low and be pleasantly surprised when people don't disappoint."

They carried on downwards, reaching their destination before the sun touched the horizon. The cave was impossible to spot from far away, large boulders and a natural recess hiding the entrance. Outside, the ground bore signs of successive fires, circular stains of grey cinder and black charcoal. Narrow, pillar-like rocks adorned the entrance, positioned upright against the walls, like doorposts. A haphazard pile of man-made objects stood on top. A gas oven. Cooking pots. Lanterns. Buckets. Shovels, tins, jars, knives. Blankets and pairs of used trainers. Ula went inside the cave, her footsteps echoing. Hildr followed. At the back of the grotto, further cavities and crannies, and a sour smell in the air.

"Hey old man, are you sleeping?" Ula called. "Comb your scruffy hair. You have visitors." She couldn't see who Ula was talking to.

Hildr noticed a neat pile of faded biscuit tins, labelled with small handwritten stickers. Each sticker had a date, scribbled in Icelandic. "May to August 2140", "September 2140 to April 2141", and so on. Dozens of biscuit tins formed an inventory stretching over years. Hildr touched one of the tins.

"What are these?" The steel plate cover gave a mournful crack as her fingers released their pressure.

"Arrgghh."

Hildr nearly jumped at the guttural sound coming from the back of the cave.

Ula ambled to the corner and stared at a recess.

"She's not going to damage your precious boxes, old man. Get on your feet. Have you been out for your run already?"

A long sigh. Scratching noises. The man walked out into the light, dragging his bare feet. He looked like a real hermit, gaunt, with a wiry, grey and white beard, long greasy hair and bushy grey eyebrows. Quite old but he still had a straight back, and he wore a blue tracksuit that was in surprisingly good condition.

"What do you want?" he asked in staccato English, visibly annoyed. His eyes were dark and evasive, meandering along the rock by his feet.

"I brought someone to meet you," Ula said. Only then did the hermit raise his eyes to Hildr, who was standing near the wall, in the way of a shy, unannounced visitor. The hermit's face muscles shifted from apathy to profound interest. He trotted towards Hildr and stared at her as if he had encountered a new species.

"Is it her?" Ula asked.

With bulging eyes and sky-high eyebrows, the hermit gazed intently at Hildr, examining her features in great detail, and even inspecting inside her nostrils. Hildr took a step back, grinding her jaw.

"Maybe," he said. "She's so tall. She looked tall in the videos, but I didn't expect something like this. Astonishing."

"Something? You mean *someone*," Hildr said.

"She says she became a Dev," Ula said.

"Can you both stop talking as if I'm not here?"

"What's her name?" the hermit asked.

"She says it's Hildr, but her story doesn't make sense. She claims she has amnesia."

Had she never believed her?

"Amnesia?" he repeated. "Hmm. Where did she come from?"

"Iceland," Hildr said, before they put more words in her mouth. "And my story *does* make sense. I tried to sabotage the algorithm. USK erased my memory before sending me here to be deported."

"We've already established the sabotage was *our* idea," Ula said. "Not yours."

"Who are you?" Hildr was looking at the hermit.

"Gunnar Grimsson. I was tasked with finding you, or a kid who looked like you, about twenty years ago."

Hildr smiled. "Is this the girl Liz mentioned? You think I might be the girl?"

The pieces were finally slotting into place.

"All kids look the same to me." Gunnar had a monotonous voice, as if he was sleepy, or holding back. "Damn you women and your snotty little children. Especially the brown ones. No food for you here."

Hildr was aghast.

Ula shrugged. "Sorry, I did warn you. Please Gunnar, don't rile our guest with your despicable views. There's no point harassing people of any gender or colour, when the rich have more than they need."

Gunnar crossed his arms and turned aside. "You're stupid, if you think that. Why would anyone have kids? They eat more than adults. At least I never fell into that trap."

His spite was so extreme, it was almost a parody of hate.

"He's just saying this to badger me," Ula said, looking at Hildr. "I haven't come to visit in a while. He's lonely and upset."

They sounded like an old couple bickering.

Where was the bracelet?

"Can either of you explain why this girl is important?"

Ula spoke first. "She was the daughter of a friend of a friend. She ... they ... were separate matters but unfortunately became ... entangled."

She avoided Hildr's gaze as she said this, looking almost embarrassed. What could embarrass the great grey dame? Hildr stepped around Gunnar and stood in front of Ula.

"What matters became entangled?"

Gunnar pivoted on his feet, glazed eyes flicking between the two women, following the interaction.

Ula's silence was unbearable.

"The girl was one of the citizens we removed from the AI model," Ula said. "We deleted several chips from their data centres. The error was randomised, you see. We didn't pick specific citizens. We had nothing against them. The girl had a history of running away, apparently. When her tech stopped working, no one could track her down."

"Ula is admitting the farmers messed up," Gunnar said, "back then and ever since. I was used to finding scum, but it was a shock to come across the kid's case."

"Were you a Finder?" Hildr asked.

Gunnar looked blank again, dropping his chin as if chewing bubble-gum.

"He was a fierce USK supporter," Ula said, "until he got busted. The old man never got used to living without his tech. He still logs his daily activities on toilet paper, keeps them inside those tins. Why don't you show them to her, Gunnar?"

He repeated the grizzly bear grunt they'd heard earlier, then grudgingly grabbed a biscuit tin from the top of the pile. As he opened the lid, a few squares of toilet paper flew out and landed on the ground. There were hundreds of sheets of toilet paper inside the tin, each one covered in scribbles. The black ink added interest and texture to the soft toilet paper, making it look like parchment from an alien civilisation. Gunnar collected the stray papers from the ground and showed them to Hildr.

"I don't log everything any more, only my running times." His withered, reddish hand was holding a piece with entries in black ink. "Day, time of start and finish, approximate distance, pace, route, related comments." She glanced at the comments. 'Oppressive heat made me slower.' On another entry: 'pain on my left knee again, had to take it easy'. Further down the page: 'good run despite the dancing cunts everywhere'.

"You're the jogger from the beach," she said. "I saw your footsteps. Where do you get the energy to run every day?"

"Gunnar is a friend of the guards at the removal centre," Ula said. "He reports new illegals arriving, in exchange for food. Disgraceful misogynist, racist, xenophobe, and a snitch too. Sometimes I feel sick remembering there are people like him in the world. I wish they all lived in a cave."

Hildr's eyes darted back to Gunnar, waiting for a nasty reply.

It never came.

He just pressed the toilet paper back into the box, closed the lid, and placed it back on top of the pile.

"I have spare New Food cartons," Gunnar said. "Including Ula's favourite, oat biscuits. Will you ladies stay for the night?"

Form for Fyr residents applying for residency on another island

Thank you for applying to move to another island covered by the USK software. This option is only available if you have a contact who can host you. Please complete the form below.

Your contact's citizen-chip number: _________

Can they host you immediately? Yes/No

Are you currently a carer for underage or elderly citizens? Yes/No

Are any goods or credits being exchanged? Yes/No

Once you press 'submit', we'll get back to you within 5 working days.

It's the first time we're discontinuing an island from the algorithm. Housing, food and healthcare continue to be completely free for USK citizens and this requires us to manage resources in a sensible and proactive way.

Chapter Twenty-One

(Axel) Shadow town

Axel and Pat ran up the mountain, led by the man with the pointy beard. Cumulus clouds hung over dark hills. On the slope overlooking the Arctic Ocean, the terrain changed. The steep ground segmented into sections covered in mud, a mesh of connected ovals waving into long patterned rows. The new texture pulsated up the mountain, like the back of a giant armadillo. Axel thought it was an optical illusion until one of the mud structures stood directly in his path. Mounds of dirt had been pulled around the oblong shape, revealing an entrance. The underlying structure was made of a soft, malleable material, covered in layers of mud. He touched it. Pliable, but firm. The entrance was big enough for a person to go in.

Axel popped his head inside.

An egg-shaped room, darkened by deep, blunt shadows.

In the darkness, something moved.

Axel jumped backwards.

He stared into the distance, unable to move, stunned, feeling like an idiot. What were these structures all over the mountain? They looked like nests. Egg-shaped nests covered in mud, with circular entrances and tight dark rooms inside. He passed more nests on the way up, disturbing burrows camouflaged by the thick skin of the mountain. Pat had stopped further ahead. He saw her turning left, into another row. A head peeked out of a nest. Then another. There were people inside the eggs. Even children in some of them. They all popped their heads back inside when they saw him.

Madness.

Pat and the man with the pointy beard had disappeared. Axel was alone in the freak town. He spun around, looking towards the valley. Gef and the housemates were somewhere down there, making their way up to them.

Another notification popped up.

> URGENT. *Leave FYR as soon as possible. Do NOT attempt to bring residents with you.*

"Turn it off!" someone yelled behind him.

Axel looked around, within his tab. The result was disorientating. The nests had disappeared. He was back in anonymous, uncharted terrain. He closed the tab. The shout had prompted a wave of heads to emerge from the egg-shaped structures, undulating up the mountain. Nearby, Pat went inside one of the nests.

Axel ran up, following her. He stood outside the structure, peeking in. The room stank of garlic and synthetic fat. He scanned the darkness. Blankets. Carrier bags. Clothes. Sausage leftovers. A stool made of the same rubbery material as the walls.

"Welcome to my home," the man with the pointy beard said. "I recommend you don't use your tabs here. You won't find our streets on your maps. USK quit sending drones a long time ago. We shoot them down." He had an accent, with closed vowels and a soft lisp, but perfect English otherwise. The pretence only lasted a moment. Axel didn't care how well-spoken he was.

"What *is* this place?" he said.

"A submarine," Pat said. "Most migrants arrive on Fyr in one of these and convert them into homes afterwards. Will you please come inside and wait until it's safe to leave?"

He was not going inside this hole.

Like a devil.

Wiry snout of a ravenous dog.

"I'm Ivan," the devil said, extending his hand.

Panic showed on his face. Panic was expected. Panic was natural. Ivan should have thought of that before messing up with a kid.

"What did you do to her?" Axel said.

Pat tried moving his arm. When that didn't work, she hit Axel's chest, grabbed him by the waist, attempted to pull him away. She failed.

Axel kept pressing Ivan's jugular.

The devil's eyes widened in terror.

"Axel, stop!" Pat yelled, yanking at his arm.

Ivan opened his mouth. A pink tongue slithered out of his lips.

"What did you do to her?" Axel repeated.

"You're choking him!" Pat said.

"Did you kill her?" Axel said.

"He can't speak," Pat said. "You're suffocating him. Please stop."

"He was the last one to see her alive."

Pat jumped on Axel's shoulders and climbed over his face. More people were grabbing his arms, punching his chest, stomach, back. He was pulled sharply backwards. He lost his grip on Ivan's neck and fell to the ground. They held him down, immobilising his arms and legs, shadows against the bright pastel sky. More people came out of their nests, forming a circle around the group.

Ivan massaged his throat. "Why have you brought this animal with you?" His voice faltered. His neck was covered in red streaks, his eyes bloodshot. "The other one almost got himself killed. The farmers took pity and let him come with them."

"You're joking?" Pat said. "Gunnar's with Ula?"

"You know what happens when people are not being tracked?" Axel raised his voice from the ground, despite the feet pressing on his chest. "Impunity. Voids can rape, steal and kill, without a single witness. He was the last one to see Hildr alive. He's your main suspect. Ask him where the kid is."

"I didn't lay a finger on the kid," Ivan said. His eyes wandered back to Pat. "I swear. She wanted to go to the port. She wanted to watch the big container ships. She wanted to meet her real family."

"The port?" Pat repeated. "Let's check the port. Maybe you can collect more data for your triangulation?"

She was desperate to believe the kid wasn't dead.

"He's lying," Axel said.

"There's more than five hundred of us," Ivan said. "If you try to touch me again, we'll leave you for dead in the valley."

"Miserable leech," Axel spat.

Pat kicked him softly on the chest. "I'm afraid we have more trouble."

Axel couldn't open the notification.

She opened hers and read out loud.

URGENT. You are in a danger zone. Please head back to a mapped area NOW.

She looked at the crowd gathered around them. "We've been getting messages since this morning. They're shutting Fyr off from the algorithm. It's a purge."

A murmur rose.

People translated the message into other languages.

German, Italian, French.

Ivan looked at Pat. "Is it legit?"

"The algorithm knows there are citizens down here," Axel said. "They wouldn't do anything while we're on the mountain."

Pat made eye contact with everyone. "I think we'd better take the warning seriously, and leave."

The bust-up with Ivan was drowned by the uproar. The news spread like wildfire through the mud-covered homes. Many doubted the threat but could not gather the courage to stay. Best to leave and come back later, if the danger proved unfounded. The whole shadow town came out into the light. Hundreds of illegals, dirty, harassed, forming a long procession between rows of subs, marching down the mountain with bags, rags, blankets. Pat, Ivan and Axel followed a group of loud Germans, rescuing relics at the last moment. A watch. A scarf. A teddy. The valley was filling up fast with the displaced crowd.

Then the noise started.

First, a faraway whirring, above, around, surrounding them. As the noise circled nearer, they looked upwards, expectantly. The waiting seemed harder to stomach than whatever came next.

"Doesn't sound like a mapping drone," Ivan said.

Army drones.

Gunshots echoed across the valley. One of the illegals was shooting at the drones with a rifle. A yellow light flashed in the sky, like a shard reflecting a ray of sun. The drone had gone down. Brief shouts of celebration.

The relief didn't last long.

A louder detonation shook the ground.

Shouts, cries, clouds of dust, people trampling over each other. Men, women, children, running for their lives, down to the valley. Axel stopped, trying to withstand a human wave running in the opposite direction, pushing him down. Where was Pat? He couldn't see her bright yellow clothes anywhere.

Another explosion.

The army drones were dropping bombs. It was a bloodbath. Had the algorithm gone mad? They knew there were citizens down here, him and Pat at the very least. He saw a spot of yellow among the mob and followed it blindly, immune to the detonations and shouts. Pat was covered in blood and dust, clutching something against her chest. He put his arm around her. She handed him a small bundle of fabric. Trousers. She had found trousers. They were too short, but they held on fine to his waist. Trousers. Madness. They sprinted through the valley, people scattering in every direction, towards the beach, towards the city centre, towards nowhere.

Axel and Pat stopped at the end of Birgit's street, looking at the mountain behind the commune. Columns of dust and smoke billowed upwards. The shadow town was burning. They watched the mountain smouldering against the pink sky, unspoken horror pinning them to the ground. Pat let go of his hand, then sat on the pavement, staring ahead, with the vacant eyes of the bereaved. She pressed her knuckles against her muddied cheeks.

"How can they do this?" Under her eyes, her tears had left two white lines. "They can't get away with this, can they?"

"I don't know," Axel said.

"We're watching," she said. "Everyone is watching."

The streets smelled of burned rubber. People stood outside communes, hands on their hips, watching the smoke spiralling, wondering what came next. They'd all been getting the messages from the software. Preparations for departure became apparent. Man-sized rucksacks rested by open doors. E-bikes hovered along the streets, cables hanging loose. Tables, beds and chairs piled up outside homes, tied with sisal ropes, hoisted onto trolleys and scooters. Pat dragged her feet, ankles pink and raw. Trousers on, but still no shoes. She leaned against Axel, picking at scabs on her feet. He put a shoulder under her arm, lifting her feet in the air.

They reached a house with familiar pistachio-green walls.

The Haunted Shipwreck.

"I need to speak to her," Pat said.

She knocked at the door, opened it.

The inside had exposed wooden beams and shelves, and corners filled with marine items, like the cabins in an old Arctic exploration ship. Anchors, oars, fishing nets. A bald man in blue overalls came down a short flight of stairs, greeting Pat with a hug. Two women joined him – Ula, in wellington boots and overalls, and another woman, younger, plumper, in a blue tracksuit. Her head was shaved too. It was like watching a convention of bald people, greeting each other after a long gap in the proceedings.

"Were you caught in the attack?" the bald man asked.

"We just kept running." Pat shivered, as if the retelling made her panic again.

"Are you receiving the messages?" the younger woman asked. "The algorithm found out what we did. There's no other explanation."

"Of course they found out." A new voice. A man came down the stairs. Gunnar Grimsson. Browbeaten, but still full of stamina. Muscular type, head full of thick brown hair, wearing a camouflage suit open to the middle of his tanned chest. "Before the scum removed my tech, I saw it with my own eyes. Thousands went void. The algorithm issued new finding jobs, then cancelled them. USK is shutting off the island."

"Too many disconnected," Axel said. "It tipped their contagion model."

"You're handing them our heads on a platter," Ula said with a firm voice. "Stop your rampant speculation."

Gunnar came down the last few steps and stood near Pat, narrowing his eyes.

"Are you the bitch who attacked me at the madhouse?"

He was almost as short as her but twice her width.

"I was one of those who helped you," Pat said, taken aback.

"Helped? I know you sold my tech to crooks at the port. Hey, is that the spreadsheet wanker?" Gunnar raised an eyebrow to Axel and puffed up his chest. "Never liked your videos. Keep playing data scientist and leave the hard work to those with real training." He tapped his tanned chest with a closed fist. "Army reserve."

"Stop squabbling right now," Ula said. "I won't tolerate this behaviour in my house. Who is this?" She was staring at Axel.

Pat's cue. "A Finder. Looking for Hildr."

Ula stared at Axel with her mean, blue eyes. "Another one? The kid's not here. I thought that was obvious." Thin lines stretched from her nose down to her mouth. "Things are changing fast round here, Mr Finder. I'm sure you've noticed. You have two options. Live the way the software wants you to live or make up your own way of living. A life begging for food, or freedom. Which one do you choose? For those who dare to leave the tech behind, a revolution is coming. A community packed with old food, jobs and infrastructure, unlike anything you've seen before."

"*Much more sophisticated,*" her bald friends repeated in unison.

"I'm getting the salvage ship out of here," Axel said.

"Suit yourself," Ula said. "The rest of you, come to the kitchen and help with the packing."

He couldn't believe it. This crew of clowns were the famous farmers. Announcing their collective stupidity with their shaved heads, like a bunch of thick matches about to catch fire. He couldn't care less about their plans to build a farm at the top of the Beranger, but they were a bad influence on Pat.

"There's a new clue," Axel said, pulling Pat aside. "On the day Hildr disappeared, a container ship left for the Hebrides. The times align. Will you come to the port with me?"

"I can't go right now."

He followed them into the kitchen. Bags of sugar, flour, synthetic cheese, pasta, and New Food cartons from all colour labels piled on the tabletop. This was their third week of hoarding, the baldies explained. The rest of the stock had already been taken to the camp they were preparing at a secret location. Soon, they'd start a new community and leave the town behind. Their conversation was stilted, full of half sentences. Unwilling to speak in the presence of mics and cameras, they retained a mysterious faith that the algorithm didn't already know about their shitshow.

Axel grabbed a carton of New Lasagne and sat on a high stool, relegated to a corner, eating. A drip of notifications kept arriving on his tab. For residents who wanted to move to another island, more forms and bureaucracy. For those with nowhere to go, a monumental kick in the ass. How could he convince Pat to leave with him? The farmers were coming in and out of the house, loading the food onto e-bikes.

"The salvage ship is leaving at nine in the evening," he said. "From Spitsbergen there are routes back to Iceland and the Hebrides. Do you have anyone outside Fyr who could host you?"

Pat grabbed another box of non-perishables, following the farmers out of the kitchen.

"People will starve," he tried again. "It's a death sentence."

"We will have food on the farm," Pat said.

She was joining the baldies. He still couldn't believe it.

"Why did you shave your head?"

"Shorter hair will be easier to maintain," she said. "There are no showers on the mountain."

Ridiculous. It was troubling him more than it should.

"It's going to get nasty, when the food runs out," he said.

"We will be prepared."

In normal circumstances, he would step away. Not his problem. Yet there she was, with her bare feet, her soft hair stubble, her yellow pyjamas covered in mud. It was as if they had a bond. He was helping her find the kid, and Pat was helping him get over the trauma he had experienced on Fyr. New memories had replaced his nightmares.

"I can ... I can host you at my place in Iceland," he said.

"We're very different," she said. He couldn't decipher this comment. "We just have business to finish. What's the new clue?"

Business. He could take a hint. Avoiding her gaze, Axel pulled the tab with the triangulation back into focus. The large bell-shaped graph had flattened out into a wider base, with more vertical bars than earlier.

"See these?" he said. "They represent more sets of co-ordinates for where the kid might be. After adding the new data, the likely position now extends from the Hebrides to the illegal town."

Ula arrived next to them. "You've searched long enough," she said. "We don't know who the kid met on her way. Let's accept the consequences of our radical action. It was for the greater good. We can't let this affect our plans. It's time to remove your chip and come to the mountain."

Axel was stunned. Wasn't Pat going to kick back, explain they wouldn't quit until they found the kid? All perky with him but didn't have the guts to go against Ula. The group of baldies went into the kitchen, discussing preparations for departure. Pat joined them.

Axel pranced about the reception room, words stuck in his throat. Four hours until the salvage ship.

Pat came out, carrying a pile of yoga mats.

"I guess this is goodbye then?" he said.

Her eyes were sad.

Excruciating.

She wet her lips with her tongue, looking up at him.

Did she want a goodbye kiss?

He waited for a clearer sign.

"Wait," she said. Axel blinked, confused. "I'll come with you to the port. Maybe I can get her bracelet back. Let me speak to Ula."

A minute later, Pat returned. She wasn't alone.

"I'm coming to the port too."

Gunnar Grimsson had a talent for being at the wrong place, at the wrong time.

Where is everybody? An interview with the woman who claims she's solved the Fermi paradox

At the age of four, Dr Shyla Patel could name over two hundred stars in the Milky Way. At nine, she differentiated between planets by the way their brightness dipped when crossing in front of a star. Now, Dr Patel has surprised the world by announcing she's solved the Fermi paradox. Probability suggests intelligent alien civilizations are abundant in the universe. So why haven't we seen any evidence of them?

Dr Patel replies: "When Enrico Fermi found no evidence of intelligent life, he thought a terrible destiny must be awaiting us. Extermination events had stopped intelligent life from travelling and communicating with other planets, and the same was about to happen to humans. We now know there is a different explanation. In fact, our senses have evolved to suit this little corner in the solar system. We see and hear only the waves relevant to our survival and taste the flavours of the food available to us. This means we are deaf and blind to vast swathes of seemingly irrelevant chemical and physical phenomena. With the help of fermion computing and AI, we're now finally decrypting those phenomena. And we're finding that the universe is filled with evidence of highly intelligent life, albeit very different from ours."

Chapter Twenty-Two

(Birgit) Corn

Ms Holm's living-room is filled with books. She hounded me before sleep time, insisting that I should take the bedroom, but I wouldn't miss the opportunity to lie surrounded by old paper books. There are two shelves below the windows, which overlook Adventfjorden's Bay, holding an eclectic collection of European classics. Fyodor Dostoevsky. Simone de Beauvoir. Jane Austen. Henrik Ibsen. The midnight sun is a welcome intruder, not just to spy on book spines. If there was total darkness in the room, the little voice in my dreams might send me back into a terrible state.

What have I done?

Then I remember: you left me first.

My efforts to become a mother were in vain.

Plants suit me best.

At the beginning, Ms Holm thought I was in Spitsbergen for the protocol. When germinating rates drop, we take the seeds out of the vault, plant them, and harvest fresh seeds to replenish the sample. The protocol keeps seeds safe. But this time, it's not the protocol that brings me here.

We couldn't imagine life without cells and DNA. Cells are the essence of life. The genome passed from living organisms to their offspring contains the biological in-structions that makes each species unique. No living spark has been found outside eukaryotes, archaea and bacteria. Even viruses rely on cells to gain life. How else could molecules organise to become intelligent? How could life emerge and evolve if not through DNA?

Another story.

The oldest fossilised corn cobs were found in a cave in Mexico, dating from six thousand years ago. People in the Americas preferred tall, weedy grasses with a muta-tion in a gene called tga1, which guides silica formation around the seed. As a result, corn lost the hard shell from wheat and rice and gained a cob. Corn's thirty-two thousand genes have suffered a great deal of selection. If the plant hadn't been favoured by human palates, we wouldn't have the corn we know today. It was all about taste, what people preferred to eat.

Corn is resilient, growing fast in different weather conditions and soil types, and making good use of natur-al resources. Even nowadays, we add corn starch to New Food to make sweets, sauces and syrups.

When I started working in the seed vault, a committee from the University of Pavia arrived in Svalbard to deposit a precious variety. *Otto file*, an heirloom deep in colour and flavour, used to make polenta. Our previous *otto file* sample had been lost. We discovered the seeds weren't viable when we took them out to replenish. Finding a new copy was a pleasant surprise. Corn had been given another chance. I was to meet the delegation from the University of Pavia outside the harbour at Longyearbyen. When I got there, a woman in a fur-lined parka was waiting in the rain, seed box under her arm.

"Ms Olsen? Such a pleasure to meet you. I've read all your papers. I'm Chiara Giudice. I lead the Plant Genomics department at the University of Pavia."

Chiara had beautiful brown eyes, long eyelashes turned upwards with clumps of black mascara, and honey-coloured hair escaping from her furry hood. She smelled of roses and had rose-pink lips. I wondered if she tasted of roses as well. We set out to the vault together, me driving the Trust's jeep through snow-covered lanes, Chiara sitting in the back, cradling the box of seeds like a child, despite its layer of coolant. Ms Holm would meet us outside the vault's portal building, a five-minute drive from the harbour.

"Do you know how lucky we are," I asked Chiara, "to find *otto file*? Mondo are thrilled. They're preparing a whole New Polenta series."

"I'm sure their highest-paying customers know the difference between cornflour and polenta. How can they stand gross New Food impostors?" She sighed. "Mondo's donation to the department will be well received. We're struggling. The Italian state has stopped funding universities. Our corporate sponsors are only interested in research that delivers quick results. We've been able to continue a few projects in genetics and in natural sciences. Humanities are not doing so well." Through the rear mirror, I saw the loose honey curls jumping on her shoulders.

"Who cares about humans anyway?" I meant it as a joke, but her expression stiffened. "I much prefer plants," I said.

My autopilot comment.

"Plants don't have a soul," Chiara said. "We live in mad times, Ms Olsen. We've lost our humanity and replaced it with extreme utilitarianism." Her eyes found mine in the rear-view mirror. She may have sensed my unease. She tapped the box beside her. "Do you want me to tell you the story of these seeds?" I slowed down and indicated left. I expected some tedious minutiae about her academic work, but instead she said, "A witch gave them to me."

The jeep's indicator flashed and ticked.

"A witch?" I repeated, unsure if her Italian accent had camouflaged a technical word I was meant to recognise.

"La Befana. Heard of her?"

"No."

I turned left, up the narrow road leading to the vault.

"She comes on Epiphany Eve," Chiara said, "on 6th January, in Italian folklore. She leaves gifts for the children. Sweets for well-behaved kids, a chunk of coal for those who have been bad in the previous year."

My foot found the clutch. "Your corn seeds were a gift from the witch?"

"Yes. A piece of coal, more precisely. We play with genes and think we have life all figured out." She dropped her head forward.

We lost eye contact.

The jeep slowed to a halt.

Chiara lifted her head. "What's wrong? Why have you stopped?"

"We're here."

We got out of the jeep, Chiara pale as the snow crunching under her boots. Ms Holm hadn't arrived yet. The rugged coastline of Longyearbyen Bay was drawn out from the sky in grey charcoal. Settlements by the water glowed, out-lined by yellow halos against the blue twilight. Behind us, more blue and yellow, atmospheric auras and the Newtoppen mountain with the light sculpture, *Perpetual Repercussion*, above the vault's portal building. A sliver of violet arrived from beyond the mountain. November's faint suggestion of sun.

"Are you religious, Ms Olsen?"

Chiara wasn't done yet.

"Certainly not. And I don't believe in witches either."

She rubbed her gloved hands together. "I know we are scientists, but there is so much that science can't explain."

"We'll get there one day. If we last."

A cynical smile formed on her lips. "Your determination scares me. My father was a Catholic priest. He led a small congregation in the north of Italy. He also made the best polenta in the world. His mother, my paternal grandmother, cultivated her own corn and tomatoes, before New Food and the farming restrictions."

"Italy took a while to comply."

"We have a rich food tradition. You're Swedish, aren't you? If you'd lived in Italy all your life, you wouldn't be able to stomach New Food either. The Mediterranean diet, do you remember it? The healthiest, simplest, most wonderful food. Olive oil. Handmade pasta. Sun-dried tomatoes. The whole world looked up to us." She had a haunted expression. "Our family's farm is gone, anyway. When I was a little girl, criminals broke in, occupied the house, stole the annual harvest, and burned it to the ground."

I froze. "I'm so sorry."

She waved her hand, dismissive. "There are many stories like mine ... I'm not telling you this to win pity. The fire happened almost fifty years ago, but La Befana came last year. On Epiphany Eve, while I was away, someone broke into my home and left a ragdoll on my Nativity scene, next to Jesus's crib. A dreary brown sack with a string tied around the neck, large round head, hair made from yarn, and two smudged black blobs for eyes. Dozens of needles had been pinned on the ragdoll, like voodoo. I squeezed the rough fabric between my fingers. Inside, I felt a thick, crunchy filling. I removed the needles, tore the sack apart and found ... corn kernels."

"*Otto file?*"

She nodded. "Low germination rate. I planted the viable kernels and managed to revive the sample. The five hundred seeds needed for the vault."

"Unbelievable. Is that true? What a story. And you never found out who left the ragdoll? It was a wonderful gift, despite the voodoo nonsense."

She wrapped her arms around her chest and shoulders, against the piercing chill. "La Befana, the witch, left me the gift. You see, I was a bad woman last year. The university was reviewing its decision to keep free places on some courses. After much thought, I voted against. We can't maintain half the projects as it stands. I know poor students can't afford a place, but how will we survive without funding? No amount of studying can get them a job anyway." She turned her face to me, her curls bouncing over her shoulders. "Oh God, I keep justifying myself, don't I? If the intention was to make me feel sick about that decision, the witch succeeded. I haven't been able to face any more students since then."

"You think the ragdoll was an act of intimidation by the students?"

"Yes, I'm sure it was. Who else could it have been? My photo is everywhere in the department. The yarn on the doll was the same colour as my hair, the eyes probably a bad joke about my makeup." Another jeep progressed along the road below, a shiny blue spot on the desolate landscape. "Everyone knew my opinion about the free university places. They also knew I was out of the house that evening, attending dinner with one of our main corporate sponsors." Her forehead was frozen into two deep creases. "I sleep badly, Ms Olsen. I keep having the same dream. In my dream, my students have turned into witches and goblins, and they're running around in my old grandmother's farm, shrieking, filling sack upon sack with charred corn cobs."

The blue jeep parked next to us and Ms Holm stepped out onto the snow.

Chiara didn't mention La Befana again.

I haven't been able to forget the Italian professor – her fantasy about the witch, and the guilt she felt about her decision. It always amazes me when scientists confess to superstitious beliefs. Most religious claims are incompatible with what we know about the universe. So religious scientists must cherry-pick the claims that don't put their professionalism at risk. It's an awful lot of work, for no clear benefit. Sometimes I wonder what Chiara would do in my place. What would she think about the creature at the bottom of the vault? Would she call it a miracle from God, or a trick by the Devil? I wonder if she would feel elated, or betrayed.

I wonder if she would give it a soul.

Aniara, my beloved – old Scandinavian poem about the fishing ban

Aniara, my beloved, we'll never sail to the high seas again
Days of wind and exertion are behind us
Fish we caught back to the streams of never-after
I'd cast my hook into the past
If it could bring back the lucid brightness of our mornings
Out in the Arctic Sea,
When we were foolish and happy,
Foolish and free.

Chapter Twenty-Three

(Axel) The port

Axel spotted the salvage ship from a distance, broad-bellied, with a stack of cabins at the back. It was moored offshore, its bulk too big for the dock. An orange dinghy travelled between the ship and the port, carrying passengers in puffy lifejackets. On shore, the port building had been inundated with citizens. Long scruffy manes, bright shirts, flowery dresses, sandals and trainers, looking like the crowd you'd find at a folk festival, plus enough luggage to party for a lifetime – suitcases, oversized rucksacks, piles of furniture. The migrants he had seen on arrival lurked in the corners, wrapped in blankets, doubting the evidence of their eyes.

Pat bit the skin around her nails. He still hoped she would change her mind, but he didn't know how to broach the subject. Gunnar was with them, slithering along the walls, like he was on a fucking stealth mission. Someone should tell him that camouflage suits were for the jungle, not the Arctic tundra.

A call arrived on a new tab. Axel sidestepped towards the window overlooking the bay. A group of citizens followed the shadow of a helicopter outside the building. It was moving across the sea, its chuff-chuffing masked by double-glazing.

"Any news, Sherlock?" Oscar Frias sat under a diffuse fluorescent light. Behind him, photos of dilapidated colonial buildings. Caribbean archives.

"I may be close to finding the kid's chip," Axel said.

The other half of the payment would come in handy.

The Mondo manager arched his eyebrow. "Is everything okay in the North Pole? There's smoke coming out of the mountain behind you."

Sunglasses on, Gunnar was leaning against the panoramic windows, tapping his foot on the floor.

"Yeah, everything's fine. Have you heard from Birgit Olsen?"

"I'm afraid I'm not allowed to share that information," Oscar said.

Something had changed since the last time they'd spoken.

"Did you intercept her at Longyearbyen?"

"I'm not allowed to answer that either."

He remembered the entries in Birgit's lab, next to dates leading up to the previous week. *MExAI, USMES, MDA, SJLYR, SGSV.* That first acronym must surely be related to Mondo's space programme.

"Was Birgit working on the MExAI project?" Axel said.

"Am I speaking in English?"

Pat touched his arm. "We don't have much time."

"I'll call you when I get Birgit's messages," Axel said, and hung up.

Coming out of his tab, he saw what was causing the bustle. A side door had opened, and the crowd was leaving the building, rushing towards the dock. On the water-front, diesel fumes filled the air. A long platform extended in front of them, sloping towards the sea, helicopter roaring above. The orange dinghy was taking on more passengers, an endless queue. There was no guarantee he would be able to board. Gunnar, Pat and Axel squeezed through the crowd, running along the outside wall, towards the dock's storage area.

A new call rang in his headphones.

Carla's pretty face appeared on his tab and his gut twisted. Some dogs died like this. The vessels around their stomachs twisted, strangling them from the inside. Axel walked slower, letting Pat and Gunnar get a head start.

The sky was clear June, the air stale Arctic balm.

"I'm glad I caught you, Mr Jóhannsson."

"Why didn't you warn me about the drones?"

Carla's virtual face mimed embarrassment.

"Your memory is failing," she said. "Didn't I tell you to finish the case before the evening?"

"You didn't explain why."

"The last ship out of the island still has space."

"Don't fuck with me. The place is being blown to pieces, and the official USK channels mention only a new wave of voids. No word about the pestering notifications, the army drones, the big purge."

Carla smiled. "Once Fyr is closed off, information will flow on a need-to-know basis. Citizens are bombarded with news all the time. No one wants more than they've signed up for."

"Why did you send army drones?"

"We've been prevented from mapping a large part of the island. Casualties and injuries were kept to an absolute minimum, using thermal radars. We targeted only the submarines. Voids could use them to reach other islands."

A crane hung over the loading bay. He waited in the shade, under the crane, squinting.

"You've murdered people. More will die, if you stop New Food shipments to the island."

"Losses at the top of the food chain are expected, Mr Jóhannsson. Did you not pay attention at school?" She had the flattest tone in the world. "Thank you for all the footage. I probably don't need to tell you this, but Hildr Olsen's citizen-chip is USK's property. Mondo Foods have no claim over it. Please bring the bracelet to Iceland."

Axel cursed, walking out of the shade, back into the summer sun.

"I'll handle it on a need-to-know basis," he said.

"We can track the chip," Carla said.

He had almost hung up.

"What did you say?"

"We're working on the fix right now. We'll be able to re-enable the tracker and find the bracelet."

Bots weren't spiteful. Carla was simply making a faulty assessment, assuming this revelation would convince him to cooperate and hand the bracelet back.

They were out of sync.

"I'm a freelancer. I don't work for the algorithm."

He should never have taken the assignment.

Axel pulled up the tab.

Pat and Gunnar had reached three faded containers on the wide expanse of cement, next to a hydraulic platform.

Half a dozen workers pranced about, manning crates and two big yellow machines with oversized pincers, moving them between the containers and the loading dock.

"It's him," Gunnar shouted, finger in the air.

The docker directly in front of his finger spotted them approaching, looking around, assessing his chances of a quick escape. Gunnar got to him first.

"Remember me?" He pulled the docker by the collar. "I'm looking for what you stole from me, shithead."

Pat and Axel reached them. Axel's sheer size and Viking tattoos seemed to intimidate him.

"I'm not a thief," the docker said. "I'm just an intermediary … you know, opening a door between those who offer and those who seek … like an old grocery shop, or a massage parlour." He half smiled, two teeth missing, looking at Pat. "Nice to see you again, sweetheart. Can you please ask your friend to let go of me?"

"What's inside?" Pat asked, nodding towards the closest container.

"Empty," the docker said. "Those two over there … discarded cartons, old furniture, rubbish, whatever citizens throw away."

"How long do containers lie around here, before they're loaded into ships and sent off?" Axel asked.

The docker scratched his head. "Dunno … a couple of days maybe? I just follow numbers on the schedule, help the drones to load and unload. No point wasting energy doing their job."

"How easy would it be for a kid to jump into one of the containers and end up being taken on a ship by mistake?" Pat said.

The docker chuckled. "By mistake? Illegals do it all the time, but it's a death trap. They can get stuck inside for days. They need another person to get them safely out the other side."

The ship's horn bellowed, a blast churning inside his stomach.

"This is going nowhere," Axel said.

Pat kicked the ground with her heel. She was wearing a pair of winter boots lent by the baldies. "Do you remember a kid's tech suite I sold you a few days ago? One with a green bracelet?"

Gunnar grew impatient. "Show us your loot right now, you stinky walrus. Can't you see we're in a hurry? My set was silver and black."

"I've got work to finish, man. And I need to pack like everyone else and get out of here. I'll tell the lady 'cos she asked nicely. Stock is low, there's been a huge demand for second-hand devices since the warnings started. But I remember a green bracelet, yeah. Kid's size. Not easy to sell, even after fitting in extensions."

Pat perked up. "Where is it?" Her voice was filled with hope.

They followed the docker past a long line of warehouses and sailboats moored by the old pier, to the hoist-lifting dock at the far end of the port. Old vessels appeared to have run aground on a black sandy beach, including a decrepit fishing boat which would sink if she got anywhere near the water. A cursive font on its side spelled the name *Aniara*. The docker climbed aboard and pulled out a massive suitcase from under the rotting deck. Gunnar and Pat leaned in to get a good view of the loot. Opening the suitcase, the man removed handful after handful of broken integrated circuits, health nodes, straps, headphones, portable screens, projectors, cameras, all in black nests of tangled USB cables.

"Here it is." The docker was holding a kid's smartwatch. The bracelet was bright green.

Pat was ecstatic. "It's Hildr's."

Gunnar climbed aboard the crumbling boat and pushed the docker away, digging into the suitcase's contents like a pirate looking for gold coins.

"What about *my* set? Where is it?"

"I sold it, I told ya," he said. "Only knick-knacks left."

Gunnar looked about to cry. He shook his head softly. "Stuck in this place."

The docker handed the bracelet to Pat. "Hope your kid is okay, ma'am."

Hope was all they had.

They went back to where the orange dinghy was taking on passengers. The queue extended out of sight, over the platform, through the port's building, all the way to the main road. Gunnar did a military salute, heading downtown. Pat went round in circles for a little longer. The twins from the first day were right ahead in the queue, wearing black felt hats, and carrying two square red suitcases. Helicopters still drummed above the port.

This was it.

He hated goodbyes.

"I'll find her," Axel said. "If she's alive."

"In the Hebrides?" Pat said.

"At the end of the world."

She played with the bracelet between her fingers. "Take this with you," she said. "Give it to Hildr when you find her."

"No, you keep it," he said. "Ask Ula to hide it somewhere in the mountain, deep inside a cave. Preferably encased in fiberglass or metal."

Pat frowned. "Why?"

"Neither Mondo nor USK deserve it. It's a long story. Birgit sent DNA-protected messages to the kid, which are saved in the chip's local memory."

"H ... how do you know this?"

"It doesn't matter any more. Please will you reconsider your decision? Come to Iceland with me."

Pat was clenching the fabric of her yellow top over her collarbone, as if it was strangling her. "You lied to me. You've been lying this whole time. You work for the algorithm."

Time was slipping through their fingers.

"It's finished. Think about it, please. Only voids will stay behind. It's suicide."

"You don't get it, do you?" she said. "There will be no voids, no citizens. Just humans. Plain humans."

"Humans with no food left. It's not going to end well. Please come with me. I can host you in Iceland until you find your feet."

He tried to hug her.

"Don't touch me," she shrieked, stepping backwards. "I'm not going anywhere. This is my home. You're a thug. Brainwashed by the algorithm into believing you're one of the good guys, but still a thug. Why did you attack that boy in Birgit's bedroom? Why did you attack Ivan?"

"You haven't seen what I've seen. They are criminals. Outside the law."

"I helped you. Against my initial instincts, I helped you. Maybe I shouldn't have. What kind of arsehole deports their own mother?"

Her accusation stung.

"She was nothing to me," Axel said.

"I'm judging you *exactly* by how you treat those who are nothing to you."

Pat turned around, heading up the road in the opposite direction to every other citizen, stepping so hard in her oversized boots it looked as if she was punishing the tar for how much she hated him. *Wow.* He hadn't seen that coming. He thought she wanted a goodbye hug. Why did he bother? She'd just been waiting for the best moment to kick him in the balls.

Axel watched Pat as she disappeared up the hill.

He didn't call out to her.

He had nothing else to say.

You gave them a slice.

They stole the whole pie.

Press Release: Mondo retrieves species trapped in permafrost

The DNA of three unknown species has been discovered as part of a two-year mission in Antarctica collecting old organisms trapped in permafrost. Plants existed for millions of years before humans and contain genes which have evolved to survive challenging conditions. Scientists will now sequence and study these old organisms to produce new lab varieties. Professor Gary Nunn, Lab Head at Mondo, said: "These species may hold some of the genetic diversity we were missing, and help us create new foodstuffs to feed billions affected by modern food scarcity." This fantastic discovery shows the enormous effort and financial investment Mondo put into its mission of securing food for the future and may enable them to engineer new resilient varieties.

Chapter Twenty-Four

(Hildr) The bracelet

Hildr thought Ula would refuse Gunnar's food. She was wrong. Living in a state of permanent starvation apparently led to great hypocrisy. Sitting on yoga mats in the hermit's cave, near a portable gas stove, comforted by a New Food carton and a cup of real tea, Hildr followed their account of what had happened on Fyr eighteen years before.

"Your plan was stupid," Gunnar said. "So many things that could go wrong."

He adjusted the gas valve on the propane canister until it released a low, steady hiss, burning at a slower pace.

"In a way, we succeeded," Ula said.

Red and blue flames projected an incandescent halo onto the cave walls.

"In what way?" Hildr asked.

Ula leaned backwards, elbows on the ground. "We showed the world it could be done."

Gunnar poked the flame with a long wooden stick.

"The whole plan was a bloody mess," he said. "The algorithm announced a tipping point in defections and shut off the whole island. Bloody disaster. Thousands of people left to starve, on top of those who were already hungry.

Thefts, murders, cannibalism. Why the hell would you plan something like that? I have no problem with kicking the scum out and taking the food I deserve, but at least I don't pretend to be a sweetie-pie and then shove everyone down the cliff."

"We proved it can be done," Ula said. "We survived without New Food."

"Your scraggy friends on the volcano? How many have thrown themselves off the cliff?"

Ula ground her jaw. "It hasn't happened for a long time."

"I thought the software had evacuated all citizens," Hildr said. She wouldn't believe any other version. Ula's recollections had made one thing clear. The farmers were at fault.

"Citizens who managed to get the last ship left," Gunnar said. "I stayed behind. Fucking bastards."

Ula looked at him. Her eyes showed no indignation, anger or surprise. Hard to guess what was going through her head.

"We succeeded," Ula said. "We proved it could be done. Growing our own crops. Producing our own compost. People were inspired by us, weren't they? We still have supporters on many islands."

"The algorithm doesn't care either way," Gunnar said. "They don't see you as a threat. They leave you to your own devices."

"We don't need any devices," Ula said.

"No one gives a shit," Gunnar said. "Why do you want to prove anything?"

Hildr sipped her tea. The first proper meal she'd had in days was settling nicely in her stomach. She was curious about the details of what had happened, but mostly she wanted to know where Ula had hidden the bracelet.

The tip couldn't arrive fast enough.

Ula placed her chipped cup on the ground. "My demands have always been simple. Reveal the location of the secret farms. Share what's left of old food. Farming is our collective legacy."

Gunnar crossed his arms over his chest, trapping the end of his straggly beard. "What makes you think there is food, when for years we've been told it's running out?"

Ula stared at him coldly. "Don't get me started. The elites and their corporate lobbies shape the news to their interests. There are other ways out of the crisis."

"What about the girl?" Hildr said. "How does she fit into this?"

Ula chewed her crumbling oat biscuit slowly, methodically. "One of our collaborators knew a scientist working for Mondo Foods. She lived in the same commune. Turns out one of the chips we deleted from the model was the scientist's daughter. We got involved in local searches, looked for the kid everywhere. Makes life hard, having a conscience."

"What was the girl's name?" Hildr asked.

"Hildr," Ula and Gunnar said in unison.

This was why she had come, why she had climbed the Beranger, why she was still speaking to them, despite their horrible deeds. Why hadn't they mentioned the bracelet yet?

"My mother was a corporate citizen too," Hildr said. "Her name was Birgit Olsen. What was the scientist's name?"

"I don't remember," Ula said.

"Olsen rings a bell, but I didn't write her name down," Gunnar said. "Bloody old fart brain, I don't know how anyone can remember names without tech."

"Do you remember a bracelet?" Hildr asked, at a loss.

"A bracelet?" Ula repeated.

"I left behind a bracelet with my old citizen-chip, when I ran away from Fyr. Did you see the bracelet?"

"Why do you care?" Gunnar said. "The chip didn't work anyway."

"I want to get it back," Hildr said.

"Why would the farmers find a bracelet, when they couldn't find the bloody kid? It's even smaller," Gunnar said.

Ula was staring into the distance, lost in thought. "Sometimes there would be a sighting, a girl of the right age. After a while, we gave up. Lost hope."

Gunnar smiled, yellow-stained teeth surprisingly still in place. "Bunch of incompetent clowns."

Ula threw him an angry look. "I found her in the end, didn't I?"

"I actually spotted her a couple of days ago, sleeping with a chap down at the beach. So, technically, I found her first."

"You told me you were alone," Ula said accusingly, turning to Hildr.

"He's just a boy," Hildr said. "I met him on the beach, helping migrants."

"Bloody nutters everywhere," Gunnar said.

Hildr got up, pacing back and forth across the cave, casting a long shadow, aware of them staring at her towering figure. She put her hands on her head.

"Let's think this through together. My adoptive mother was called Birgit Olsen, and you think this might be the name of the scientist working for Mondo Foods. She lost a girl called Hildr, like me, just before Fyr was removed from the algorithm. And I ran away from Fyr, before the events you described." She looked around the cave. Piles of old crap everywhere. The recess at the back, where Gunnar slept. Ula was supposed to have hidden her bracelet inside a cave. So many hiding places here. Where was the bracelet? They were staring at her, waiting for her to carry on. "I know this sounds crazy, but I ... I think I'm the girl?"

Ula blinked. "Possibly. It was so long ago. And with your amnesia, it's impossible to be sure."

Gunnar shrugged. "Plenty of water under that bridge."

Hildr looked at them, mystified. Did the algorithm have the wrong information? Had her mission been a mistake, a misunderstanding, a mirage?

"What about the story Liz mentioned?" Hildr said. "The girl with the key to endless food?"

"That's just a fairytale," Ula said. "A story we tell the kids, to give them hope for the future."

"You mean a lie," Gunnar said.

Hildr was still pacing back and forth.

"But Birgit ... my mother ... she was working on a research project for Mondo ... I heard rumours ... about something underneath the vault."

"Sounds like you heard some fairytales too," Gunnar said.

"I don't care for Mondo's food," Ula said. "They just churn out lab junk. No, thank you."

Hildr strolled to the cave's entrance. The sun tinged the sky in deep reds. A full moon floated high in the sky.

"Where is the bracelet?" she wondered, out loud.

"Pat probably took it with her," Ula said.

Hildr turned around.

"Who is Pat?"

"I remember now. The nasty thing seemed alive," Ula continued. "A little bell would come off every now and then. Pat is the collaborator I mentioned before, the one who befriended the scientist."

"Where is she?" Hildr asked. "Where is Pat?"

"She left years ago," Ula said. "Life at the farm wasn't for her."

Hildr felt her head spinning.

She was in the wrong place. The journey had been in vain.

Gunnar turned off the gas hob.

"I don't know about you ladies, but my eyes are closing."

Hildr watched Ula and Gunnar put away cups and bowls, preparing their sleeping bags, huddling together in a corner at the back.

"Where did Pat go?" Hildr asked, following Ula.

"Spitsbergen."

Not Fyr. Spitsbergen.

She had to get there.

A memory popped into her head, a recent one, a graspable one, of a cheerful Bas jumping along the beach, after they'd met. *Have you seen one of the subs in real life? The most amazing and scary piece of equipment I've ever seen. Honestly. I'm learning to pilot one. Call me Captain from now on.*

The Multi-Exoplanet Artificial Intelligence (MExAI) programme, interview in AI News Channel (extract)

AINC: Everyone is talking about the MExAI probes sponsored by Mondo Foods, but the space mission seems to have little to do with food. Why does Mondo have such a large stake in a space exploration venture?

Mondo: Producing food for our times is not just about investing in lab innovation. We must be visionaries. Current models predict billions of habitable worlds in our galaxy, and they might give us valuable clues about creating new sources of nutrition. A probe using AI is a great way to gather more information. The findings will be transmitted back to us at the speed of light, but the information-gathering exercise can be conducted in real time.

AINC: Has anything interesting arrived from the two hundred probes already launched?

Mondo: Nothing conclusive, but we're optimistic. We must be patient.

Chapter Twenty-Five

(Axel) Spitsbergen

Axel's last hours on Fyr were a blur. He couldn't figure out the order of events. How the purge had started. The people he'd met. Who had fucked him up first. The tide had got ahead of his stroke, and no matter how much he pushed, he was still dragged to the bottom. After Pat left him at the port, chaos reigned. A crowd of residents protested the algorithm's decision to shut off the island, demanding to know what would happen to those left behind, threatening to take over the ship. Departure was delayed by almost five hours. USK cleared the last batch of citizens and sent drones to guard the lifeboat tenders as they squeezed into the salvage ship. Many were left behind. A whole island disconnected.

He hadn't found the kid. The outcome bashed against the walls of his tired brain, over and over, like an animal trapped in a cage. He couldn't go back home, accept his meat delivery, leave the case unsolved. He had to find the kid. It wasn't about money any more, but basic decency. He would go to the Hebrides, follow the ship Hildr might have boarded. Sitting near the toilets, Axel watched the staff crossing off shifts on a piece of paper, until the shit was too much to handle.

Longyearbyen.

He felt like a soldier returning from the frontline, no fanfare waiting. Dinner, loneliness and a good night's sleep. Patterns of pinks near the sunset. Endless ponds zigzagging the low land, the only sign permafrost had ever existed at this altitude. No trees, but plenty of grass and small patches of purple wildflowers. Arctic summertime. He looked for a place to crash. The Wild Reindeer, a local inn. He crossed quiet streets of dark-red box-like homes with small windows, old RIB boats and snow scooters parked by the doors. No voids in sight.

At The Wild Reindeer, the walls were covered in stuffed animal heads and oversized photos of reindeers, grouse and whales. He ordered flipper pie and found chewy black bits under the pastry, alongside fake seal lard. Almost like the real thing. The dining room was desolate. A handful of Arctic researchers, two stuffy Russian expats, and an unpleasant hostess with thick rimmed glasses and a frilled white apron. Bliss. For decades, the island had been closed to tourism and real estate development. In Spitsbergen, the future took time to arrive. The lingering stuffiness contrasted with the boisterous character of Iceland, Scotland and the bigger islands. He could live here.

The hostess gave a loud sniff and glanced at his empty plate on the bar.

"One night?"

She sounded pissed off.

But he was feeling replenished enough to chat.

"I might, if you have blackout curtains."

"Put a pillow over your head." She dangled a stinky cloth under his nose. "We're closing. Do you want a room or not?"

He downed his last sip of water and got up, hands in his pockets. Nothing to carry. He stood by the reception desk, which had one of those little mushroom-shaped bells that you're supposed to tap for attention. He felt compelled to hit it continuously until the shrill noise drowned his thoughts. Forcing himself to stay put, he stuck his hands in his pockets and looked at a set of framed documents on the wall. Cargo ships, diplomas, certificates, pompous crests of arms.

"Is the seed vault nearby?" He wondered if Birgit was still in Spitsbergen.

Another loud sniff. "Few minutes' drive up the mountain," the unpleasant hostess said, bending behind the desk.

His eyes were drawn to a detail on the wall.

"What's that?" he said, pointing at one of the framed documents.

The hostess placed a pile of white towels on top of the reception desk.

"Bills of lading," she said. "Old shipping forms."

"That acronym on the corner. SJLYR. What does it stand for?"

"It's the port's code. Longyearbyen. No shit on the towels, please. Use toilet paper."

"Is this how you treat guests?" he said.

"I'm not a drone," she replied.

Axel walked up to the first floor, wooden staircase creaking with each step. His room was the second on the short corridor. Marine decoration, including cushions shaped like ships' helms. Lying on the bed, Axel reviewed the footage from Birgit's commune, paying attention to every detail his consciousness might have skipped. The annotations about Japanese rice. The seed boxes scattered everywhere. The intimate moment in the lab. He rewound the footage, looking for the acronyms. MExAI, USMES, MDA, SJLYR, SGSV. If MExAI was Mondo's space programme and SJLYR was Longyearbyen's port, what could the other letters be? Maybe locations. With dates next to them. Schedules for rendezvous.

He fell asleep with his clothes on.

In the morning, he had a long shower and ordered fake pancakes with a mug of cof-e. The hostess seemed even more irritated than the night before, rushing between her chores.

"How do we visit the vault?" he asked.

"You don't," she said. "Not in the summer."

She dragged a bucket of water into the hall and started mopping the floor.

"Is there a porter, or a security guard keeping an eye?"

"There is a digital application form on the Trust's website. They offer limited spots for tourists every year." She mopped his feet with dirty water.

"I'm not a tourist. I just want to ask a few questions."

She leaned on the mop looking pensive.

"Ms Holm. Try her. She's been a clerk at the vault for twenty odd years. She lives down the road. Number 56."

"Thanks. That's ... surprisingly helpful. I'll leave this place a good review."

"Don't bother. I'm closing in a month."

"Fed up with the job?"

She dropped the mop against the reception desk and stepped over the wet floor. "With waking up every day," she said, going into the toilet.

After breakfast, Axel headed to Ms Holm's flat. New tab. *Svalbard seed vault.* He read that the current building had opened in 2008 to host crops from plant gene banks around the world. Before the tunnel was finished, the seeds had been kept in a coal mine shaft. The vault's bio concluded with a nonsensical statement. *The DNA samples inside the vault have become essential for our food security.* What food security?

The clerk's address was at a two-storey box with dark-red walls, two lines of windows and no bell. An old man let him in, pointing at a separate flat upstairs. Steep, narrow staircase. A snug dolls' house. Gentler footsteps from inside the top flat. The door opened. A middle-aged woman, short, stocky, with narrow, deep-set eyes angling up at the corners, and an almost perfectly round face.

"I'd like to ask you a couple of questions about Dr Birgit Olsen."

Ms Holm invited him in with a gesture.

The flat smelled of coffee and cinnamon. Axel followed her into the lounge, a long room with low bookshelves under wide windows. She made him sit on the sofa facing the windows and left him alone, listening to an old pendulum clock, which was in another room but so loud and crisp it felt as if it was inside his head. His eyes drifted to the houses across the road, to the slivers of sea and mountains visible between buildings. Ms Holm came back with a plate full of cinnamon biscuits, which smelled delicious. Axel plucked three from the plate, building a stack on his hand. She put the plate on the table and sat next to him, facing the windows, her hands fidgeting in her lap. Her hair was dyed black and cropped short.

"I've already spoken to Mondo Foods," she said in a gentle, low voice, barely rising above her breath.

"I don't work for Mondo," he said.

"How do you know Dr Olsen?"

"I'm a Finder. Birgit asked me to find her daughter, a seven-year-old girl who disappeared before she came to the vault."

"That explains her state. I've known Dr Olsen since she started working with the Trust. Two days ago, she wasn't well."

"Did she go to the vault?"

"Would you like something to drink Mr Jóhannsson? Coffee, tea, water?"

"No, thank you."

A few sideways glances. Ms Holm sat upright, clasping her hands more tightly together.

"I'm afraid it's not in my power to let anyone inside the vault," she started, "especially outside approved visiting times. All visitors need authorisation from the Trust. I have physical keys to the doors, but a central application generates the digital codes to go in. Depositors, Mondo Foods, the Trust's staff and emergency services personnel can request entrance within pre-agreed parameters. I follow the instructions to the letter. We must protect the seeds at all costs."

She hadn't answered his question.

"Did Dr Olsen request authorisation to go inside the vault two days ago?"

The clerk looked out of the window. Her silence lasted long enough for him to finish his third biscuit.

Ms Holm's steely expression morphed into a serene smile.

"Did you know," she said, "that when we ask people their favourite number, they usually choose number three? One is too lonely, two is too even, three is just perfect. Bewitching, isn't it?"

Her eyes kept jumping between him and the window.

Was she trying to tell him something?

The words eventually arrived, calmer than the sea rolling between the houses across the road.

"You might not be aware, Mr Jóhannsson, that when the vault's builders excavated the tunnel under the mountain over a hundred years ago, they decided to make the complex much bigger than it needed to be. Call it prescience. So there's only one entrance, but there are *three* vaults underground. For one hundred years, only room number two was in use, the middle one. When the middle room filled up with seeds, we started using room number one, to the left of the main tunnel. There was still an empty room to the right, until recently." A subtle nod. "Room number three."

"Three is a good number," he said.

Her eyes became narrower, and bags bulged beneath them.

"Two weeks ago, Mondo requested to use the third room. What I'm telling you is available in the Trust's public logs."

She was choosing her words carefully. Nothing she was telling him could be traced back to her alone. Ms Holm was protecting Mondo's confidential information, making sure the contract with the Trust wasn't breached.

Axel followed the bait, her logical thread. "If there's still space in the other rooms, why did Mondo need the third one?"

"Whatever they need it for, they paid a generous rent to USK to use the room. That's in the Trust's public logs too. The seed vault is in Uskanian territory, a legacy from the Norwegian government, and USK charges rent on top of the Trust's depositor fees." She leaned towards him, putting her hand on the seat in between. The sofa's cushions sighed and sank, edging them together. "If you look carefully at the Trust's logs, they wrote the name of a research project. MExAI. That's what they're using the room for."

The space probe programme. He had been right about the initials in Birgit's lab.

"Do they have one of the space probes in there?"

Ms Holm peered nervously out of the window.

"That would be pure speculation, Mr Jóhannsson. How would I know such a thing?"

And yet he was sure she did.

"Was Birgit's research related to the MExAI programme?"

Ms Holm shook her head gently, pressing her lips shut.

"I don't know," she said.

"Are there cameras inside the vault?" he asked, changing tactic. If Ms Holm couldn't tell him, he could at least try to check.

"Plenty. Two of the video streams are even publicly available. One outside the portal building, another at the top of the tunnel. There are more cameras inside. Mondo watched the recordings two days ago."

"Why did Mondo watch the recordings?"

A subtle nod.

"Dr Olsen went into the vault. When you knocked, I thought that's why you were here. The videos show her going inside the third room. I find it baffling that Mondo have done nothing for two days. I'm sorry, Mr Jóhannsson, I'm not sure how much more I can tell you. I hope you understand."

She looked pained.

"Where is Birgit now?" Axel asked.

"Inside," Ms Holm said.

"Inside the vault? Still? For two days now? This whole time? Are you sure she didn't leave?"

She nodded.

"I watched the recordings myself. After going inside the portal building, Dr Olsen went down the tunnel. At the end of the tunnel, she exited the portal building and went into the mountain section, crossing in front of the office and the two rooms with electrical equipment. There are cameras above all of those. She opened the double airlock doors in the middle vault. She covered the camera inside the middle room, stayed for eight minutes, uncovered the camera and left. Then she continued to ..."

"Wait, you said she went into the *middle* room? What did she do in the middle room?"

A shallow breath. "I don't know. She got something out of her backpack, moved the ladder used to reach the seeds, and covered the CCTV camera near the ceiling. The video shows a blue-tinged stain during the full eight minutes."

"Where did she go afterwards?"

"To the third room."

"Did she have clearance to go in? Isn't the vault supposed to be closed in the summer?"

Ms Holm tilted her head. "I don't have that specific information but can only assume so. They open on exceptional occasions, and she told me it was an emergency. She got the codes from the Trust. I opened the main gate, lent her the keys, waited outside the portal building. I had no reason to doubt her."

"And after she went inside the third room, what happened?"

"The Trust doesn't have access to the video stream from the third room. The restriction was part of the contract with Mondo. Their research is classified. After watching the recordings, Mondo said the cameras were malfunctioning. The videos from the preparation room show Birgit going inside the third room, but Mondo say she never went in."

"They're lying."

"I'm afraid you might be right," Ms Holm said.

"Where is the preparation room?"

"It's the main lobby outside the three rooms, where we prepare the seed boxes before bringing them out and putting them on the shelves. We do it to minimise the time the airlock doors stay open."

"Could the camera in the preparation room be compromised?"

"They filmed me without any issue, when I went inside to check on her. Dr Olsen went in at 9.30 in the morning. I waited for her inside my car. At 10.30, when she still hadn't come out, I raised the alarm with the Trust, and they called Mondo. She could have felt dizzy, fainted, had a heart attack. She was wearing a snowsuit but could easily have gone into hypothermia, if she was knocked unconscious. Mondo asked me to go in and check on her. I got the codes for every room except the third one. I banged on the door, called her name. Nothing."

Axel's mouth had gone dry. He swallowed, hiding his shock. "Despite knowing she went inside the third room, Mondo didn't give you permission to go in?"

She offered him a strange smile. Commiserating. Ms Holm seemed more worried about Birgit than Oscar Frias had ever been. Why wouldn't they give the clerk access to the third room, if Birgit was in danger?

"What's the temperature inside the seed vault?"

"Minus eighteen degrees Celsius," Ms Hold said.

"Could she survive for two days, in a snowsuit?"

"Maybe." Ms Holm reached towards the table, grabbed the plate, swung it towards him. "Would you like another biscuit, Mr Jóhannsson?"

The cinnamon-flavoured biscuits were finished. Ms Holm convinced Axel to join her for lunch, saying he must taste her Suaasat (seal and potato soup). As Greenlandic as it gets. Her kitchen was a glorified cupboard tucked between a bedroom and a toilet cubicle, with a square table and two stools. When Axel went past her bedroom, she apologised about an old bathtub behind her bed. An odd design from a botched flat conversion. During lunch, they chatted about Longyearbyen, the Svalbard archipelago, and the seed vault.

"Each box contains five hundred seed packets," Ms Holm said. "The Trust keeps track of aisle, shelf and position for each DNA sample. I print the barcode labels for the boxes in the office at the end of the tunnel."

"And the third room? No seeds in there?"

"Only Mondo knows what's inside, as per the contract."

"What if they put a bomb in there?"

Ms Holm looked at him crossly. "Our depositors share a duty of care for the seeds."

"If someone wanted to damage the vault, I suppose they could just stop the cooling system," he said.

"That wouldn't work either. There's still permafrost. Much less than before, but if the cooling equipment fails, the rooms will slowly warm up to minus two degrees Celsius, and the sensors will warn us before any seeds become compromised. The Trust receives live updates from the closed network system."

"It's a safe."

"A safe for the seeds. A tomb for any humans trapped down there."

"Understood."

After lunch, Ms Holm saw him off at the door.

"Safe journey to the Hebrides," she said. "I hope you find her little girl."

"Thank you for the Suaasat."

She gave him a brief hug. Axel patted her back awkwardly, enjoying the sudden warmth of feeling. Going down the steep staircase, real cinnamon cookies and fake seal meat weighing in his stomach, he made a promise to himself. He would find Hildr and what Mondo were hiding inside the vault. He would leave no stone unturned. Even if this was his last case.

How come the subs used by migrants don't sink more often? Thread on GreyIt forum

Question: How come the subs used by migrants don't sink more often? They literally have a hole at the bottom.

Top answer: They are glorified diving bells, produced by a consortium in the Netherlands. The concept has been around for ages. Since the fourth century, to be precise. The physics is simple, you can try it in your own bathroom. Fill the bathtub with water, get an empty cup, turn it upside down, and push the cup vertically into the water. You'll notice the water won't fill the cup. The liquid pushes the air upwards, and because the air is lighter, it generates an air pocket. On top of that, the submarines are fitted with air tanks, controls for buoyancy, navigation tools, CO_2 pumps, wiring and oxygen refilling. The physics is solid. Only a few sink, when something goes wrong.

Chapter Twenty-Six

(Hildr) The submarine

Ula and Gunnar slept at the back of the cave. Morning arrived. A different tinge of light. Gunnar went for a run. Ula said they'd wait for him. The two women exchanged brief glances, eating leftovers from the previous night, tidying up their sleeping bags, clearing their throats as if they were going to speak, then saying nothing. Eventually Hildr could no longer keep her thoughts to herself.

"How can you sleep next to him? The man is abominable."

Ula sat across from her, knees raised, feet flat on the ground.

"We've lived on the mountain a long time. People who spend time together develop a natural kinship, even if they come from opposite worlds." She loosened and rearranged her hair, reining in the grey frizz, pulling it back into a tighter knot behind her head. "Plus, he's Liz's father. Life is complicated."

Gunnar reappeared by the cave's entrance in his blue tracksuit.

Hunching his shoulders, Gunnar grabbed a pen, collected a toilet roll from one of the rocks, ripped out a square, scribbled, and pressed it inside one of the biscuit tins. He removed his trainers and placed them neatly at the end of a long row of footwear, collecting a different pair of trainers from the middle.

"So ... are we going to meet the South Asian kid?" he asked.

Hildr clenched her teeth. "He's from Fyr."

"I don't have time for a bath, do I? Not that you stinky farm people would notice anyway."

"You don't need to come with me," Hildr said. "Neither of you. I will find my way."

"We want to," Ula said. "It's the least we can do. You have some guts, if you can pull this off."

The three descended into the dunes behind the ruins of the old weather station, not far from the dancers' camp. Gunnar hiked ahead, hands swinging along his lean torso. Hildr saw them first. Silhouettes dancing by the water's edge, torsos connected, feet in the water, long shadows extending from their calves. More dancers sat on the sand. Behind them, tents and capes hanging from ropes, people opening and closing their legs, jumping, moving their arms in synchrony. She squinted. A figure approached them, features blurring against the bright sky.

"I spotted you way back there," he said.

A warm feeling swept across her chest.

Bas.

His beard looked longer, his hair pulled up in a ponytail. He took three steps back. She thought he'd changed his mind. Then he stretched his arms in the air and ran forward four more steps, bringing his hands to the ground and propelling his legs over his trunk. He was doing cartwheels. Returning his feet to the ground, he stood upright in front of her and smiled.

"I thought about you," he said. "I even walked back to where I left you, but you were already gone. I see you managed to find Ula." The old woman had stopped a few metres behind Hildr. "Is that the runner standing next to her?"

"They're friends." Hildr extended her hand towards Bas. "I'm sorry for saying what I said. I was a fool. I've never met anyone as generous as you. Thank you."

"You came back to thank me?" He seemed chuffed. "I couldn't stop thinking about what you told me either. The research in the vault. The stuff spreading underneath Svalbard. Is it true?"

Hildr smiled. "I need your help to get to Spitsbergen."

Bas's eyes lit up. "S...s...Spitsbergen?" he stammered, jumping, as if the sand had become too hot. "I know exactly who can help us. I hope he hasn't left yet."

The four of them ran along the beach, Hildr and Bas at the front, Ula and Gunnar struggling to follow. Bas pointed at a ramp leading down the mud hill to the sea, with brown sludge leaking between two boulders, like a mudslide after the rain.

"Do you see the path? That's where we roll the sub for our lessons."

They climbed the hill.

When they got to the top, Hildr put her hands on her hips, staring. A submarine was resting at the top of the dune. Someone had dabbed the dark-blue walls with mud and thrown chunks of moss on the roof, perhaps in an attempt at camouflage. The egg shape still looked out of place.

"Sea-borne just two weeks ago," Bas said. "In excellent working condition. Santiago looks after it like a baby."

"Isn't it too small?" Hildr asked.

"It can take up to eight people," Bas said.

"Small people."

A man emerged from behind a bush, zipping up his trousers. Santiago. In his twenties or early thirties, with tight brown trousers tucked inside black boots, and a belt around a loose white shirt. Dark hair padded the shirt, a carpet extending from his chest to his neck, matching the full beard and long curly hair on his head.

He looked like a pirate. A hairy one.

"Mate, I'm so glad you haven't left yet," Bas said. "We have a favour to ask you."

Santiago grinned. "Whoa, you brought your 'ole family? You should've warned me. I would 'ave polished the silver-ware, eh?" Spanish accent, with soft, rolled *rrrs*.

"What?" Bas looked confused. "Sorry," he gestured to the others, as if excusing Santiago's bad joke. "Aren't you head-ing to Nordaustlandet to meet your brother? We need a lift, mate."

"A lift?" Santiago said. "I couldn't convince you to come with me, but lady friend asks and *ka-boom*, you're in. Fine, fine, climb aboard. I 'aven't crossed 'alf the continent to get stuck on a beach with black mud."

"I need to go to Spitsbergen, not Nordaustlandet," Hildr said.

"Volcanic islands," Bas said. "All our beaches are like this."

Santiago looked as if he hadn't understood. "All your beaches are made of black mud? In that case, I'm going back to Ibéria right now!" He dropped his head backwards and let out a wild roar, half laughter, half war-cry.

Hildr watched open-mouthed as the Spaniard scuttled over the egg-shaped submarine, reaching the top and balancing there, knees bent, arms stretched, feet wide apart, like a performer showing off a circus trick. Applying strategic pressure on the vessel, he slowly rocked it forward, until the submarine tipped down the ramp and over the slippery mud, gaining momentum, rolling at unexpected speed. Santiago bounced on top, until it stopped at the edge of the water with a splash. Jumping to the ground, he kicked and rolled it a few degrees further, exposing the circular hole in its base.

"Ladies and gentlemen, move to the back and sit against the wall. Seat belts on. Please keep your 'eads above the white line. Water will rise when we're at sea."

Hildr peered through the entrance. The door jamb revealed four distinct layers, two soft membranes hugging a thin metal core. The rubbery outer coating had a subtle pattern of extruded octagons interrupted by circular portholes.

"Can this get us to Spitsbergen?" Hildr asked doubtfully.

The Spaniard touched her shoulder. "Fear not with Santiago, eh? My name means 'saint' in my country. I'm a big angel with furry wings."

Stooping, she found the depression she was meant to sit on. With the vessel tipped on its side, this meant she was almost lying down. Domed windows revealed views of the sky and the beach. The walls were encrusted with pockets bulging out of the sub's inner membrane, like a strange skin disease. Inside the pockets, she found clothes, tools, and bottles, fastened and secured. Every inch of the vessel had a function – it was undeniably impressive.

Bas stepped in, squeezing himself against Hildr, back towards the left wall.

The beard and ponytail suited him, she thought.

"Are you sure … about coming?" she asked.

"It's the second time you've asked me that," Bas said. "Yeah, I've had enough of Fyr. Or maybe I just like you." He winked.

His presence filled her with optimism. Together, they could cross oceans. Santiago jumped inside the sub, placing himself in the middle, on a swivel seat. The front panel was covered in switches, buttons and levers outlined in white phosphorescent ink. A single white line went around the bottom, over a protruding ledge, marking about two-thirds of the sub's height. From pirate to pilot, Santiago swung his hips, orchestrating his instruments.

"Ballast and air tanks. Check. Pressure regulator and batteries. Check. Fly-by-wire, buoyancy control. Check. Ready to sail. We need to pull her up to the right position."

"Where are our oxygen tanks?" Hildr wondered aloud.

Santiago spun around and let out a loud roar. "Plenty of air in the sky! Air tanks are for controlling the ship. When we run out of air, we come up to breathe, like the tasty seals you eat here." He licked his lips.

"What about the seaworms? Won't they spot us?" Hildr asked.

"Arctic seaworms are tasty too," Santiago said. "They only attack when they're scared."

A spot of red appeared through the entrance. A rucksack. Hildr grabbed it against her lap. Then Ula's face appeared.

"There's food in there," the older woman said. "We will prepare more before winter. Safe travels. When you arrive, go to The Wild Reindeer in Longyearbyen. That's where Pat went." She looked at Santiago. "How long will it take you to get there?"

"Longyearbyen is full of drones and citizens," Santiago said. He leaned towards his passengers. "Nordaustlandet close enough, eh?" He looked back at Ula. "Ten days, maybe. Sailing is a breeeeeze without glacier. Double that if wind is west-southernly. Bye-bye!" He waved his hand in front of Ula's face, then put his head through the hole and called back again. "Hey, can you give us a little push? The hole needs to be facing down, or we'll get very wet!" He laughed.

Hildr felt the vessel shake, move and tip over. Santiago removed the pirate boots and put his feet on the pedals protruding from under the front panel, crossing two straps over each foot. She pressed her face against the domed bull's eye window. Ula and Gunnar were pushing the submarine further into the sea, trousers heavy with water. Gurgling noises echoed inside. Water was coming in at the bottom. The air became moist with saltwater. A chill crossed the width of the vessel. More water gushed through, flooding the room under them. The submarine submerged further, but they were safe in the pocket of air at the top of the upper chamber, white phosphorescent line shining above the surface.

The porthole was half-submerged when Hildr got her last glimpse of Ula Svenson's profile against the imposing Fyr mountains. Ula's thin grey hair, usually pulled back in a slick bun, fell over her face, making her look older. She was waving goodbye. Hildr's apprehension morphed into something else. Hope.

Bas put his hand over hers.

"Are you scared?"

"No," she said.

They were on their way.

PART THREE: THE VAULT

How our food chain is changing: lessons for school children

There are three types of organisms in our food chain: producers, consumers and decomposers. Plants produce their own food, using sunlight, carbon dioxide, water and minerals. That's why they're called producers. Humans eat plants and animals. That's why they're consumers. Bacteria and small organisms are decomposers because they decompose producers and consumers into minerals, which are absorbed and released back into the food chain. A great deal of energy is lost in this cycle. Animals need more energy than plants to move, digest and reproduce, so the food chain looks like a pyramid – a few large consumers at the top, with many small producers at the bottom to sustain them. In simple energy terms, we cannot remove producers from the food chain and expect all consumers to survive. When plants die, the top of the pyramid collapses and the food chain readjusts itself, until energy is rebalanced in the ecosystem.

Chapter Twenty-Seven

(Hildr) Underwater

Hildr ran her fingers over the delicate fissures and bulging pockets. The sub's inner membrane seemed alive.

She noticed Bas's face close to hers, watching.

"Are you still having memory issues?" he asked.

"Yes." Better this way.

Her stomach groaned.

"We have to be efficient with calories," Bas said. He emptied his pockets of New Food energy bars, stuffing them into the sub's wall pockets.

"That's very generous," she said. "You asked me if I was scared. What about you? Are you scared?"

"Nah. I like new adventures."

Hildr rummaged inside Ula's rucksack, counting the protein bars.

"I don't think we have enough food for ten days. There's an adventure for you."

"When food finishes, we fish," Santiago said. "My beauty has 'arpoooons." He pointed at one of the phosphorescent dots on the control panel. "I push this button and it goes *whoooosh*." He moved his hand in the air, like a cowboy throwing a lasso. "We pull the line and eat sushi."

"I'm a Jain," Bas said.

Santiago shrugged. "That's a woman's name."

"A religion," Bas said. "I don't eat animals."

"I think some of these don't have worms." Hildr fiddled through Ula's foil-wrapped packets. "We can keep them for you. Santiago and I will handle the harpoons."

Bas unwrapped a doughy dark-green lump. "Wow, are these from their farm? They look like biscuits." He bit off the edge and bounced the mush around in his mouth. "Vegetables are over-rated," he decided.

They reached deep sea and the atmosphere became darker. Santiago moved his feet on the pedals, huffing with effort. A permanent low hum filled the chamber.

"I can't believe we're pedalling all the way to Nordaustlandet," Hildr said.

"Safer than a dinghy." Santiago heaved as he spoke, long curly hair wet with perspiration. "Buoys, drones and ships 'ave 'ard time spotting subs underwater. Cheap models are upside-down cups. My beauty is special edition." He pointed at the phosphorescent outlines on the panel. "Sonar. Electronic fly-by-wire. Flood valves. Even propellers. We can't use them most of the time, so we pedal." He looked over the shoulder and gave Hildr a thumbs up. "Nice long legs."

Bas had a smile on his lips. She couldn't help but smile too.

The submarine travelled between four and six metres below the surface, basking in pale rays of sunlight filtered by the ocean. Sea creatures wiggled past the portholes: ghost-like snailfishes, spotty eelpouts, spiky angry-looking sculpins, indifferent cod. The water was thick and murky with sediment, but the propellers created millions of bubbles that swirled around them, like schools of tiny fish.

"Do you ever dive down there?" Bas pointed at the black pit under their feet. "I mean, besides relieving yourself." They had already done that a few times.

Chirps from Beluga whales reached them from the depths.

"*Si*, on long journeys," Santiago said. "To catch fish, 'ave a bath, swim."

"This equipment must cost a small fortune?" Hildr was looking at the control panel.

"Eh, if you 'ave the money, better than giving it to filthy smugglers." Santiago kept pedalling, leaning forward, like a cyclist pushing towards the finishing line. "*Oliveras*. 'Eard of them? Olive trees. My family is one of the last landowners in Ibéria, but here in your islands I'm nothing, eh?" He lifted his index finger in the air, like a teacher pointing out the obvious.

"Why did you leave?" Hildr asked. "Couldn't you get enough to eat, even with the olive trees?"

Santiago sat upright again, slowing down on the pedals. "Land and money buys food, protection from gangs, air conditioning, but slums and refugee camps were right outside our home. No jobs, no income, no citizenship. Those with nothing died on the streets. Not a good place to live."

"Uskania has no slums because we deport migrants back to the continent," Bas said. "The algorithm sends them to die somewhere out of sight."

Santiago kept swaying his head sideways. "*Mira.* We're growing food on the moon, but on Earth people keep pointing finger at each other. Our planet is doomed like this, no?"

The temperature inside the sub was cold, but bearable. The top chamber trapped most of the heat generated by their bodies, despite the freezing water splashing their feet. Every three hours, an automatic pump emptied the ballast tanks and filled them with air, pushing the vessel almost to the surface. When the sub glided at about one metre deep, a long instrument rose slowly out of its bulk.

"*Tam-ta-da-dam.* 'Ere comes the periscope," Santiago said.

The whole operation took about twenty minutes, during which the vent renewed the rarefied oxygen, filling the room with fresh air.

Despite this, the lack of food made Hildr dizzy.

"Only six energy bars left," she said on their fourth day.

Santiago hit the control panel with his knuckles.

"Damn ...'arpoon supposed to go out and catch fish, but ..." He pursed his lips and made a sputtering noise. "*Nada.* Must be stuck between inner and outer hulls. System is boosted."

"Do you mean *busted*?" she said.

"No, *boooosted,*" Santiago said. "*Bastard* is person who sleeps with your wife."

"What is a *wife*?" Bas asked.

They had some of Ula's farm food. After that, only scoops of krill, which they caught with a tight net attached at the bottom. The drowsiness got worse. Hunger. Dehydration. They sucked on empty foil wraps, sipping water from the condensation tube.

Santiago and Hildr did most of the pedalling.

"I can't do it any more," Bas said. "My lower back is killing me. I need to dance. I'm going mental inside this room."

"I will do your shifts," Hildr said. Pedalling helped her keep the cold and her impatience at bay. The lack of space bothered her more than the lack of exercise. She couldn't stand upright or lie down straight. When she wasn't pedalling, her legs were constantly folded. Her muscles ached and she started feeling claustrophobic.

"Who knows Bad Sailor song?" Santiago asked.

He shouted the out-of-tune lyrics.

Bad Sailor doesn't like pedal
Bad Sailor doesn't drink wee
Bad Sailor doesn't win medal
Bad Sailor sinks in the sea

Bas pouted, suspecting the verses were aimed at him. During the day, they chatted, laughed, sang. Silence was their worst enemy, inviting unwanted thoughts. Would they ever reach their destination? At night, when it was Hildr's turn to pedal and the others slept, a crippling panic took over. Fast heartbeat, cold sweats, cyclical thoughts. The Devs' school. Fyr. The bloodied pin coming out of her head. Being dropped at the beach. Bas. Finding Ula. Failing to find the bracelet.

Hildr closed her eyes.

She missed the breeze on her face.

"Are you okay?" Bas had woken after her, and he was looking at her anxiously.

"Yes. Just tired."

"I bet you regret inviting me now." His hair was soggy and greasy, framing a dark beard which kept getting longer.

Hildr forced her mouth into a smile and kept pedalling. "I'd have felt very lonely without you."

"Shut up, lovebirds," Santiago mumbled. "I'm trying to sleep."

"What about you, Santiago? Why are you going to Nordaustlandet?" Hildr asked.

"My brother and his friends started a fishing community there. A new beginning, away from everything."

"Fishing is illegal in Uskania," Hildr said.

"Fish don't care about borders," Santiago replied.

"Maybe we should check it out," Bas said, looking at Hildr with an expression she didn't want to decipher. Instead, she looked ahead, outside the sub, pedalling into the darkness.

There were no close encounters with ship hulls, no whale or seaworm sightings. Just long, cold boring days in the dark, the three of them stuck in an egg, unlikely triplets, forced into an intimate friendship. Taking turns to use the wonder instrument, a shovel with a tube and an articulated lid, emptying their business in the lower chamber, splashing water on their private parts, skinny-dipping in the freezing Arctic. They rubbed each other's arms, exchanged massages, shared body heat. The submarine gained a perpetual bouquet of toilet, sweat and seaweed. They barely noticed.

On their eighth day at sea, Santiago spent a long time looking at his mechanical compass. They were two metres below the surface, waiting for the chamber's air to renew.

"Dead batteries can't find their north," Santiago said. "That's why I always carry this beauty."

Hildr was doing her arm exercises. "We must be getting close. Can we take a peek?"

Santiago shot her a dirty look. "Take peek? The closer we get to Nordaustlandet, the more dangerous to *take peek*. Sonars, radars, drones, they're all looking for us."

"It's too risky," Bas weighed in. "USK have satellite technology. They might already suspect we're not a big fish."

"We keep low until Nordaustlandet," Santiago said. "No peeking."

"So how will we know when we're approaching the buoys?" Hildr persisted.

Santiago raised the compass in the air. "With this." He turned it round, showing a window with a red needle bouncing between the numbers. "And luck."

"Luck?" Hildr looked at him, stunned.

They had left Fyr over a week ago – and it felt more like a year. She couldn't fake optimism or light-heartedness any more, couldn't pretend to be amused by their jokes. Relying on luck was the last straw. The submerged room provided an illusion of agency. Her life was a long, dark tunnel between events that occurred eighteen years ago, and a mythical future she was forced to believe in. Attempts to clutch at hope and blind faith were revealed for what they truly were: the ravings of an amnesiac.

Hildr unstrapped her seat belt and put her hand inside one of the wall pockets.

The two men exchanged glances.

"I need to get out," she said. Legs, sleeves, torso. Hildr slid the wetsuit on. The garment was too small and tight to accommodate her muscular chest, the top of her wide back. "If I'm not back in a few minutes, please keep going without me."

Bas helped her. "That's not an option. We will wait for you," he said, zipping the suit up as far as possible, forced to leave a gap at the top.

"You look like seal," Santiago said. "Tasty."

Hildr squatted near the white phosphorescent line, dropping her legs inside the water. A chill rose up her spine. Freezing cold. She lowered herself into the black hole. Her whole body went through, long fingers grasping the ledge, head emerging from the liquid void.

"Please take care," Bas said. "Look out for seaworms. They spawn around Spitsbergen, near the vault. In and out, as quickly as you can, okay? Like a winter dive after the sauna." He stroked her cheek with his fingers. "Remember I'm waiting for you." The touch felt more intimate than usual.

Hildr took a deep breath and plunged into the Arctic.

'Can we grow food on the moon?' Sci-Fi Newsletter, article sponsored by Mondo Foods International

New Food has split public opinion and raised social unrest in many countries, but everyone acknowledges that agriculture's carbon footprint is unsustainable. What if we could grow our food on the moon? That's exactly what the UArtic Institute in Nuuk and the multinational conglomerate Mondo Foods are looking to explore, in partnership. In a ground-breaking mission, bacteria are being seeded by rovers to clean and fertilise swathes of lunar soil. "It's the initial step," says Dr Jean-Luc Ghent, one of the leading scientists working on the project. "We don't know how life started on Earth. Some scientists speculate an asteroid with bacteria from another galaxy hit us early on. Now we're doing the same with the moon, but in fast-forward. The initial stage will take between twelve and fifteen years." We'll keep our forks ready.

Chapter Twenty-Eight

(Birgit) Tomato

When I get underground, I won't be able to reach you. The tunnel leading to the vault was built between the rock seams of the Newtontoppen mountain, under layers of sandstone, siltstone and claystone. Please don't judge me too soon. Sometimes the details can't be gleaned from the surface. We must dig deeper.

Shall I tell you one last story?

According to the Incas, our solar system was formed four billion years ago when Inti, their golden deity, became a ball of fire in the sky. Inti taught his daughter and son the arts of civilisation, and the siblings came to Earth to pass on their knowledge. They built the Inca capital in the ancient city of Cusco, Peru. Magnificent buildings and roads stretched across the empire covering Ecuador, Bolivia, Argentina, Chile and Colombia. The siblings taught their people to plant and tend amaranth, quinoa, potato, corn, peppers. They also gave them small, glossy red fruits, never mastered by humans before.

Tomatoes.

Spanish convoys decimated the Inca people, but their farming legacy endures to this day. Scientists believe that the genes of tomatoes tripled seventy million years ago, around the time dinosaurs went extinct. This versatility may have saved tomatoes from the same fate as the dinosaurs, allowing them to adapt when a rogue meteorite unleashed devastating climatic and tectonic activity on Earth. The skies of the late Cretaceous period were obscured for a long time, but the great Inti would soon return and bless the highlands of Peru with hard, flavoursome tomatoes.

When the Svalbard seed vault opened, delegations visited from around the world, and Peru deposited wild varieties similar to the first harvested tomatoes. The ancient fruits from the Incas can grow and blossom in cold or heat, rain, drought, unlike today's mutant relatives, grown for their size and sweetness. Plants are nothing if not flexible. Tomatoes would continue to adapt to climate change, if only we let them. Instead, producers got rid of genetic diversity and selected traits to maximise profit. Bigger and sweeter fruits, easier to transport and store.

We've sequenced the genome for over twenty tomato varieties. When you were a baby, I used to take you with me into the lab. You loved seeing me fiddle with the instruments. I explained the regions associated with certain phenotypic traits, the polygenic effects of two or more genes, the way they interacted with the environment. It was like building a puzzle together, even if you couldn't understand a word.

Our play evolved. For your seventh birthday, I gave you a special gift. Pot, bag of compost, and a handful of tomato seeds. You were ecstatic. Running around, giggling, jumping over pots and buckets, opening the water tap, hose wiggling and hissing, an untameable snake. We got wet. You did it once, twice. *Are you sure you're responsible enough to look after a tomato plant of your own?*

We brought the pot inside the greenhouse and filled it with compost. We watered the soil. *These are your special tomato seeds, from the best tomatoes in the world.* You were so proud. You usually helped me for a few minutes, then lost interest, and moved onto something else. This time you sat on the floor next to me and paid attention. You met me at the greenhouse first thing in the morning, observing the seeds germinate, the sprouts coming out, the tender bulbs forming, the soon-to-be leaves. *Look, it's even bigger today.* After six weeks, we removed the seedlings and planted them in the garden, in a spot by the wall, where they could enjoy the great Inti and also some shade. Now I realise how much I enjoyed those moments. The time I spent with you and our tomato plant was an oasis.

Seven years old. The same age I was when my parents left for Canada. Maybe I'm repeating a pattern. For decades, we've been taught to loathe the plague we've become on the planet. There I was, worrying about a tomato plant.

Who was going to look after you?

Before I left, Pat came screaming into the bedroom. *She removed her bracelet.* Such a twisted turn of events. We ran down the street, climbed the mountains, split the ground in two. Neighbours formed search parties, went to the town centre, the beach, the port. In the evening, I walked to the dune where I had found you as a baby and sat on the sand. I was stunned, numb, catatonic. My efforts had fallen short, they were inadequate. Why was this happening? How could I still think about coming to the vault? Isn't a child worth more than anything? The waves continued moving to and fro, mocking my despair.

According to the legend, Inti instructed the siblings to create the Temple of the Sun, to mark the start of the great Inca dominion. Ayar, their reckless and cruel brother, helped them gather stones for the temple. He killed a tribe on his way. The siblings were furious. The great Inca rulers would not tolerate needless suffering. They gathered a handful of wild tomatoes and called Ayar into a cave. He ate one, two, three. Sweet, sharp, delicious. He couldn't stop eating them. He didn't notice when the siblings left the cave, or when they pulled a large rock over the entrance, sealing him inside.

Ayar died inside the cave, screaming into the darkness.

By the wall, our tomatoes were coming out. Small, shiny, pea-sized, like the first variety from the Incas. I plucked one, wiped it against my vest, put it in my pocket, brought it with me to Svalbard. My dear child, our old food is dying. To survive, we need fundamental changes. We've been waiting so long for a breakthrough. My actions might look crazy, but this is the best chance we have.

I hope one day you'll forgive me.

I'll always love you either way.

What abandoning farms means for our genes, article in The Buff Post

A new study confirms that human genes are changing to adapt to New Food. The city of Surat Thani, Thailand, was one of the first in the world to implement a diet totally composed of New Food and is home to many labs providing food for neighbouring Asian nations. Eating a New Food diet for two generations has caused the population of Surat Thani to display a higher frequency of a specific mutation on the FADS3 gene. This mutation allows them to process New Food more efficiently, converting it into nutrients essential for health, and is not present in groups that still eat farm-based diets. Subjects in the study also tended to have a lower body temperature, and taller and lighter bone structure, than the average Thai population. Humans are expected to keep evolving in novel ways.

Chapter Twenty-Nine

(Hildr) Nordaustlandet

*T**he breeze. I need to feel the breeze.* Hildr swam past the antechamber. Seen from the outside, the submarine looked like a sunfish incubating eggs. She went around it, peeping through the portholes. Bas. Santiago. They were smiling. She smiled back. Trapped air escaped from her mouth, dozens of bubbles rushing to the surface. Turning from the deep, Hildr kicked to propel herself upwards, legs undulating, arms extending, fingernails guiding the rest of her body, like tiny anglerfish lamps. She swam up, an eel wriggling towards the light. The sky was getting closer. Right there, above her.

She pierced through the surface, wiped the excess water off her eyes. Hands gliding, legs twirling, Hildr brought her stomach to the surface and lay flat, floating, under the sky. Long, deep breaths. Cirrus clouds hovered over the expanse of sea, thin and wispy filaments the sun had coloured red. The sunset glistened over the Arctic Ocean, a slight breeze pricking it with dots of light. Gentle waves rolled inside her ears. She wanted to stay like this forever.

A rhythmic noise.

Her abs contracted.

She spun around in her cold bath, retreating inside the water, looking up. Where had the noise come from? Near the horizon, a long hump extended against the sea. Hildr squinted. Too wide for a whale. She dived down, swimming fast towards the submarine.

The room shook and groaned as she burst through the hole.

"Drones," Hildr said, breathless. Bas helped her rise to the top chamber. "There are drones above us, following the sub." The whole room swayed, splashing them.

"Big shit," Santiago said.

"Can we dive deeper?" Bas asked.

"I saw something else," Hildr added. "Land, ahead of us."

"Really?" Santiago looked at his compass and at the control panel. "Must be Nordaustlandet. Not on radar yet. We arrived fast. More legs, I s'pose. We never stopped for sleep. Always pedalling. We must be right outside the buoys. I will 'alt assisted propulsion, stop the noise, and go deeper."

"How deep?" Hildr asked.

Santiago raised four fingers in the air.

"Four metres?"

"Forty," he said.

Hildr gasped. "*Forty* metres? Underwater?"

"Can the sub take it?" Bas asked.

Santiago's shoulders rose, more involuntary convulsion than shrug. "Eh ... *si, claro.*"

Bas was biting the neck of his bottle, a tic he returned to when nervous. "We'll be in for a laugh though, and that's the best-case scenario. Nitrogen narcosis. The pressure poisons you."

Hildr sat in her usual place, peeling the wetsuit off her legs, slowly regaining her normal heart rate and body temperature. She placed a hand on Santiago's shoulder.

"You know what to do?" she asked.

Santiago nodded. "Nets and sensors from buoys don't go deep. We turn assisted propulsion and sonar off, and we go under nets, like fish." Santiago held one hand in the air and moved his other hand below it. "Buoys will have 'ard time knowing we're not beluga. Flying drones won't spot us either. This is what my beauty was made for."

"What about the pressure? How long can we last down there?" Bas said.

"A while," Santiago said. "We must 'old tight till we reach land."

Bas looked puzzled. "We'll have less than a couple of hours until we need to come up for air again. And we can't come up too fast. We'll need to decompress."

"My beauty adjusts speed," Santiago said. "We just follow her."

"Have you done this before?" Hildr asked.

"Only dry run." Hildr and Bas looked at him in shock. "I mean, in the water, but not in real situation. The buoys around Fyr were never finished, they were *easy pizza*." Santiago's big, brown eyes filled with melancholy. "My friends, you asked for lift, didn't you? You're in the shit too. No citizen-chip. No life. Why did you come if you're scared of dying?"

"Do you mean scared of *diving*?" Bas said.

With the propulsion off, gurgling sounds echoed louder.

"We're not scared," Hildr said. "Tell us how we can help."

"Yeah," Bas added quickly. "Let's do this."

Santiago pressed a few buttons. The air in the room renewed. Ballast tanks filled with water. The control panel showing their depth started changing – six, seven, eight, nine metres, numbers going up as they went down. Hildr felt giddy. Nitrogen narcosis already? Perhaps the adrenaline playing tricks on her. Eighteen metres. Nineteen. Twenty. The water in the antechamber rose higher, pressing the air against their ceiling. Hildr and Bas sat quietly in their assigned positions. Outside the portholes, the deep blue grew darker, until it was almost black. The control panel illuminated Santiago's face, making the pores on his skin shine like fireflies. He kept pedalling. With the sonars switched off and the darkness outside, it was like cycling blind. If they hit rock, they would never know what had struck them.

Thirty metres. No one dared speak. Saving oxygen. Avoiding detection. Gurgling and Santiago's breathing was all there was to hear. The water line stood three fingers above the phosphorescent ledge, projecting a white translucent aura under their feet.

Forty metres.

Pure black.

Were they finally swimming among the Arctic seaworms? Were the belugas outside as scared as they were inside? Humans were never meant to come this deep. In seconds that felt like hours, and minutes that felt like weeks, Santiago's vessel kept them safe.

Until Hildr felt a lash on her chest.

The submarine roared.

Nausea touched the pit of her stomach, like a lift going up too fast. A long shaft with concentric rings tightened and loosened around her body. Her head dropped.

A metallic taste. Was this what death tasted like?

How much time had passed?

No gliding motion.

Struggling to hold her head straight, Hildr turned towards the white blur at the edge of her vision.

Daylight.

One of the circular portholes of the submarine showed a fragment of sky. She uncrossed her arms from their stiff position. Where the seatbelt had stopped her, a painful wound remained. The white ledge was a good two palms above the waterline. They were floating. Hildr stretched her legs and found that moving them was less painful than turning her head. Bas was wriggling out of his seat, moaning. She helped him. They both turned to Santiago, who lay inert, head over his hands, on top of the instrument panel. Hildr put two fingers on his neck. His skin was cold, but she could feel a pulse. She leaned towards the porthole on the other side of the sub, wiping it with her arm.

"We're near an island. Let's get out of here."

They wrapped Santiago's arms around their shoulders, lifted him, and dived into the flooded chamber, dragging his limp body through the opening. Beneath the chamber, the sub's outer layers contorted above a rock. Underwater, they felt Santiago waking, arms twisting and fretting, pushing back up.

The three surfaced together.

Santiago flailed his arms, grabbing at Bas's T-shirt.

"*Joder*, are you trying to drown me?"

They dragged themselves ashore, Hildr pulling Santiago by his shirt collar. "The submarine crashed," she said, hauling him over a boulder and laying him on his back. A drone circled above them, maintaining distance. "We need to get out of here, before we get caught."

Santiago shook his mass of soggy brown hair. "I'm not leaving my beauty behind." He raised his head above the boulder, looking at the ruined sub. The front had been whacked, smooth membrane ripped off, revealing a silver metal plate jammed against the rock. "I'll fix her. It will be a good chance to get 'arpoon working. Then I'll continue to the south of the island. My brother's waiting for me there."

"We'll go with you," Bas said.

Bas looked like a wet bird, skinny and fragile, no feathers puffing him up.

"*You* should go with Santiago," she said. "The fishing community sounds like a good plan. I'll find my way to Longyearbyen."

Bas jumped between rocks, joining her. "Are you trying to get rid of me?"

"Spitsbergen is too dangerous," she said.

"Don't lecture me on danger. What about that one?" He pointed at the sky, towards the faint rhythmic noise. "It's been following us for a while."

Santiago coughed, spitting water. "My friends, make up your minds. I only gave you a ride."

"I'm coming to Longyearbyen," Bas said. "End of discussion. Santiago, we'll meet you afterwards."

The Spaniard smiled. "Yes, my friend. It will be my pleasure to welcome you."

He got up, put his arms around Bas's shoulder blades, and squeezed tight.

Hildr and Bas followed the dark landmass of Nordaustlandet, a lump of volcanic rock with a flat surface and horizontal ridges carved on the side, like a giant slice of chocolate cake. No beach to speak of, only scattered groups of boulders following the line of a wall that was too steep to climb. They walked for miles, jumping from rock to rock, picking their way along the base of the 'cake', constantly checking for the faint rotor noise above, only to confirm the drone was still there, following them. They had nowhere to hide.

A cliff came into view, like a fortress of natural turrets perched above the sea, with straight-cut rectangular steps carved into its face, offering a route upwards. The wind wept and howled. Tufts of pale green moss broke the grey mass of straight angles, disappearing into a spectral mist. Gulls and guillemots circled above the menacing towers, below a dim, leaden sky. The fortress continued along the coast, beyond the horizon. The steps, though abrupt, were their first chance to reach higher ground. Hildr used her hands and feet, deciding the next move from an infinite network of trails. She climbed slowly, methodically, a cat keeping count of its nine lives, followed closely by Bas. Gulls cried and flapped around them, provoked by their intrusion.

They reached the field at the top. The vast mountaintop, a rough platform of blurred edges, was a podium between layers of water above and below. Cloud and sea. Here, the Arctic sang a song of silence, broken only by the howling wind beneath an overcast sky and a drizzle that barely touched the ground. Hildr's ears hurt from the cold. As they walked deeper inland, the landscape changed, the edges of the podium crinkling, folding, rising like a piece of cloth. Far in the distance, she noticed a vague shape against the mist, tall, slender, with a dark waving tip, like a flag. Bas's legs stiffened.

"Is it a drone?" he asked.

"I don't think so," she said.

They kept walking, noting how the tall shape also seemed to be moving in their direction. The more they walked, the more it looked like a human figure, a twisted reflection of Hildr, strolling towards the invisible mirror between them.

"A man?" Bas said.

A friend. She felt a certainty she couldn't explain. The man walking towards them had white trousers, a padded vest, and a white pouch at the front of his waist. His skin was the colour of hazelnuts, his eyes a striking olive-green. His dark, long hair fluttered with the wind. Yet the most notable thing were not his features, or his clothing, but the synthetic snake climbing from under his vest and coiling around his neck – an impressive tech suite attached to his skin with hundreds of tiny suction cups, like an octopus's tentacle.

Almost instinctively, Hildr touched her own neck.

I had one of those.

The man had the fixed, blank stare of a blind person. It was so disconcerting that Bas moved to one side, checking if the man's eyes followed him. They did.

"Look at his tech," Bas whispered to her. "He's a Dev."

Like a machine taking aim, the man's pupils moved to focus on Bas. He unzipped the pouch at the front of his vest and reached into its opening with his slender fingers. Black and white speckles fell on the ground.

"Sunflower seeds," the man said. "For the seagulls." He smiled. "My name is Gabriel. I'm a birdwatcher." He had the warmest voice she'd ever heard. "Can I help you?"

Hildr felt compelled to trust him.

"We're heading to Longyearbyen," she said.

Gabriel smiled deepened. "Perhaps you would like a ride. My speedboat is moored fifteen minutes away. It's nice to see you, Hildr."

Bas covered his mouth with his hand, a hint of terror in his eyes.

"How does he know your name?"

"A lift would be excellent," Hildr said.

The trust settled nicely in her chest.

Bas glanced at her, eyebrows edging together. He followed them reluctantly, wincing with each step. Their podium of rock wrinkled at the edges, and a mountain emerged from the mist.

The tale of Hildr, the giant – the part in the middle

"Hildr never stood still. Every day, she would ask the farmers to let her go outside the glass domes. They explained it was safer to stay there, where they had wonderful vegetables, water, and enough to eat."

"Did Hildr run away, Mama?"

"Yes, she did."

"Like me."

"That's the story, anyway. One day, she escaped."

"What happened?"

"She walked for five days and five nights and almost died of hunger."

"And then?"

"Then ... she fell in the Arctic Ocean and swam straight into the mouth of a seaworm."

"Did the seaworm eat her?"

"No. She was expelled by the sphincter at the other end."

"Seaworm poo! And then?"

"Then ... she found the vault, hidden under a mountain."

Chapter Thirty

(Axel) The return

Spitsbergen, Svalbard archipelago, June 2149

Eighteen years after Axel had closed the kid's case, a mail drone tapped softly at his window, like the beginning of a hailstorm.

"It's for you," he said.

He knew the drill. Ever since she had got back into the model, she was sending supplies to Ula and her farmer friends. Flour, sugar, oil. The farmers depended on donations while pretending to be subversive, and the algorithm didn't care any more. A bunch of hippies counting clouds on an abandoned rock.

Pat disagreed, as usual.

"Who gave you permission to open my fucking post?"

"I didn't open it, I just let it in," Axel said.

"Give me that!" She snatched the parcel from his hands. "You shouldn't even look at it. You'll make it shrivel and burn."

Pat tolerated him for practical and sexual matters, but when it came to politics, he was the Antichrist. She never forgave him for being right. "I'll be more useful in the model, supporting the farmers from afar," she'd said when her dreams of freedom collapsed. After the purge, she'd spent five years in low-calorie lock with the farmers, at the top

351

of the Beranger volcano. Axel never stopped sending messages. He flew the drones himself, testing new coordinates month after month, until the letters landed on her head. After many farmers threw themselves off the cliff, she finally agreed there was no point in suffering. Axel sponsored her new citizen-chip and she offered to help him run the inn. Thirteen years of infighting and false dead-ends, and here they were. The mismatched hosts of The Wild Reindeer, still clashing their antlers.

Inside the drone was a message from their old friend Ula Svenson, saying they had found a woman collapsed on the mountain. Birgit's daughter, supposedly.

Alive.

Hailstorm unleashed.

"I knew it," Pat said through gritted teeth. "I never believed your *triangulation*."

They were in the kitchen, in the middle of their daily production line, turning New Food Breakfast Surprise cartons upside-down onto stoneware bowls, and adding two squishes of fake carrot syrup before serving them to guests.

"Can't be her," Axel said.

"I should never have listened to you," she said. "Just because your clues led nowhere, didn't mean she was dead."

He didn't feel bad. Why would he feel bad? He had only lied to spare Pat.

"Wishful thinking," Axel said. "A random woman collapsing from hunger. Why does Ula think it's Hildr?"

His lie had given her hope.

"How many times will we have this argument?" Pat said.

Now hope was coming back to bite him.

"The kid disappeared eighteen years ago." Axel squeezed the last drops of carrot syrup from his bottle. "Doesn't make sense for her to show up now, does it?

"How can you be so mean, so negative, so nasty?" she said.

Mean, negative, nasty.

He should have been used to her accusations.

"Ula wants you to feel guilty, to regret leaving Fyr," Axel said.

Did she regret it?

"Can you hear yourself, how toxic you are?" Pat wailed. "How can you accuse Ula? You *always* think the worst of people."

"Where was the kid hiding for eighteen years?" Axel said.

"She obviously didn't go to the Hebrides. You said you turned every turd on the island looking for her. You couldn't find her in the Hebrides because Hildr was on Fyr all this time."

"Impossible," he said.

"We must tell her what happened to her mother," Pat said.

"We don't know if it's Hildr."

Pat halted her carrot dressing in mid-air, sneering at him with half-closed eyes.

"Why can't you admit you were wrong?" She slapped her bottle down on the table, orange-coloured syrup squirting her face. Axel cleaned her chin with a cloth and grabbed a syrup refill from the shelf. Pat stood rubbing her chin with the back of her hand. "I just *know* it's her ... I know it's Hildr. Shall we give her the bracelet?"

Their eyes locked.

"Stop," Axel messaged.

They had hit the compromise demanded from well-fed citizens. The software was always listening. They couldn't reveal the bracelet's location, after all the effort they had put into hiding it. They must stay quiet. They must trust each other.

The hardest task of all.

Axel's natural inclination was to analyse data, not people. If understanding people came naturally, he'd have started with himself. He had spotted the chink in Pat's armour early on. Fighting for her principles no matter how gullible. Trusting strangers, despite all evidence showing they were not to be trusted. After Pat had agreed to come to Longyearbyen, Axel finally understood why she behaved the way she did. She had a constant need for validation. But not from him, nor from anyone in the world of the living.

Six months after she'd moved into The Wild Reindeer, they had received a package from a memorial site. Dried flowers, handwritten messages, candles, photographs, flags from thirty nations paying homage. From then on, a similar package arrived every year. Pat's father had been one of the activists in the Clair oilfield explosion. She had tried hard to abide by the godly vision of the man she had barely known, enlisting in endless political campaigns, botched revolutions, crazy ideas. She couldn't relax, get by, live like a normal person. Bringing down the oil industry was a feat she couldn't match. No matter how hard she tried, she couldn't please her father's all-seeing eye. She never talked about this, of course.

The worst demons were the ones you couldn't see.

Events took a radical turn before they had a chance to make it up after the argument. A few days after the mail drone had arrived with Ula's message, someone knocked at the door of the inn at three in the morning.

Axel sat up, gulping from the water glass by his bedside.

"Out-of-hours check-in?"

"I didn't take the booking," Pat said.

She seemed wide awake, despite her unpreparedness. Rushing out of the bedroom, Pat followed the inn's ambient spotlights under the embellished ceiling friezes. She sped up by the portraits of Roald Amundsen and Erik the Red, eyes watching from the walls. Axel followed her, shoes on, socks off, stepping carefully on the carpet, careful not to disturb their guests. He didn't have a good feeling about this out-of-hours visit.

An eerie silence filled the main lobby. Axel stopped in the semi-darkness behind the reception desk, watching from afar. Pat opened the inn's front door, only a crack, and held it against her chest, like a shield. Whispers. Gestures. The door opened wide, and two figures came in, heads bowed, scurrying along by the wall. The first figure was a very tall black woman with short, braided hair. The second was shorter, long haired, slender, with the gait of a teenager. Their profiles receded into the darkness as the front door squeezed out the midnight sun. Three figures tiptoeing into the kitchen.

He heard chairs scraping on the floor. More whispering. Glasses clinked on the countertop. Drinking and chewing noises. Axel walked into the kitchen, standing in the doorway. The shorter figure was a young, bearded man. The woman was practically a giant next to him, neck thick as a log, hair braided into cornrows, a sort of mohawk at the top. She froze when she saw Axel. She even stopped chewing. Pat's lack of reaction reassured her. Yes, his presence was expected.

"Is this place like a hotel?" Hildr asked in a throaty, choppy voice. "Can you order extra food for guests?" She was guzzling down Breakfast Surprise directly from the carton.

Pat nodded, tapping her fingers on the countertop. "We can order more next week."

"You can't storm in here without a booking." Axel's voice was loud, commanding attention.

"Ula said you have something that belongs to me," Hildr said.

She must be joking. Straight down to business, no time for niceties?

"Who are you?" Axel asked.

"Hildr."

"Hildr who?" he asked.

"Olsen," Hildr said.

He scoffed.

"Please, Axel. Not now," Pat said, eyes pleading.

"We need proof," he said. "She can say she's the Queen of Norway."

"How can I prove my name?" Hildr said. "I don't have tech."

"We'll give her the bracelet," Pat said. "If the messages work, it's the same DNA."

Axel stood next to the table where they sat eating, looking down on them.

"You were on Fyr only a few days ago," he said. "How did you get here?"

"We got a lift," Hildr said.

"A *lift*?" Axel repeated, incredulous.

"Two lifts, actually," Bas said. "A friend and a foe. It's a long story. Can we get more food, or would that be a problem for your guest allowance?"

"They're hungry," Pat admonished him. "Can we please stop the hostilities." She removed two more cartons from the fridge. "Let them eat in peace."

"I'm not holding their mouths shut," Axel said. He wished he could. Pat was so gullible.

"I'm Birgit Olsen's daughter," Hildr said, noticeably annoyed by his presence. "Ula believed me, and she had more reasons to doubt."

Who had sent her in the middle of the night?

"Are we talking about the same Birgit?" he asked.

Hildr seemed briefly taken aback. She closed her eyes. "When the house was full, she would stay inside her cubicle, working non-stop. On that day, she sent me away. She thought the others could entertain me, but I wanted *her*. I was so disappointed. I don't know why I left. She was the only mother I ever knew. I should never have removed the bracelet."

Axel did a double take, observing her.

"What happened, after you ran away?" Pat asked.

"I was rescued. They took me in a big ship. To Iceland."

"Rescued by whom?" Axel said.

"I have memory issues," Hildr said. "Post-traumatic stress disorder."

"How convenient," Axel said.

Pat looked as if she were ready to kill him.

"It's obviously her," Pat said. "We know Hildr went to the port. Instead of the Hebrides, she went to Iceland, and now she's here. Tell her what happened to Birgit. Tell her what you found."

Axel took a deep breath.

"There was a list of initials in Birgit's lab," he started, "with dates next to them. The initials referenced MExAI, the space probe programme sponsored by Mondo. They also mentioned the port at Longyearbyen, the Svalbard seed vault, the Port of Minneapolis, and a lab in Minnesota, where Mondo have a high-security research facility. The dates align with a shipping contract from a Canadian biotech handler carrying a consignment from Mondo. They picked up something from the lab in Minnesota and took it to Svalbard. A few days after they had deposited the goods inside the seed vault, Birgit stepped into the same room. She never came out."

Hildr was transfixed.

"She's still down there, for all we know," Pat said. "The clerk who looked after the seeds retired. Until that moment Birgit hadn't stepped out. The place is covered in cameras."

"That's insane," Bas said. "Isn't it freezing cold in the vault?"

"Birgit died," Pat said, "and Mondo and USK covered it up, to keep their secret intact. Whatever they brought from the MExAI expedition is hidden deep inside the vault. Tell them what you found out from the cleaners in Minnesota."

"You spoke to them?" Hildr said.

"He used to be a Finder," Pat said.

"The cleaners weren't allowed on one of the floors," Axel said. "A red alert was raised in the lab. Biological contamination. That's when the biotech handlers were called in."

"And the nitrogen narcosis," Pat said. "Tell her."

"Cleaners in other floors reported people feeling dizzy and collapsing into comas. Mondo staff were taken to hospital as well."

Bas's eyes lit up. "Nitrogen narcosis ... like what happens in deep diving? I've never heard about it happening on the surface."

Axel nodded. "Their blood showed an increased concentration of nitrogen. Symptoms included intoxication, poor judgement, dizziness and euphoria, but their condition must have been caused by a different mechanism. There was no change in air pressure inside the lab."

"He spoke to the American doctors too," Pat said. "He went as far as he could, but he hit closed doors with Mondo and USK." She placed her hand on Axel's arm. "Let's take her to the bracelet. Please. We don't have much time. The algorithm already knows she's here."

Still so trusting of strangers.

Hildr dragged her chair backwards and got up from the table. Her size was menacing, a good two palms taller than him.

"Shall we?" Hildr said.

"Can we bring food for the journey?" Bas asked.

"*Her story doesn't add up,*" Axel said, voice-free. "*She is a freak.*"

"*Young people are tall. New Food is affecting their genes,*" Pat said.

"*Two voids strolling around Spitsbergen? Finder drones would have been all over them.*"

"*They came in a submarine,*" Pat said. "*They risked their life.*"

"*She's lying. She told you exactly what she needed to convince you. Doesn't it remind you of the algorithm?*"

"What are you waiting for?" Hildr asked.

Pat walked to the lobby and grabbed two yellow raincoats from the rail, the ones with the local museum logo they kept for unprepared guests.

"Put these on," she said, handing them to Hildr and Bas.

"*What if she was sent by USK? They will keep Mondo's secret for themselves. Only USK citizens will have food. Is that what you want?*"

Pat held the front door open, shooting him a look of disapproval. "*Don't you fucking gaslight me! You know perfectly well that's not what I want. We don't have any other option. Let's give her the bracelet and figure out the rest later.*"

Axel leaned over the reception desk, plucked the boat keys, threw them in his pocket.

"*You're taking full responsibility for this decision,*" Axel said. "*Fine.*"

He was only the expedition guide.

Autotrophs vs heterotrophs, Philosophical Science

We divide living beings into autotrophs (producers) and heterotrophs (consumers). Autotrophs can feed themselves without requiring other living beings. They produce their own food using sunlight, water, carbon dioxide and other chemicals. Plants, algae and some bacteria and fungi are the only autotrophs on Earth. Heterotrophs, on the other hand, eat other living beings, like plants or animals, to survive. Humans are heterotrophs. The distinction falls apart at quantum and cosmic scales. Go small enough, and living beings are merely a shifting configuration of elemental particles and chemical processes. Go big enough, and they're a scrumptious meal being cooked up for a hungry black hole.

Chapter Thirty-One

(Hildr) The mine

Early dawn. Empty streets. Hildr zipped up her raincoat and slid the hood over her head. Since they'd arrived, she'd felt as if she was approaching the steepest part of a rollercoaster sim, the part where her stomach lurched backwards and she plummeted into freefall. Pat had believed her straight away. Her boyfriend not so much, but it wasn't up to him. Now they were both guiding her through the empty streets of Longyearbyen, towards the marina. At the end of the pontoon, a neat grey and white powerboat bobbed gently on the water.

"This is the *Isfjorde Explorer*. We use it to shuttle guests to the old radio station," Pat said, stepping on board. "Our main tourist highlight, along with the seed vault."

Low clouds rose from the water, a thin fog filtering the view of the bay. Axel assumed the steering position in the cockpit while the others sat at the stern. They soon reached cruising speed. On the other side of the bay, dark horizontal streaks marked the thick land crust, Spitsbergen's hardened skin. Above the waterline, a wall of rock. The boat followed the coastline until they reached the shore with its cracked boulders. Axel stopped the *Explorer*'s engine, anchored it, and jumped into thigh-deep water.

"We're close," he said. "It's four miles inland."

Hildr jumped out, gasping with the shock of the freezing water.

They reached the shore and climbed, then started walking.

"Where are we going?"

"There are nine coal mines in the Svalbard archipelago," Axel said. "While they were allowed to burn fossil fuels, Russians and Norwegians explored the Arctic's natural resources as best as they could. After the ban, most of the old mines were dismantled and closed. A couple became tourist attractions. The one where I hid the kid's bracelet isn't even officially listed. The complex under the mountain became visible after a methane deposit exploded in thawing permafrost. I came across it by chance, on a trek. The locals say it used to be a Gulag."

The kid's bracelet. He was still talking about her as if she was a different person.

"Smart," Bas said. "And the algorithm didn't see you hiding it?"

Pat came between them. "Axel paid a void to hide the old chip where Mondo and USK wouldn't be able to track it." She turned towards Hildr. "I never forgave myself for what happened …. Where have you been, all these years?"

Hildr kept quiet. She didn't want to risk saying anything untoward and setting off her boyfriend's doubts again.

"Her memory is affected," Bas said. "Are you an original Fyr citizen? What was the island like, back then?"

Saved by small talk.

Pat nodded. "After the purge, I lived with the farmers on the mountain."

"And then you put a chip back on?" Bas sounded genuinely intrigued. "I hadn't heard about anyone changing their mind."

"Takes guts to wear the chip too," Pat said. "The farmers are amazing and inspiring, but the real work is at the intersections. It's easy to shut yourself off from opinions you disagree with. But when you lose your shared sense of reality, you dry up the spaces between people."

Bas mulled this over. "Migrants don't have a choice, do they?"

They had reached the crest of the hill. From there, they could see only highlands, flattened ridges, brown, grey, dull, no snow left on their tops.

"We're on the same side," Pat said. "Those bastards from Mondo let Birgit die inside the vault."

"We don't know that for sure," Axel said.

"The farmers mentioned an underground place with endless food," Hildr said.

"Ula is a dreamer," Pat said.

"Ula is hungry," Axel said.

"Where's the vault?" Hildr asked.

"Three kilometres' drive from Longyearbyen," Axel replied. "But they don't open in the summer."

They stopped walking.

The four stood in front of a dark, narrow hole reinforced by rotting wood and rusty metal beams, a mere cat flap into the featureless grey slope.

"Did it collapse?" Hildr asked.

"The entrance is pretty much the same size, but the tunnel seems unstable." Axel inspected the opening. "One of the walls is almost gone."

"And this is where you've hidden the bracelet?" Hildr said.

Axel probed the dried edges around the entrance. Dust and sand streamed to the ground. "About twenty metres into the tunnel, there's a recess on the wall down to your right, like a boarded-up window, except it's not a fucking window, it's just a hole underground. If you stick your arm through it, you'll find a metal safe with a copper box inside. Bring it out here, we'll open it together. The kid's citizen-chip is in there, with the bracelet. Pat can lend you a projector and headphones."

"Will the old chip work?" Bas asked.

"Once we get it out in the sunlight," Axel said, "the tech will power up and connect to the central logs. She'll see the old files and messages. The GPS will work too."

"That means the algorithm will be able to track the chip," Pat pointed out.

"We'll listen to the messages and dump the bracelet back in the same place," Bas said. "After that, we're joining our friends in Nordaustlandet." He looked at Hildr. "Right?"

Hildr kept silent.

Pat cut in, noticing her unease. "Wearing a chip doesn't mean you agree with the algorithm."

Axel smirked. "I thought the chip was drying out our *... shared sense of reality.*"

Pat pinched his arm, throwing him a stern look. "Not funny. You sound like a fascist pig."

"What's fascist about what I just said?"

Stooping, Hildr walked into the coal mine.

"Please be careful," Bas said. "Don't touch the walls."

Easier said than done. Her arched back scraped the top of the tunnel. A flurry of dust fell on her head. She held her breath. Nothing else gave.

"Are you okay?" she heard Axel asking.

She kept walking into the mountain, taking side steps, keeping her head low, her back bent, until she reached a wooden frame on her right. She couldn't see any hole, only a slight depression, which might have been deeper in the past. She kneeled and thrust her arm inside. Dust puffed out. Hildr coughed, grabbing at what she could, fighting her instinct to run out of there. Finally, her fingers scratched something metallic but there was no gap to grip it. She scraped the walls around the object, pulling each side with her nails, slowly releasing the sturdy box from its grave, loose bits clinking inside. She held it against her chest.

Bas let out a sigh of relief when Hildr emerged from the tunnel.

She dropped the safe at Axel's feet. "Open it."

He clicked in a 4-digit combination. All there, as promised. The citizen-chip with its silicone prongs, the bracelet, even a couple of health nodes.

"Don't worry about the sensors," Pat said. "You can pair the old chip with my projector."

"Share the tab with me," Axel said.

"They're private messages," Hildr said.

"We will listen to Birgit's messages at the same time," Axel said. "That's the deal. If you don't agree ..." He held the chip from his pointer and thumb, above his mouth. "You can fish this out of my toilet."

"Axel, please," Pat said.

"Is he nuts?" Bas said.

"Okay." Hildr gave in. "Where shall we do it?"

A lake twinkled on the horizon. No drones in sight, just the occasional buzzing of mosquitoes.

"Why not here?" Axel said.

She sat on the slope. Pat helped with the tech, going for minimal setup: chip, ear canal, fingertips. She removed the silicone protection and inserted the three pins on her wrist. Hildr recoiled at the prickle, before sealing the strap around her wrist. The adult extension came in handy. Hildr opened a new tab, navigated the initial boot, and accessed the main applications.

"Share the tab," Axel said.

Hildr unfolded her legs and lay down on the ground, eyes open, inhaling the crisp cool air of the mountain in short bursts, afraid of missing something important by breathing in too sharply. Her hands were shaking. The projected tab was there, in the water particles above her face. Birgit sounded frazzled and lost. The messages followed her journey from the house on Fyr to the ferry to Spitsbergen, and from a different house to the vault, until she finally walked into the heart of the mountain, words floating like clouds, surrounded by dark meandering ridges, hovering over the mountaintop where Hildr now stood. Her mother had sent six short messages before going inside the seed vault. They took less than fifteen minutes. When the last message had finished, Hildr sat up and made eye contact with the others.

They waited expectantly.

"What happened?" Pat said.

Hildr was still searching for the meaning.

"They're bedtime stories," Axel replied. "About crops. Why were Mondo and USK so keen to get their hands on these? Was Birgit taking the piss?"

"It's a code," Hildr said. "Rice, potato, wheat, corn, tomato. She was giving us a code. She hid something inside the seed boxes." Hildr rose to her feet. "Can you take me to the vault?"

Axel and Pat looked at each other intently.

They stayed like this for a while, making faces at each other.

Bas shifted his weight from one leg to another, as if he was trying not to pee.

"You're using voice-free between you, aren't you?" Bas said. "I don't miss it, to be honest. It was like people were sucking thoughts out of my head."

Hildr noticed the noise first.

Bas called it out. "A drone."

They craned their necks towards the sky.

"No. Different frequency," Axel said. "Powerboat."

"The Dev who gave us a ride to the hotel," Bas said. "He's following us."

Bas was right. They were talking voice-free behind their backs, and she didn't need them any more. Hildr started trekking down the mountain. Gabriel's powerboat, a newer and faster model, was moored just a few metres from the *Isfjorde Explorer*.

"Hey, they'll take us to the seed vault!"

Hildr turned around. Bas was running behind her, catching up, breathless.

"You'd better stick with us," Axel said, following close behind. "We have the only jeep on the island. It's parked by the town hall. We'll get the *Explorer* back to Longyearbyen and switch to the jeep. We'll get to the vault much faster that way."

Hildr stopped.

"Let's go with them, please," Bas said. "Gabriel is creepy."

About the Svalbard Global Seed Vault, CropTrust.org

The Seed Vault is the ultimate insurance policy for the world's food supply, securing millions of seeds representing every important crop variety available in the world today and offering options for future generations to overcome the challenges of climate change and population growth.

As of May 2024, the Seed Vault holds more than 1.3 million seed varieties originating from almost every country in the world. These range from unique varieties of major African and Asian food staples such as maize, rice, wheat, cowpea and sorghum to European and South American varieties of eggplant, lettuce, barley and potato. The Seed Vault already holds the most diverse collection of food crop seeds in the world.

Read more at https://www.croptrust.org/what-we-do/programs/svalbard-global-seed-vault/

Chapter Thirty-Two

(Axel) The vault

They boarded the *Isfjorde Explorer*. A distinctive hum followed them across the bay. The algorithm's vigilantes. Axel sniffed the drones like meat on a bone. They were hovering above the powerboat, never close enough to point his finger at them.

"*Her story doesn't make sense.*"

"The DNA is a match," Pat messaged back. "*It's Hildr.*"

"*What if USK cloned the kid?*"

Pat arched her eyebrows. "*Ridiculous. Why would they wait eighteen years to send a clone?*"

He shrugged. "*Kids are not good actors. They had to wait for her to grow up.*"

Pat puffed and whistled like an old kettle. "*Too convoluted. Reality is always simpler than that.*"

"The evidence is right in front of you," Axel said. "*How does she know Birgit hid something inside the seed boxes? We never told her that Birgit went into the second room.*"

"*Stop playing Finder,*" Pat said. "*You're a thousand times better than your old job.*"

"Can we go any faster?" Hildr asked.

Axel pushed the powerboat to maximum speed.

At the marina, Axel and Pat jumped out of the boat, flanking the two guests. Hildr and Bas kept their eyes on the ground. Drones followed them the whole time. They couldn't always hear them, but the invisible eye of the algorithm was always there. Why didn't the authorities stop them? Axel couldn't think of any explanation other than that this had been USK's plan all along. A twisted way of finding what Mondo had brought in the probe. And Pat had fallen straight into the trap, first giving them the citizen-chip, now driving them to the vault.

Near the town hall, Axel unblocked the hire, and they shuffled inside the jeep. Hildr and Bas sat at the back, Pat next to him.

"What if it's an ambush?" Bas asked.

Even the boy was more clued up.

"There's a camera outside the portal building," Pat said. "The livestream is publicly available. I'll check if anyone else is around."

Axel started the engine, sighing loudly. Years of washing dishes at the inn had taken a toll on Pat's stealth techniques. To think she used to make him scribble with blunt pencils. The tires screeched. Three kilometres to the vault. Pat looked at her tab, giving them the rundown from the livestream.

"I can see the end of the road in front of the vault, the mountains across the bay, the bollards outside the entrance. All clear. I will be able to see our jeep arriving, as soon as we turn into the road leading to the vault."

Not so easy.

A three-wheeled taxi with dark windows and flashing indicator lights had stopped before the crossing, blocking the road.

"Who's that?" Pat messaged. *"Why did they stop right there?"*

"I guess we'll find out soon." Axel slowed down. He went around the vehicle and pulled his window down. "Looking for directions?"

A man came out of the taxi. Androgynous, slender, unnervingly tall, wearing beige trousers and a matching vest, eyes covered by dark glasses. An impressive tech suite surfaced from inside his clothes, a silicone snake covered in sensors and nodes, twisting and bending around his torso and neck. Axel had seen pumped-up tech, but this one was quite the show-off.

"I'm looking for the doomsday vault," the Dev said, lips opening to reveal a row of perfect white teeth. The name *Gabriel* appeared below his stilted smile. "I've always heard about this fantastic place with our seed relics. Do you know how to get there?" He spoke as if he had learned English from an Oxford pronunciation guide. Someone coming all the way to Svalbard and not knowing the seed vault was at the top of this road? Preposterous. There was even a little road sign.

"What a coincidence," Axel said. "We're heading to the vault. Why don't you follow?" Bas had frozen on the back seat, googly eyes staring through the rear mirror.

"Excellent idea," Gabriel replied.

He got back inside the taxi.

"It's him," Bas said as they drove away. "It's the bird-watcher. The Dev who was near the place where the sub crashed. The one who gave us a ride to Longyearbyen."

A Dev chauffeuring voids. Made no fucking sense.

"What do we do now?" Pat said.

"*It's a trap,*" Axel said. "*Hildr was sent by the algorithm. Why would a Dev give them a lift?*"

They were rolling up the hill towards the vault, Axel's manual steering relying on visuals, Gabriel's taxi hovering behind.

"*Stop doubting,*" Pat replied, straight into his headphones. This was what telepathy felt like. "*The Dev is following Hildr to find out what happened to Birgit, like us. I can see the portal building. We're almost there. Wait ...*"

Pat leaned towards the back and twisted her torso, looking behind them.

Axel's eyes jumped between her face and the road ahead. "What is it?"

"*Weird,*" Pat messaged, jerking her head left and right. "*I'm looking at the vault's public stream. The video is showing our jeep coming up the road, but not the taxi behind us.*"

"Maybe the portal's camera is at the wrong angle?" he said.

"*No ... the video should have shown the taxi, but it's like ... it's like the taxi is invisible.*"

"Our tabs are being doctored," Axel said.

No one was supposed to see the Dev or what was going to happen at the vault. Why else would the taxi not show on the video? The algorithm controlled what played on their tabs.

No shared reality.

Bas grabbed the back of their seats and pulled himself forward, leaning between them. "I don't know what you're talking about, but it doesn't surprise me that the algorithm is manipulating your tabs. That's the whole point. To stop you thinking for yourselves."

Axel parked next to the vault's portal building. "Can you see the taxi next to us?" Bas was the only one not wearing tech.

"Yeah ...why?" Bas said.

"We're not crazy," Pat said.

"Shall we get out?" Hildr asked.

Axel turned back to her. "Care to tell us what the fuck is going on? The vault is one of the most secure places on Earth. Four locked doors down to the seed rooms. Keys coded to different levels, requiring numbered combinations. The place is riddled with motion, fire, smoke and gas detectors, cameras and alarms. A log is automatically generated for every person who enters, and the police and coast guard are instantly informed of any unauthorised access. Shall I go on? We already told you the vault doesn't open in the summer. You can't walk in and out as you please. You need the Trust's permission to get in, and Mondo's sign-off to go inside the third room. And your friend's vehicle is not showing on our tabs. What exactly are we doing here?"

Pat looked pained. "Please guys, we're here to find out what happened to Birgit. We're real, the vehicle is real. Maybe the camera outside the portal building has a technical problem ... What if I play the video from my logs?" She brought her head down to her hands. "This is making my brain hurt."

"Let's get some fresh air," Bas said.

One by one, they stepped out of the jeep. An insidious wind swept over the treeless mountainside. The taxi's door remained closed, Gabriel inside. What was he waiting for? The four walked to the portal building, a tall, narrow concrete wedge sinking into the mountain, set against grey rock and coral skies. A short metal bridge led to the north-facing door, thick reinforced metal fending off the heat and unwanted visitors. Their heels clinked on the bridge's metal grid, over the ditch, dug to allow for melting ice underneath. Above them, blue and yellow reflections glittered from the art installation at the top of the portal building. Light in a place of darkness.

That's when Axel noticed.

The door to the portal building was slightly misaligned from the frame. At an angle.

Open.

He pulled the heavy door towards himself. The metal scratched the ground with a moan, opening onto a long tunnel. A breath of freezing cold spilled from inside, wrapped in the scent of mould. Guiding the way down the tunnel, a line of blue lights flickered along the low ceiling. Axel could just about sense where the tunnel finished, opening into a wider area with another metal door at the bottom.

A subtle hiss sounded behind them. Gabriel got out of the taxi and removed his sunglasses, revealing thin pupils, like a devilish cat. He placed the sunglasses inside the pouch at the front of his waist in a leisurely way, as if he didn't have a care in the world. He walked slowly towards them.

"Only Hildr is allowed in the vault," Gabriel said, in the tone of a vending machine telling you it doesn't accept coins.

Hildr stepped inside the vault and sprinted down the tunnel.

"Wait for me!" Bas said, running behind Hildr, as if he were afraid of missing his turn.

Pat looked at Axel. "Shall we?"

She dashed down after Hildr and Bas.

Axel's legs stayed glued to the spot, eyes squinting into the depths. The ramp sloped down for one hundred metres. Ms Holm's descriptions played in his head, like an old movie. Stairs to the right led to a loft with the cooling system compressor and the electrical networks powering the light art on the portal. Hildr, Bas and Pat were jogging madly, heading deeper underground. Whatever Mondo had put inside the third room, which had caused scientists to collapse from nitrogen narcosis at the lab in Minnesota, was still lurking down there.

"Pat, stop!" Axel's shout echoed on the bare walls.

At the bottom of the ramp, the three disappeared through another door. He heard Gabriel's steps on the metal bridge and turned round. Gabriel hesitated for a second, staring at his trimmed, polished nails. Axel's reaction was delayed, but sharp. He stepped into the tunnel and shut the door forcibly. Gabriel jerked forward, grabbing the door handle as it was being pulled away from him. His complaints were silenced by the thick metal door closing.

Inside, Axel strained his eyes, forcing them to peer into the sudden darkness. Behind the stairs leading to the portal's loft, he spotted a concrete closet. Letting go of the door, he ran to it. Machinery, electrical cables, backup generator. He grabbed a reel with an electrical extension, wove the lead through the door handles, pulled hard, then wrapped the thick cable round the closet's knob. Even if Gabriel had the code to get in, that should hold the door for a while.

Axel walked down the tunnel, into the mountain. When he realised how long it would take him to reach the others, he started running. Pipes with cool air followed the length of the passage, blowing and hissing. The entire vault felt alive, slumbering, heaving around him. Flickering lights created an unsettling blue aura. His summer clothes were unsuitable for the cold inside the vault, but the running helped. As Axel reached the wider area at the bottom of the tunnel, he saw a door ahead signalling the end of the portal building. A pump and another backup generator leaned against the wall. Thumping noises could be heard from the top of the tunnel.Gabriel.

Axel opened the second door and stepped into the mountain section. Another tunnel extended beyond sight, encased in a heavy steel tube, with a slighter downward slope. He saw Pat, Bas and Hildr at the bottom of this new tunnel, going through another door.

"Pat!"

She never listened.

After the steel tube section, the corridor turned into rock chiselled out in irregular shapes and covered in a coating of white ink, bright and austere. He passed more rooms on his right. The office. A storage room for electrical equipment. At the end of the corridor, another set of double doors. Axel pulled hard but they wouldn't budge. He pushed instead. Still nothing. He knocked loudly at the metal. Behind him, at the top of the tunnel, Gabriel's thumping continued, persistent, echoing his own despair.

"Pat, please open the door."

"Can you hear me?" Her voice arrived faint from the other side. "It's stuck."

He pushed harder. The metal moved. Pat jumped into his arms, pressing against his chest. "It's so cold," she said. He smelled her gardenia shampoo.

They were alone in a vast, cavernous area, a monumental hall in the heart of the mountain, raw rock emitting a glacial aura. The high ceilings were covered in glistening crystal, bright and sharp as a summer day, but painfully and unbearably cold. The skin on his face burned. Moisture solidified inside his nostrils. They couldn't linger in there, not in these clothes.

Pat pointed to a door on their left. "They're looking for the seeds."

They opened the first seed room. Metal shelving units lined the walls, each shelf stacked with carefully labelled containers, colour-coded and stamped with barcodes. Over one million seeds in this room alone. Bas was at the end of the third row.

"This will take ages," Bas said. "There are thousands of samples. This whole section is just rice. How are we supposed to find rice from Japan? I can't stand this cold."

Hildr had taken the ladder, to search one of the higher shelves, at the back.

"San Marzano, Roma, Green, Sweet, Cherry, Heirloom." She pushed box after box, making some crash on the floor. "None from Peru."

"Bas is right, we can't stay," Axel said. Among the crashing echoes, he heard a faint chime and frowned. "What's with the Tinkerbell noise?"

"What noise?" The freezing cold made Pat shake as if she was sobbing.

"The little bell," Axel said. "Can you hear it?"

Hildr jumped from the top of the ladder, moaning as she hit the ground. Bas peered from behind his row of seeds. Swiftly back on her feet, she ran out of the room.

"What happened?" Bas said. "Did she find the seeds?"

"I heard it too," Pat said. "It's coming from her bracelet."

Axel rushed to the hall. "It's the chime. From Birgit. Activated by proximity."

"The noise started when we first came into the big hall," Pat said, following. "I didn't realise what it was until now."

In the preparation room, Hildr was kneeling in front of a large airlock door encrusted in ice crystals. The third room. The chime on her bracelet was louder than ever, making the whole cavern jingle like a Christmas grotto. Bas approached the third room and crouched next to Hildr. They exchanged whispers.

"No seeds in that room," Axel said.

"Shhh." Bas put a finger to his lips. "She's receiving a new message."

"From Birgit?" Pat asked. "How can that be possible? Is she alive?"

"There's no reception down here, only the vault's closed circuit," Axel said. "Birgit sent a message on the same day as the others, but it was only delivered now, once the bracelet got within reach. Either way, we need to get out of here."

The sound of footsteps echoed underground, coming from the main tunnel. Gabriel was already there. Axel heard him approaching the final set of doors that stood between them, tension thick in the air. The Dev entered the cavernous hall, calm and deliberate, making his way towards the third room. He squatted next to Hildr, willowy fingers brushing against her worn bracelet, touching her wrist.

"Congratulations," Gabriel said. "I thought you wouldn't get this far on your own. I was wrong. The model was right." He enunciated each syllable as if he were an actor performing lines in a tragedy.

Hildr looked mesmerised, staring straight ahead, at the door.

"Who are you?" she said, as if she had only just become aware of the Dev's presence. "Why do you keep following us?"

Gabriel turned to the rest of his audience. "Unfortunately, she doesn't remember me."

"Who am *I*?" Hildr said, growing into her role in the tragedy.

"You're Hildr Olsen," Gabriel said.

Axel interrupted. "Hildr Olsen is dead. She died inside a container ship, along with others escaping from Fyr. This Hildr is a fake."

A high-pitched sob escaped from Pat's lips. "That's not true ..."

"USK found the body, in the Hebrides," Axel said. "They must have cloned her in one of their halls."

Would Pat finally believe him?

Would she hate him for telling the truth?

Gabriel seemed unimpressed. "She *is* Hildr Olsen."

"How do I know which memories are true?" Hildr's eyes filled.

"I know this comes as a shock," Gabriel said, "but you consented to the plan from the beginning. You helped us figure out the best way to get the bracelet. You grew up watching the videos recovered from her central logs. You preferred to believe you were her."

The others waited for her rebuttal.

Hildr buried her face in her hands.

"If I agreed to this, I regret it … The purge on Fyr, did it really happen? A whole island starved to death?"

"We did the right thing for the planet, with the data we had at the time," Gabriel said, as if repeating a psalm. "Did Birgit explain how to get into this room?"

Axel scoffed.

"You cloned a dead kid, but you can't open a bloody door."

"I can try to send her a message," Hildr said.

"So she's alive?" Pat said.

"I'll go in with you," Bas added.

A crack appeared in the Dev's poise. "Only Hildr is allowed in. You shouldn't be here. None of you." He looked down at the crouching Bas as if he was a pebble in his shoe. "Get out." Bas rocked backward from the unexpected push, heels sliding, centre of gravity shifting.

Axel grabbed the Dev's arms and locked them behind his back.

Bas dropped onto his rear with a soft thump, looking more embarrassed than hurt.

"Why don't you pick someone your size, ice queen?" Axel said, still locking his arms.

"Can you please let me go," Gabriel said.

"Four against one," Axel said.

"Violence is superfluous."

Axel breathed down his neck. "We all want to know what's inside this fucking room. Either we all go in, or none of us goes in."

"Alright," Gabriel said. "Let me get the snowsuits."

Was he bluffing?

"Fuck off. I'd rather wear you as a neck warmer," Axel said.

Gabriel's expression stiffened. "The snowsuits are in the second room. It's too cold to go in without wearing one. Can you *please* let go of my hands."

Pat approached, shaking like a rattle. "Let him get the snowsuits."

Axel released him with a groan.

Gabriel rubbed the red marks on his wrists, looking cross. He paced along the hall, stopped in front of the middle door, typed in a code, and disappeared inside. In the preparation room, the others waited. They heard screeching noises. A solid metal platform crossed the threshold of the middle room. Gabriel was wheeling a trolley towards them, a mound of bulky clothes piled on top. Snowsuits. He hadn't lied. Reaching the group, the Dev put his hand inside the white pouch he carried around his waist. Sunflower seeds chinked on the floor. Swiftly, graciously, Gabriel removed a small object from inside and pointed it at Axel.

A whooshing sound. Axel fell on the ground with a loud thump. A feathery rainbow flag stuck out from his trousers, prickled with blood. A dart had perforated his right thigh. He pulled it out, rainbow flag and all, wincing with pain, rolling onto his stomach. Lightheaded, he started crawling. Pat clambered on top of him, feet on each side of his hips, hauling him from his chest.

"Get up. Get up!" she was shouting. He wished he could obey. His leg had frozen into an icicle, but it was pulsating like hot coals. The cold-hot effect was spreading upwards fast, to his groin and torso. "Get up." Pat struggled and fell on top of him. She tapped his thighs, his glutes, his lower back. "There's no blood. You're alright. Please get up. You're too heavy for me." She huffed with the effort.

He felt terribly woozy.

"I can't gghh ... urmf ..."

Axel's voice slugged into an incomprehensible mumble. He could still hear Pat berating him, panicking about his stiffness. Bas shouting at Hildr. And Hildr shouting at Gabriel. His head was spinning like a carousel. Next thing he knew, Pat and Bas were on each side of him, grabbing him under the arms, dragging him towards the main tunnel. He opened his eyes, just a crack – his eyelids weighed a ton now – enough to see Gabriel standing next to Hildr, by the third room, aiming at them with the dart gun. Then he heard the tunnel door close, and he was gone.

Most famous Viking runestone returns to Uskania

We're pleased to announce the return of the famous Viking Rök to the Uskanian Archaeology Museum, living proof that our ancestors worried about climate change almost as much as we do. The period known as the Late Antique Little Ice Age (536–660 AD) registered exceptionally low temperatures, food shortages and mass extinctions, with drastic climatic changes wiping out 50% of the population in the Scandinavian peninsula and devastating communities across Europe. Erected after this, the Rök stone expressed fears of a new climate catastrophe. Such events are cyclic and expected. We can prepare.

Chapter Thirty-Three

(Birgit) The last message

I'm not afraid. We're half-dead when we're born, destined to become food for more resilient creatures. Now, I can't feel pain or hunger. Just an endless stream of thoughts coming in and out of focus, like a train I was supposed to catch which keeps blurring past the horizon. How long have I been here? I've lost track. Of the days. The endless days. It was my choice. I would have it no other way. This is our story. Hunter-gathering to farming. Farming to New Food.

At the beginning, Mondo didn't tell me where it had come from. *An exotic autotroph producing carbohydrates that can be used as food.* Nothing more than a speck of translucid slime, about three centimetres across, growing in height. I thought they had found it in the Newfoundland meteorite. They asked me to lead the project. Explore the possibilities. What a bright and exciting discovery. A new energy source. The sample was stored in the US. An assistant smudged it on a petri dish, so I could analyse it from my lab. Our attempts at automated DNA sequencing failed. The autotroph wasn't based on DNA, or RNA. The organism relied on an entirely different chemical structure replacing the usual sugar-phosphate backbone. What could be more shocking?

Initial reports were full of promise. Novel molecules made from carbon, hydrogen, oxygen and nitrogen seemed to work as unconventional replacements for our sugars and proteins. We mixed the molecules into New Food compounds. Our lab rats ate it with glee. No adverse health effects, other than an unexplained dizziness. The autotroph was based on a new biopolymer and harnessed free energy sources. It could grow and expand, maintaining a constant inner state. We didn't find traditional cells, but it was carbon-based and able to use water as a solvent, though not efficiently. My guess was that it was using water as an alternative to a more common molecule found in its natural environment. Could the organism learn and adapt to our planet, like DNA-based plants? We were unsure of what was feeding it. Initially, we thought it relied on energy deposits that would continue to deplete, until one day it would perish before our eyes.

The prospect filled me with dread.

Two weeks into the project, I got a clearer answer from Mondo. The autotroph had been found inside a rock collected from an asteroid, near Europa, Jupiter's moon. An alien organism. One of the MExAI probes had brought it back. On the same day I learned this information, I received a phone call. My colleagues were panicking. Overnight, the organism had grown and flattened itself, stretching across the whole lab floor.

The change was too quick, too radical.

Plants didn't behave like this.

Bacterial cultures didn't behave like this.

My colleagues weren't keen to host it any longer. Mondo had no reason to believe the autotroph was dangerous, but it's only human to fear the unknown. The plan to transfer the sample from the US to the vault in Svalbard was expedited. There it would be locked away from human contact – and it would be closer to me, the lead scientist on the project. Five people in bulky protective suits scraped it from the floor, using a special mop attached to a long pole. The substance became volatile, changing into a translucid, low-viscosity liquid. At a whim.

They put it in a box. The autotroph contracted, becoming a thin veneer on the inner walls of the box. They brought the box into the seed vault, deep underground. We thought it would be safe here. We predicted the low temperatures would tip the autotroph into a dormant state. I wasn't there for the transfer but I was supposed to access the room once the weather cooled, and the vault reopened. From the lab in my home, I kept rigorous logs, analysing real-time readings from the mirrors, cameras and sensors. Radiation detector, pressure gauge, lasers, spectrographs, UV cameras, gas chromatographs, temperature and humidity sensors, X-ray spectrometer, chemical and mineralogical analysers. I spent hours observing it. Feeling it breathe. The idea of seeing it in real life made my mind cloud over, my hands shake.

At that point, we thought it fed on microwave radiation. Minimal amounts seemed to sustain it, as little as the residual cosmic background reaching our planet from the beginnings of the universe. Under certain circumstances, it expanded to absorb more heat. Since arriving at its new home in Svalbard, it had spread to every nook and crevice inside the box, and acquired a milky tinge, with light-grey strokes, thicker at the bottom, next to the ground, implying it was perhaps no longer relying on cosmic radiation, but preying on the warmth emanating from the Earth's core.

I was restless, sleepless, in a permanent state of euphoria.

Some nights, I didn't sleep at all, drifting into a state of semi-waking trance, opening my eyes when I was meant to be sleeping, and finding myself next to it, in the vault.

The autotroph kept expanding. Space ran out. One by one, sensors stopped working. I carried on with limited chemistry experiments, annotating the behaviour, making sure I had thorough records. What a discovery. A self-replicating, nutritious, freely available energy source. We might be able to rely on it. Perhaps we could farm it and eat it? What better news could there be for humanity? The lack of sleep gave me a headache stretching from my temples to my spine, throbbing and stinging as if a giant scorpion was perched on top of me. If I could get my head around how the alien organism worked, it would be ground-breaking. When inert, it was close to known carbohydrates. Large amounts of carbon, hydrogen and oxygen. In periods of expansion, it released nitrogen. Less promising. The initial hope had been to grow it in vertical labs, but without understanding the expansion cycles, it was unpredictable. A new beast.

Would we be able to survive on it?

One night, the worst possible thing happened. I lost contact. I checked the CCTV cameras. In the middle of the room, the cameras showed an amalgam of irregular edges. Polycarbonate. The remnants from the box were hauntingly quiet. The container had given way to the pressure and cracked wide open. No other signs of disturbance, no debris, no apparent leakage. I couldn't move my eyes off the screen.

Where was it?

The walls inside the seed vault have a distinctive silver-white colour, rough textured rock covered in ice crystals, like a magical twinkling grotto. I scanned the walls inch by inch, hoping to find a darker tinge, a smoother corner, any sign of its presence. On one occasion, I thought I had spotted it, hiding in a depression. Another time, I saw it stretching into an invisible layer over the rock, thin and brittle as frozen skin. After hours staring at the video, I noticed the autotroph seeping into the pores and cracks of the vault, excavating a tunnel under the mountain, longer, wider, deeper.

Was I going mad?

Mondo had to grant me access. Only bureaucracy stood between me and the alien. I wasn't due to visit the vault until weeks later. The Trust managing the vault denied entry, blocking us with their security and access policies. *Too hot outside.* The only exceptions allowed were emergencies, including threats to the seeds. A contractual nightmare ensued, with lawyers on both sides trying to bully the opposition into accepting defeat. We couldn't even tell them the truth. The MExAI project was confidential. Mondo had to put pressure on the Trust without revealing the real reason why we needed urgent access.

What if it was dying?

I knew the risks of coming. This was the largest expansion cycle I had seen it perform; and in periods of expansion, the autotroph released nitrogen. Lab rats had remained in a petrified daze for weeks when we increased the dose in their New Food rations, little brains still working, showing low-amplitude, high-frequency waves, like REM sleep. Attempting to relax only worsened my anxiety. I had palpitations. Uncontrollable shaking. Hallucinations. The Trust had to let me in. If I couldn't tell them the truth, I would tell them a lie that was equally bad. I blamed the farmers. I told the Trust we suspected Ula Svenson and her allies had slipped a ticking bomb into the box. I offered to go underground and retrieve it. The Trust had known me for years. They relented.

I got Ms Holm to open the main portal. I unlocked each level on my own, rushing underground. When I opened the airlock to the third room, everything was like it was in the CCTV video. Bare walls with ice crystals, a cracked box in the middle. Then I stepped into the room, and I felt it. A clear, warm substance, pressing against my body. The autotroph filled the entire space around me, inside the room, like an invisible plasma. It didn't leak when I opened the door, it simply welcomed me in, seeping into my ear canals, leaking into my eyes, squeezing inside my lips.

The smell.

I never thought it would have a smell.

The taste.

I could never have imagined the taste.

Freshly baked sourdough bread with a dollop of butter. Roasted new potatoes dipped in olive oil and sprinkled with coriander. Sweet rice pudding with a dusting of cinnamon. It came in through my nose. When I inhaled it slowly, it was sweet and sour soup. When I took in big breaths, it tasted like fresh salad, rocket, honey-glazed walnuts, a punch of balsamic vinegar. I closed my eyes and thought of fruits. The taste instantly shifted into the sweetest, most pungent fruits you could ever imagine – figs, oranges, pears, strawberries, filling my mouth, my nose, my stomach. The autotroph dissolved on my tongue and climbed the roof of my mouth, filling every passage in my skull. I couldn't feel the cold any more. My throat felt funny, but I could still breathe. My stomach was bloated, but I could eat more.

How can I convince people to let go? Isn't this everything we had hoped for? The world will finally forget about old food. This is better, so much better than our dreams.

Mondo Foods International, Senior Scientist job spec

Mondo Foods International are looking for a Senior Scientist for our European Hub. The role will report to the Head of Human Resources for European Research and Low Latency Projects and support our Lead Food Scientist on innovative research into New Food compounds and ecosystems, progressing and reporting on key strategic projects with a focus on novel approaches using applied plant genetics. Typical tasks include carrying out field work, collecting samples, analysing DNA data, planning and conducting experiments, writing papers and executive summaries, supervising junior staff, and keeping up to date with relevant scientific and technical developments. This is a corporate position, fully sponsored by Mondo Foods and with a flexible work location, with a preference given to candidates living within easy access of the Svalbard seed vault.

Chapter Thirty-Four

(Axel) Unravelling

Axel woke up in one of the guest rooms, leg swollen and stiff. He tried to sit up. His head felt as if it had been bashed by a log. Pat was sitting on the edge of the bed.

"A medical drone is on its way," she said. Her voice was soothing as sunrise.

"How long have I been sleeping?" His came out croaky, as if there was a toad living in his throat.

"Almost six hours. You passed out at the vault, with a sedation dart. Can you call the Trust and tell them what happened?"

He propped himself with a couple of cushions, eyes levelling with hers.

"I'm sure they know. The vault wouldn't have opened without the Trust's permission. You checked the video outside the portal. The Dev wasn't there. It'll be our word against the algorithm. Have you checked your logs?"

"Nothing after we entered the vault," she said. "Not even our voices. It's as if those fifteen minutes never existed. Hildr stayed behind, underground. Can Ms Holm speak to the Trust?" A crease appeared between her eyebrows. "Why did you lie?"

She had switched subject.

Time to face up to the consequences.

"I changed my mind a thousand times," Axel said. "I couldn't bring myself to tell you ... You never listened, never trusted the data. You were in denial. I didn't want to put you through the pain again."

He'd carried the pain on his own.

"But did you see it ... with your own eyes?"

Sometimes he wished he hadn't.

"I was going to tell you when you first arrived."

It would have brought everything back. Fyr. The arguments.

"How do you know it was her? Maybe it wasn't her. The algorithm wanted you off their case and showed you a fake body. They can make us believe anything they want, can't they? It still doesn't excuse your lie. You did what was comfortable and convenient for you and left me in the dark."

Axel pulled her close. "I did what was best for *us*."

Pat pushed against him.

"I know you think your behaviour is normal, but it's not. You're a cynic. You've been bruised by neglect, by violence, by hate. I'm not sure I want to understand you any more. You'll never get out of here."

"Get out? What do you mean, *get out*?"

"We know nothing beyond what the algorithm tells us. They're controlling our minds with our tech, like the farmers always said."

She was losing her grip again.

"I'm realistic," he said. "Does removing the chip solve anything?"

Pat looked at him with her sad, grey eyes. Tears tumbled out. She seemed surprised by this. She wiped them away hastily, as if she was embarrassed to cry in front of him. Before any more tears could roll down her cheeks, Pat got up and left the bedroom.

A delivery with bandages, painkillers and antibiotics arrived the next day. Axel's severed leg muscle and mild infection were healing. Soon, he wouldn't need crutches. Early morning. A smattering of light. Half-asleep, he felt Pat's lips on his forehead. The gesture was endearing, but it freaked him out. He had a deep-rooted anxiety about people leaving him.

Axel turned on the bedside lamp.

"I'm leaving," Pat said.

He was too sleepy, groggy and shocked to reply.

For years, she'd refused to accept that the kid was dead. Now she blamed *him*. Would it have made any difference, if he had told her the truth earlier? Of course not. She would have believed the fake Hildr anyway, when she came knocking at their door. He couldn't win. He wanted to shout, protest, slap Pat in the face.

This wasn't the way their story was supposed to end.

"How can you even think about going back, after all I've done for you?" His voice rose with his anger, pulling strength from his powerlessness.

"I'm not going back to Fyr." Pat lowered her gaze, unable to meet his. "I'm going with Bas. He told me there's a new void community in Nordaustlandet. His friend is there, the one who brought them in a sub. He asked me if I wanted to join them. I said yes."

Her bulging rucksack was standing against his desk. She had folded her remaining clothes in a neat pile and put them on his chair. Why would she leave her clothes on *his* chair, if she wasn't coming back? Axel got out of bed, kicked the rucksack and the chair, banged the desk against the wall, turned the room upside-down, screaming at the top of his lungs.

"I'm not going to send you food! Do you understand? If you remove your chip, I'm not going to save your arse when you change your fucking mind again!" Pat pressed her lips together tightly, holding the words inside. "Did you hear me? You're on your own! I mean it. I really mean it."

He didn't know what else to do.

No tears rolled down her cheeks this time. She'd made up her mind and couldn't bear to tell him.

There was a soft knock at the door.

"I have to go," Pat said. "I don't want your help, but will you promise me one thing?"

"That would be helping you!"

"Tell the others what happened at the vault," she said. "If you don't believe in Mondo and the algorithm, don't turn a blind eye. Don't be a cynic."

He hated her for even asking.

Pat grabbed her stuffed rucksack from the floor and left.

Days flew past, hospitality duties a blur. Almost a week later, he met Ms Holm for brunch. She nodded, sympathetic, agreeing that the Trust must have known about Hildr's visit weeks before they went into the vault. They wouldn't sign-off the out-of-season permission without advance warning and a detailed explanation. Protecting the seeds was the task of a generation. None of this was new. Axel gave lectures about the seed vault, as part of the local tourist tour.

"Maybe they relaxed the rules," he said. "Mondo's ships are always around. Their people go in and out. If I put in a request and explain what happened, will the Trust let me in?"

"Mondo are a depositor," Ms Holm said. "They go in for the seeds. Members of the public are granted access only in rare circumstances. You know this perfectly well. Perhaps you should stop overthinking it all. It's making you ill. You did your best." Ms Holm gave him a furtive glance. "She left for her own reasons."

She thought he was pursuing the idea because he couldn't get over Pat.

Lying on their empty bed at night, from midnight to two in the morning, he scrolled through the logs and notifications that had come in since she'd left, day after day, the sheep-counting of his sleepless nights. Mondo and USK would keep manipulating everyone. Would he just sit there and let it happen? No, he couldn't. With or without Pat, he was going to find out what they were hiding in the third room. An hour or two later, his eyes would finally snap closed.

Every morning, he would listen to Birgit's messages during his wake-up routine. Rice, potatoes, wheat, corn, tomatoes. Until one day, after showering, he spat toothpaste straight onto the bathroom's mirror. *For fuck's sake.* Why would Birgit hide a code inside the seed boxes, when she knew it would be nearly impossible for them to access the vault?

Ms Holm sat on her rocking chair, bee camera flying above the book-lined windows.

"The code to open the room is not inside the boxes," Axel said.

"Good morning to you too," Ms Holm said.

"Birgit's messages mention five crops. Japanese rice, Dutch potatoes, wheat from Tajikistan, Italian corn, Peruvian tomatoes. The specific varieties must be important, right? We wouldn't know where to start looking if Birgit wasn't specific. I searched the vault's seed database online, using the Latin and Greek genus names. *Oryza, Solanum tuberosum, Triticum aestivum, Zea mays, Lycopersicon esculentum.* The boxes have unique shipment numbers which are added to the depositor code and recorded in their database, alongside the room, row and shelf numbers."

Ms Holm's eyes narrowed even more. "Well done. Sounds like you were the one working at the vault for thirty-five years."

"I have the positions for all the seeds Birgit mentions in her messages, including the unique identifiers." A guest came into the inn. Axel lifted his feet from the reception desk. "When Birgit went into the middle room," he continued, "why would she cover the camera? She was hiding the position of the boxes. Only Hildr could have known which boxes she used, because she had the messages with the specific varieties. The code to get into the third room is hidden in plain sight. It's their unique identifier. Can you help me get inside the vault to test my theory?"

Ms Holm coughed loudly, burying her face on her flower-patterned pillowcase.

"Wouldn't Mondo change the room's code after so many years? Sounds terribly foolish."

"There's more." He shared a tab with the graphs. "Rice, potato, wheat, corn, tomatoes. The five crops Birgit mentions in her messages. Now look at this. New Food cartons launched by Mondo around that time. The first one was rice pudding. Birgit's bedroom was filled with that crap. Four months after Birgit went into the vault, they launched a Purple Potato Bake. The following year, an Italian Polenta. Two years later, Tajik Naan, and Cusco's Special Tomato Sauce."

"Cusco?" Ms Holm repeated.

"It's an ancient Inca city, in Peru."

She cleared her throat. "I'm not sure I follow you."

"They're the five crops Birgit talks about in her messages. Mondo launched New Food simulacra of them."

"That's their line of business, isn't it? They have thousands of fakes."

"You don't understand. I looked up the small print, the list of ingredients in these five cartons. I noticed a new ingredient. L-274. There's a whole list of *E* additives from the old European Union rules, but the *L* series is a new standard agreed after the switch to New Food, with little scrutiny and no international governance. I couldn't find conclusive information. The *L* standard covers everything from DNA editing to new experimental compounds. They allow food corporations to feed us whatever crap they come up with, as long as it's not grown on a farm."

"I've never liked New Food either," Ms Holm said. "Full of preserving agents and the rest of their malarkey."

"It's not a preserving agent. L-274 has largely replaced carbohydrates in these cartons. Independent labs analysed the new substance. It's a biopolymer with a molecular structure that doesn't match fungi, bacteria or any other organism with a known origin."

"Are you a chemist, Mr Jóhannsson?"

"I'm a concerned citizen. This substance has spread to other Mondo labels since Birgit went into the vault, and not just in Uskania. What if this secret ingredient is what they found, what they brought to the lab in Minnesota, what they're collecting off the coast of Spitsbergen in their ships?"

"The ships are researching the seaworms. There are many articles on the news about it."

"They're not telling us the full story. The substance is leaking from inside the mountain and feeding the seaworms. That's why they're getting so big. Mondo found a new food source."

"Highly speculative," Ms Holm said.

"I need to go inside the vault again. We need to convince the Trust to approve entry."

"You know how difficult it is," she said.

"Please. Will you help me?

Ms Holm sighed.

"I can't promise."

"Thank you."

"I'm eighty-nine years old, Mr Jóhannsson. You should be offering me a nice cup of tea and taking me for a drive around the bay, not talking about visitor logistics."

Her eyes were full of kindness.
"I'll come round at the weekend."
Kept his mind off her absence.

Axel filed the tourist visit request with the Trust. Dull weeks lay ahead, waiting for an answer. He couldn't bear dealing with guests at the inn. He used saved-up credits to go on a little trip.

New Oslo, early afternoon. A town centre younger than him. Straight avenues, boxed residential quarters. The Museum of Cultural History stood between an alcohol shop and a charity mission, an old warehouse recycled from industrial machinery landfill. As soon as he entered the hall, he spotted it. The same colour wood, the same ridges, the same spiral, as familiar as the shape of his own hand. He walked towards the Viking ship, an oversized and more elaborate version of the old wooden toy he had owned as a kid. His miniature version had been a piece of bent wood, dark, sinuous, with deep carved ridges and a delicate spiral at one end. He had thrown it away, before moving to Iceland. Back then, he thought the bad in the world was his fault.

He grew up.

The bad in the world was not his fault.

He found no peace in knowing this.

Axel circled the podium with the Viking ship, climbed the dais. The mighty lump of oak was supported by narrow metal poles, with overlapping ridges fixed with iron rivets, and fifteen oars on each side. Interlacing serpents had been carved into the prow and stern. A mast erupted from the deck, ten metres high, like a spear. The small plaque on the dais captioned the exhibit in five languages. *Oseberg was built around the year 820, a sea-faring vessel, before being brought ashore as the last home for its wealthy owners.* Two women had been buried inside. Their profiles made him shiver. Next to the *Oseberg*, a recent item had been added to the museum's collection. A submarine. Oval-shaped, like the ones he had seen on Fyr. *The most significant human artefact found in the Norwegian Sea, since the Vikings ruled our shores.* Pristine condition, deep blue colour, soft external layers. The Vikings believed a new Ice Age would kill them. A new Ice Age never came. Their fate was sealed anyway.

He hadn't posted a video for a long time. Finders lived interesting lives. Hostel caretakers, not so much.

An overweight, middle-aged rock star, back on the stage.

"It's a fucked-up world but I don't make the rules. Are you enjoying your New Food, the entertainment on your tech, your snug energy-efficient home? No one gives anything for free. In return for your silence, the algorithm is getting away with decisions you'd never have voted for in good conscience.

"Eighteen years ago, USK made a deal with Mondo Foods to use the Svalbard seed vault. We suspect Mondo found a new ingredient which revolutionises our food production system. In Uskania, this ingredient is simply referred to as L-274. You'll find it in cartons sold in many countries, even when labels don't mention it. Why aren't Mondo sharing what they found? Is ending world hunger not a good thing, if there's no money to be made? I don't believe in stupid theories about elites hiding old food, but here I raise my head above the parapet and ask everyone: *what the fuck are we doing?* We can't wish away this situation by closing our eyes. Help us find what they're hiding in the seed vault. Don't disconnect."

Hundreds had watched the video, before USK took down his channel and deducted a fine from the hostel's credits. Two cantons in Switzerland banned New Food cartons containing the L-274, ordering further tests.

Four days after Axel had posted the video, he received a call.

"Will you please drop your little misinformation campaign?"

A woman in her thirties, dark hair, colourful scarf, walking across a golf course.

Birds chirped in the background.

"USK have already taken care of that," Axel said. He felt a pang of pride. His videos had ruffled Mondo's big feathers. "Will you tell me what the L-274 is?" He couldn't miss the chance to ask.

"We'll go straight to legal action if you continue spreading lies." She flipped a silver stick behind her back.

Swoosh. Toc.

"What was in the MExAI probe?"

The woman stared into the bee camera. "This is your only warning."

Axel smiled from ear to ear.

He wished Pat followed his videos.

Two and a half months after Pat had left, Axel was running the weekly inventory at the inn's storage room when he heard a noise. He stopped the scanning motion. *Not mice again.* Rummaging between boxes, he looked for invisible residue from discarded New Food cartons, splashing bleach behind the freezers, mopping the floor harshly. Only later in the afternoon, after checking beds and linen, while preparing for dinner, he noticed the old drone model knocked off outside the kitchen window.

It wasn't one of USK's drones. Large, clunky, with an ugly pouch embedded within the airframe, a flaky "mail pigeon" model from a collapsed German company from the early 2100s. Inside the pouch, a message that would turn his sanitised world upside down, written in what looked like graphite scribbles, in honour of the old times.

Dear Axel

I know you probably hate me. When I look back at my life in Spitsbergen, I have mostly good memories of our time together, filled with love, safety, even abundance, if we can pronounce such a word in our age of mass depletion and extinction. I could have carried on. I could have grown old at The Wild Reindeer, next to you, performing the same soothing routines, seeking a sense of service to others (even if they were rich, wasteful tourists without a clue about their role in this fucked-up situation), alternating between the same packaged meals to create an illusion of healthy variety, and performing our little acts of rebellion against the algorithm to pretend we were still in control. Decisions happen over a lifetime but also in a split second, and I don't know why my decision to leave turned so unbelievably radical when it had been staring us in the face for at least ten years.

Despite not regretting my decision to leave (I don't want to grow old in a horrible society that hides the real world from us), there is a massive hole in my life. The hole is your absence. The more I think about it, the more I wish we were in the same place on that dangerous spectrum running from cynical pessimism to carefree optimism. Because we believe in similar things, don't we? Justice, freedom, compassion. You have a good heart. I loved you from the moment you came into our house on Fyr (almost as strongly as I hated everything your old job represented). I still love you and cannot bear the thought of never seeing you again. I cannot change this, or dismiss you as a cynical bastard, although I often wish I could.

I think you would like it here. Bas, Santiago and his friends are wonderful humans. They had such challenging times before arriving at Nordaustlandet. Like you, they didn't surrender to fate or complain about bad luck. They rolled their sleeves up and got busy, building a community that, despite the many hardships, is going to thrive. We're setting up freeze-drying chambers under ice boulders, and fermentation caves for seaweed, fish oil and seal fat. We're devising our own recipe for pemmican, combining krill, cod and seaworm meat. We're harvesting water from ice, and preparing shelters inside a cave network, under the collapsing ice shelf. These caves are carved into volcanic rock, with geothermal vents in some of the lower areas. We can even boil fish in them.

As you may imagine, the simple act of communicating with you presents a big risk for our community. Once you press the return button, the drone will fly back to Nordaustlandet, to a spot far away from our cave. I won't be able to send you regular messages, as you once did when I was living on the Beranger. We never go out of the cave complex in groups larger than three, nor do we interfere with the outside environment in ways that could be recognised by USK drones or satellite cameras. But if USK decides to get rid of us, they will find a way. I can't risk too much.

Please don't reply to this message. On the back of the drone, under a protective lid, a small screen shows a set of coordinates. That's the place where the drone is programmed to return. If you miss me as much as I miss you, pack your essentials, remove your tech, and use the coordinates. I will check the place every few days, even after the drone returns. The hope of meeting you there will give me a reason to stay optimistic.

With love,

Pat

That was it. A much shorter message than the endless conversations they'd been having in his head. He stared at Pat's jagged handwriting for a long time, not reading the words any more, simply feeling connected to her, despite the vast distance separating them, mentally and physically. Through the serving hatch, he watched the first guests arriving in the dining room, sitting down at the tables, waiting for their New Food burgers. Nordaustlandet. A fishing community. In a cave complex. What would they do when winter came? He couldn't think clearly. His emotions were confounding, erratic, explosive. *A reason to stay optimistic.* Steadying his hands against his thighs, Axel grabbed the first two plated burgers and walked into the dining room.

The hunt for giant seaworms off the coast of Svalbard, news report

Local accounts mention at least one hundred sightings in recent months. The creatures appear to spawn near the island of Spitsbergen. From there, they roam the Svalbard archipelago in groups. Ships attempting to capture them have retreated under threat of capsizing. Numerous descriptions point to symmetrical muscular bodies, cylindrical digestive tracts resembling sacs, and a spoon-shaped proboscis. Some seaworms have been reported to reach four metres long. Annelid creatures, called Echiurans, have lived in the Arctic for a long time, but the size of these specimens is unprecedented, suggesting they're from a new species, or they have been affected by higher mutation rates.

Chapter Thirty-Five

(Hildr) Mission

Reykjavik, Iceland, May 2149 (three months before)

They met at the Hall of the Wizard of Oz for the last briefing session. The room had been built as an annex to the main school, ceiling three times the height of the tallest pupil, interior design loosely inspired by the Hallgrímskirkja church in Reykjavik. Through the doors with their pointed arches, covered in relief sculptures of Icelandic flora, twenty-odd Devs came in, silent, disciplined, spreading themselves evenly across the room. They sat on the wooden benches, Hildr at the centre of the group. At the far end, the vertical device of gleaming metal arranged in symmetrical, geometric patterns, with central shafts wide as tree trunks stretching towards the ceiling, resembling a church organ, or the columns in an ancient temple. The Wizard.

Surrounding them, stained-glass windows, but with a different palette from the rest of the school, casting soft pools of blue and green light. Hildr felt weirdly calm, wondering if this was an inevitable side effect of being immersed in the colours of sea and nature. She hadn't felt this peaceful for a long time. More precisely, not since she'd received the date for the mission.

She would be heading to Fyr the next day. The last briefing session was momentous, tense, charged with significance. Part spiritual metaphor, part self-conscious humour – named as it was for a user experience prototyping technique relying on humans rather than technology – the Wizard gave voice to the algorithm at strategic junctures, when the model's predictions ventured further in time. Instead of a relatable and friendly bot, pupils were confronted with this church-like room, an impersonal setup evoking power and purpose. Perhaps they ought to believe the model's pronouncements as if they were religious edicts.

The melody started, signalling that the briefing was about to begin. Hildr loved the simple, upbeat sequence. The pipes didn't visibly vibrate, but the Wizard roared with sound, filling the entire room with deep, thunderous notes on the bass lines, and a shimmering, flute-like whisper for the main melody.

"We thank all brothers and sisters for their individual sacrifices," the Wizard's voice started, above the music. "Today we thank Hildr most especially, for volunteering for the mission."

"Thank you, sister," the Devs repeated in unison.

Hildr shivered.

Sitting next to her, Gabriel offered a serene smile.

The voice of the Wizard resounded, addressing her directly. "Tomorrow, you're going outside the model. To minimise the risks, we have put in place protective measures for your stay on Fyr.

"You and Gabriel will leave on Monday morning and arrive on Fyr on Wednesday evening. You will eat a hearty meal and rest at the short-term holding facility. On Thursday morning, you will remove all your technology and undergo a minimally invasive brain surgery. You have requested this for your own comfort, to reduce cognitive dissonance and improve your interactions with locals. You will retain the memories and knowledge required to complete the mission. In the afternoon, after we're satisfied that you have successfully recovered from the procedure, Gabriel will drop you close to a climbing path leading to the Beranger."

"What if the voids intercept her?" one of the Devs asked.

"We have observational data," the Wizard said. "They are resource-deprived but highly sociable. According to the model, local voids may even help Hildr to find Ula." A sceptical murmur rose from the group. "Nevertheless, Gabriel and our stealth drones will be following her at a distance, keeping an eye. Assuming Ula hasn't destroyed the device or permanently disabled it, Hildr will recover the chip, reconnect to the algorithm, and access Birgit's messages. Gabriel will then collect her from the Beranger."

She had heard this narrative in previous briefing sessions. Repetition was important to consolidate memories. Even after forgetting biographical details, Hildr would retain the core of her mission.

"From there, a few scenarios can develop," the Wizard continued. "In the best-case scenario, the messages will provide details on Mondo's research and how to access the room. Gabriel and Hildr will travel to Spitsbergen, go inside the vault, and inspect the site in person. In the middle scenario, if the messages contain blueprints for the L-274, but no information on how to access the site, Hildr and Gabriel will attempt to reach the tunnels using the ship moored near the island. In the worst-case scenario, the messages will be compromised or irrelevant. In all scenarios, Hildr and Gabriel return to Iceland safely after the mission, carrying crucial data for our future."

The Devs produced a low, indistinct song of approval.

Hildr remained silent.

Gabriel raised his hand. "On the first scenario ..." He paused. "How far must we go underground?"

They had seen the data from Mondo's lab experiments.

"Inside the tunnels, you should venture only where it's safe to do so. Evidence collected by the Trust suggests Birgit Olsen is alive and helping Mondo with harvesting the organic substance, but we don't know what neurological adaptations she has developed after years of exposure. She may also be using special equipment, such as air filters to reduce nitrogen to oxygen ratios, or thermal pods to withstand the cold. Gabriel, you'll have access to the vault's internal network, and you will guide Hildr as needed. We'll be in close communication. The model's advice will be relayed as close as possible to real time. We thank all brothers and sisters for their individual sacrifices."

"Thank you, Hildr," the Devs repeated.

"Thank you, *all* brothers and sisters," the Wizard said. "Securing food is a critical step in the event of global collapse. We know Mondo Foods are growing new compounds in underground networks in and around Spitsbergen. The activity started eighteen years ago, just before Birgit went in. Ultimately, this is a race to control a new source of food, and potentially a new type of farming. With our data and technology, we have a good chance of succeeding.

"Our scenarios include adapting to living partially underground, in structures embedded within the tunnels, and shielded from nitrogen spikes via filtered air systems. Another option includes drone-guided explorations, or human-led expeditions with suitable equipment. A third scenario we're currently developing is to erect floating platforms on the Arctic Ocean and harvest the organic substance directly from undersea vents. We're stress-testing these scenarios and overlaying the possibility of genetic enhancements, allowing for controlled N_2 consumption and absorption. I hope this gives you an idea of the possibilities. We have a plan. The mission on Fyr is part of a long-term strategy. We just need more data."

"Data leads to the truth," the Devs said on cue.

The Wizard's catchy upbeat melody played again.

Hildr and Gabriel held hands, mouthing the closing line in unison:

"Do the right thing for the planet, and our future is bright."

Late afternoon. Hildr pressed her face against the square grid, panting into the respirator. She had been running for five hours. Was she over-exercising? She checked in with her feelings, ensuring she wasn't running away. The problem wasn't her conscious thoughts. Those pushed her to run further, to be at the top of her physical condition. Ready. The problem was the feelings that might lurk beneath, recognisable only through complex physical responses. Higher heartbeat than expected. Kicks of dopamine aligned with endless ruminations. Her tab blipped, producing the response.

You're experiencing mild anxiety generated by the upcoming mission on Fyr.

Hildr switched off the treadmill.

"Your legs must be like jelly by now," Gabriel said, approaching from behind. "How are you feeling?"

"I was asking myself the same question. My arrythmias have returned."

Gabriel's pupils reflected the light coming in through the hall's windows, black lines repeated in a pattern of bright green, red and yellow, as if his eyes were made of stained glass.

"I'm sorry. I can see the trip is causing you a lot of stress. You'll be fine without over-analysing your heart's electrical activity for a few days."

Hildr put one hand over her chest, right where it hurt.

"Will I even be the same person, if I'm not checking my sensors all the time? That scares me more than the amnesia, to be honest. Not knowing what's going on inside my chest feels more worrying."

She grabbed her towel, dried her forehead, sweat prickling against her skin.

Gabriel leaned against the leg press machine, looking at her forlornly. "Don't play it down. It'll be unsettling. To believe ... you are her."

"I *am* her."

"You know what I mean."

"This is what I'm meant to do, isn't it? Find the bracelet or feel like a failure for the rest of my life. It's better to believe

I'm her. That way, at least I'll have the best chance of finding the messages."

"We don't know if they'll say anything useful. And Ula might have thrown the old chip in the sea, for all we know. The trip is your choice. You can still change your mind."

"I *can't*," Hildr said. "Even the Trust is on board, and they have more to lose. Mondo are obviously lying. What are they doing down there? How are they excavating the tunnels? New Food production is booming, and yet prices haven't come down. We can't keep collecting their breadcrumbs."

"Your anxiety is getting worse. You're breathless even though you stopped running several minutes ago."

Hildr rubbed her face on the towel.

"What if we see her ... down there?"

"That would be great, wouldn't it?" Gabriel said. "She might tell you Mondo's secrets."

"I'm not sure I want to meet her."

"Allow yourself to feel this."

"I'm also dreading meeting voids in real life. How can anyone choose to live in ignorance?"

"It's a different world, without tech."

Hildr let out a long sigh.

"Let me watch it again."

Old files flooded her senses. Central logs from the original Hildr, and contextual files. The videos included newsreels of children leaving Rwanda, Sudan, Libya, Italy, crossing continents, escaping drought, war, hunger, with images of boats arriving on beaches, mixing with scrapbooks from Fyr's old town. The Blue Boat commune. Birgit's greenhouse. Wasn't this how memory worked? A patchwork of visions and feelings curated by technology, each file accessed on demand, clicking into place. The biographical threads expanded like a cat's cradle, weaving her fractured identity. Towards the end, the video followed the little girl on the island, after she had removed her tech, coming in and out of colourful houses, playing on the streets. USK's cameras lost sight of the first Hildr near the port. On the last image of her alive, she filled a cup by a water fountain, running back and forth, watering a patch of bearberry shrubs. Hildr would be returning to Fyr. How would she feel? What would remain of herself?

She wrapped the towel round her body, respirator blowing on her back.

"I'm cold."

"Shower, dinner and a movie? I'll wait for you at the canteen," Gabriel said.

"Will you go in with me? When we're underground."

"Of course. Whatever happens, we'll be together."

"I want to go in."

"I'm sorry," Gabriel said. "I didn't know it would be this difficult. I'll be there."

"I won't recognise you."

"We're siblings. The heart finds a way."

Gabriel put his arms around her shoulders.

A brief respite from the cold.

The tale of Hildr, the giant – the part at the end

"*Inside the vault, deep in the mountain, surrounded by sweet fruit treacle, Hildr met an old woman.*"

"*Who was she, Mama?*"

"*The Goddess of Farming. In the past, humans built shrines for the Goddess in hallowed mountain rocks. To honour their offers, the Goddess planted the most splendid foods under the mountain and kept them safe from the weather. Underground, Hildr came across the new farms, tweaked and perfected to acquire the taste of old foodstuffs, from cereals to fruits, from vegetables to nuts, from pulses to roots.*"

"*Grandma Ula told me that story.*"

"*And you must never forget. Once, humans ploughed the Earth's surface. Now, our food is underground. One day, Hildr will return and lead the farmers to the hidden farms. Please promise you won't run away again. You gave me such a fright.*"

"*I promise, Mama.*"

"*You're not saying that just to please me, are you?*"

"*No, Mama. I'll stay right here with you.*"

Acknowledgements

My sincere thanks to the team at the Crop Trust, whose vital work in safeguarding biodiversity inspired key elements of this story (although this book is a work of fiction, their mission is very real); to my partner, for his patience and support throughout the countless hours of writing; to the Bridport Prize, for awarding this book a *Highly Commended* prize and motivating me to keep going; to my beta readers, for their time and honesty; to my critiquing partners and fellow writers, for their shared passion and willingness to exchange ideas; and, last but not least, a huge thank you to everyone who supported the book through my crowd-funding campaign. Their names and pseudonyms are listed below.

Yiannis Chronakis, mdtommyd, Paul Edwards, gwendolyn-tennison, Helia Press, Zack Fissel, Zach Townsend, John, Vikesh Boodhna, Jeff Wasserman, Joao Gil, Patrick McAndrew, Walter Cardew, smvm2876, Anu Huhtisaari, RK, Marian Gossmeyer, Dan Brotzel, Helen Marsden, David Whitmarsh, Sam, Nick, Jonas Sværke, Rui, Eileen, Davina Caulker, Rui C, Eirini Gia, Travis Huyghebaert, phoenix_17, Jessie, Piotrek

About

H. B. Viegas is a new writer of speculative fiction.

For more books, visit **hbviegas.com**

Coming soon:

Valeria is an Alien *– A black comedy about gender*